Post Contact: Holding On

(Post Contact - Book 2)

Set in the very near future, this second novel of the Post Contact series finds humanity struggling with its own self-inflicted damage even while reeling under external attack.

Balanced on a knife edge to extinction, those few survivors that can still resist must stand against overwhelming odds and terrifying dangers.

Books by D. C. Macey

THE POST CONTACT SERIES
Near future SF action thrillers

Post Contact: First Days
Published October 2022

Post Contact: Holding On
Published November 2022

Post Contact: Breaking Back
Published May 2023

THE TEMPLE SERIES
Contemporary archaeological thrillers

The Temple Legacy
Published August 2015

The Temple Scroll
Published August 2016

The Temple Covenant
Published April 2018

The Temple Deliverance
Published April 2019
.

Post Contact: Holding On

(Post Contact - Book 2)

Butcher & Cameron

D. C. MACEY

Chapter 1

Base Primo

Professor Steph Simpson knew, because Weeman had explained to her several times before he died, that the sample mixing process in Earth's atmosphere couldn't change because of humanity's subsequent evolution – humans were simply a product of that process, not the final beneficiary.

Long ago, long before the emergence of humanity, Earth had been selected. Its averageness and the solar system's conveniently anonymous location in the middle of the galaxy's Orion Arm were perfect. The stars of Orion stretched out through the void to link two of the galaxy's great arms, Perseus and Sagittarius. Orion served as a highway for sample craft moving between the thousands of life planets scattered through all three arms. It channelled them all to Primo, the ancient base on lonely Planet Nine from where their atmospheric samples were distributed through Earth's atmosphere.

Earth was the planet-sized laboratory where the mixing of a common biology occurred. The resultant product was then harvested and redistributed back to all the other life planets in an endless cycle of replenishment. It was the perfect process to maintain a set of identical life-supporting atmospheres across more worlds than a single human could ever hope to visit.

Except, with Earth's atmosphere now closed to all traffic, nothing could be mixed in its atmosphere, and nothing harvested back for onward distribution.

Calamity had quickly followed on the heels of that disastrous closure. The last sample craft in had distributed a potentially lethal pathogen from a distant world. The following craft, laden with the carefully prepared tempering virus didn't get through, didn't deliver the antidote. Captain Kingston and Fay Dower had watched it crash and burn.

Earth was cut off with a deadly virus circulating in its atmosphere. Steph had calculated in excess of ninety-nine percent fatalities.

***

General Dower stared out through the viewing port into the vast expanse of the Grand Canal – the tunnel that gave access to Base Primo. It seemed an age and yet had only been days since the president had ordered him to assume direct command of Primo and all its associated activities. The weight of the world sat on his shoulders; he didn't even know if the president was still alive. His command was humanity's last hope – it *was* humanity.

The Grand Canal was half a mile wide at its gaping mountainside mouth. From there, it burrowed deep into the rock to provide craft of every size safe access to the base. Dower focused his attention on a giant sample craft that glided effortlessly past his location. Propelled by its gravdrive, the sampler used the power of gravity to move with unerring precision to some destination deeper beneath the mountain.

'That's another one, more frequent than I'd realised,' said Dower.

'Yes. Three coming in every day, sometimes more, but none are going back out. There's plenty of room though, for now,' said Steph, standing at his side. In her capacity as Primo's lead scientist, Steph was coordinating the science and engineering teams that were trying to understand the base and its myriad secrets while simultaneously striving to come up with solutions to the bigger problems that beset them all. Though not in the chain of command, she sat at the top table, and the general relied on her for the facts to inform his strategy.

'What's happening to the samples they bring in, will they keep?' said Dower.

'They'll be fine for now. The samplers are designed to safely carry the samples they collect during their journeys out along the spiral arms and back. Even using their folddrives to move at super-speeds, the trips can take a long time, many months. For now, they're holding their samples on board until we can process them through Earth's atmosphere again. It's a backlog that just keeps growing. Worse still, just as we can't feed their samples into Earth's atmosphere, none of Earth's samples are accessible for onward distribution. The sample craft are just waiting here. But that's the least of our problems, for a while anyway.'

'And what progress are we making toward solutions?' said Dower.

'Nothing to report yet, I'm afraid. I've set Celine to focus on finding a solution that will clear Earth's atmosphere of the debris field. She's sharp, so I'll let her get on with it. She knows where I am when she needs me. Oh, and she's saying very good things about your daughter too. She's sure Lily will be an asset to the team.'

General Dower nodded an acknowledgement. His younger daughter was undoubtedly the true brains of the family. He hoped both she and big sister Fay would be seen to contribute to the resolution of the base's problems. For security reasons, the original recruitment rule for Primo had been single people only, no dependants and no relationship ties.

Alone among the near six thousand people who had transferred to Primo, Dower was accompanied by his family. He was acutely aware of what others had lost and what he had saved when his wife Gail and their daughters Fay and Lily had been snatched from Earth just ahead of the atmosphere becoming blocked with space debris.

Dower grimaced as he thought about the surviving population of Earth, all facing a deadly virus and trapped beneath an orbiting cage of satellite and missile debris, created when Earth's nations sought to destroy each other's communication and defence systems. His family's rescue had been the entirely understandable and instinctive act of a family man amidst a crisis, but it had broken the rules. Nobody complained, most on Primo not giving it any thought – they all needed the general. But it did weigh on his mind.

Even as they had fled Earth, the wheels had begun to come off society. Missiles had flown back and forth; the atmosphere had filled with countless fragments of destroyed satellites and the spent killer missiles themselves. Quickly, the Earth had been surrounded by a minefield of shrapnel thousands of miles deep, completely barring any access.

That his people were unable to return to Earth was cause for disquiet. That the samples from Weeman's fleet of sample craft could not reach Earth was a disaster beyond measure. It went far beyond the simple isolation of Earth. The network of Earth-like planets scattered through the galaxy were linked by the samplers' continuous journeys, gathering life samples and bringing them all to Primo from where they were channelled into Earth's atmosphere. In turn, samples of Earth's mixed atmosphere were harvested and channelled back out to all the planets in the network – seeding and supporting a common core biology across them all.

Always hidden from humanity, far above the orbital plane of the solar system, and concealed in its darkest reaches, was remote Planet Nine.

There, Base Primo had now begun to surrender its secrets, slowly. Slower still since the death of Weeman, the last survivor of the race that had for aeons overseen the project's smooth function. His last act had been to entrust humanity with Primo's continuing operation. And things had not started well.

'The virus will have already done its worst, general. I'm sorry, it's now all about how we break through to save what few are left, if any,' said Steph.

'I wonder if you wouldn't have been the best person to try and reopen Earth's atmosphere?' said Dower.

Steph frowned. 'General, I'd love to work on that, but you know the other challenge.' Her right hand stroked down her left forearm. The sleeve glistened and shimmered very slightly under her touch.

All Primo staff received a bodysuit biometrically tailored and printed to their personal specification; it was their personal interface with all Primo's technology. Each suit contained a collar-phone communication device and provided perfect atmospheric comfort for both indoor wear and off-base activity. The collar included a flick out hood that once deployed would seal around the neck and fix rigid in the shape of Weeman's classic dome-headed alien. The suit also contained an oxygen reserve to support its dual role as uniform and spacesuit.

'Yes, I know, it feels like just too many problems,' said Dower, as he touched his sleeve. It too shimmered.

One of Weeman's last acts had been to upgrade the suits of the three humans he truly trusted: Steph, her close friend Jamie MacAulay, and the general. The new suits had enhanced functionality, layers of extra knowledge, and access to remote and hidden places within Primo that they had not previously guessed at. Every suit on the base included a standard interface within the sleeve. For their three suits alone, the sleeves almost pulsed, perpetually eager to share more, to respond to the next instruction.

'So, you need me to work on weapons. I'm doing that with the main control room's Goliath,' said Steph, matching the general's steps away from the viewing port as he set off toward his office.

The Goliath was a huge LPA, a light processing array, the advanced computing system developed by Weeman's race. A Goliath had a vastly larger volume than the regular desk-sized LPAs that were found dotted throughout Base Primo, wherever Weeman's kind had needed one. This Goliath was situated in the middle of Primo's main control room, and it dwarfed the rank of standard LPAs that surrounded it. There, Steph had been devoting her efforts and her suit's elevated access permissions to resolve the weapons crisis, searching for the lost build instructions for the warbird fighter craft. Her job was to deliver a military solution to the looming crisis emerging from the Perseus Arm.

Approaching the general's office, they found two people waiting outside.

'Sir,' said Captain Kingston, throwing an enthusiastic salute toward Dower. 'Ma'am.' He nodded politely toward Steph.

'Kingston, thanks for attending. At ease, I want to know how the training is coming along,' said Dower with a nod in the direction of the young woman standing beside the chief warbird pilot. Fay, his elder daughter had recently been added to the pilot training programme. She smiled at him.

'Sir, I've got thirty trainees engaged and as many again just starting. We're making great progress on tactics and theory. But with only one warbird available, giving our pilots hands-on experience of flying and weapons control is slow, very slow. How long before more warbirds are available?'

The general looked toward Steph. 'We're working on it. The professor has it as her main priority. What's your training timeline, as things stand?'

'Sir, I've pilots who know how to use a warbird and fire its weapons. But, sir, a brief introduction to flying and gunnery is a long way from them being combat ready. With that basic level of skill, I wouldn't bet on any returning from a combat mission.'

'That's pessimistic, captain.'

'Begging your pardon, sir, realistic. I've seen the pictures Colonel MacMillan brought back from the Perseus Arm. Those bogeys may not have a gravdrive to power them about, but there's a lot of them. Any novice pilot could be overwhelmed by sheer weight of numbers. We need more warbirds if the pilots are to get up to speed.'

'Do your best, captain. There might only have been ten warbirds in the concealed hangar Professor Simpson opened, but she'll get you more. Meantime, you must ensure we have people competent to fly when she delivers. Am I understood?'

'Yes, sir. I'll deliver you the pilots. Just, I know right now they're wondering what they'll fly.'

'Captain, you tell them again, Colonel MacMillan got the priority allocation. He took every warbird bar one with him back to the Orion–Perseus junction. If those beasts he found out there are coming into the Orion Arm, he needs all those warbirds to have any chance of fending them off.'

The little group fell silent for a moment. Each knew the truth about the numbers and the scale of the task they faced; it was daunting. Colonel MacMillan had recently left with his squadron to complete construction of Base Secundo, the planned station at the junction of the Orion and Perseus arms.

MacMillan's Perseus Squadron comprised three Leviathans, the biggest and fastest transport vessels they had. Each was powered by gravdrive for travel in normal space. Each had a folddrive, enabling them to move into and through folded space. There, they could travel at breathtaking speeds as space folded toward the travelling craft.

Previously, speed had been the Leviathans' only defence. Now each of the Perseus Leviathans carried a flight of three warbirds. Everyone recognised they were pitifully few, and everyone hoped they would be enough for the job they might face.

'Captain, let me see what I can do,' said Steph. 'Maybe I can have some of my team put together a flight simulator of sorts to help for now. I know it won't be the same as flying for real. But it might help some of your trainees sharpen up, get a better handle on things.'

'That's a great idea, ma'am. Thank you,' said Kingston.

Steph looked toward the general, saw him nodding enthusiastically.

'Make several simulators if you can,' said Dower. 'The more pilots we can put through training the better. Though pray God we don't need any of them.'

'Leave it with me. I'll see what I can do.' She turned and headed toward the main control room.

Steph knew the general was deeply troubled by the risk they all faced.

It was the same worry that had first driven Weeman to engage with humanity. He had expressed his anxiety at the loss of several unmanned sample craft in the Perseus Arm, and worse still, the subsequent failure to return of two craft crewed by his last remaining colleagues.

Weeman, how we need you now, she thought. His untimely death had left her adrift in an ocean of knowledge and secrets. An ocean that had now whipped into a storm of troubles.

They had started with nine Leviathans. General Dower had split them into three squadrons. The Perseus Squadron comprising P-1, P-2 and P-3 were now out at Secundo.

The Sagittarius Squadron under Brigadier Smith-Brown had travelled toward the junction of the Orion and Sagittarius arms. There, the proposed Base Trozos had never been founded. Of the squadron's three Leviathans, terrorism had destroyed one completely, S-2 lost with all souls. Another, S-3, under the command of Jamie MacAulay had been damaged and fell from folded space to an unknown place. If it had survived, S-3 was truly lost in space. Only S-1, the brigadier's flagship survived for certain. Now it stood off Planet Nine, providing a docking facility for the trainee pilots to practise launching and landing their sole warbird.

The three Leviathans of the Orion Squadron were under Dower's direct command. O-1 also held station above Base Primo, awaiting his orders. O-2 was temporarily in Earth's orbit with Celine and Lily on board; they were completing an inspection of Earth's atmosphere. Finally, O-3 was also stationed above Earth, searching for signals from the surface, no matter how weak. None had been detected to date.

No one knew yet how much of the radio silence was interference due to the debris field's signal disruption and how much was due to the intense solar storm that had swept across Earth just as the virus began to spread.

The sudden need for more warbirds and the consequent repurposing of Leviathans from transport craft to combat carriers had been triggered earlier when Colonel MacMillan took P-1 deep into the Perseus Arm. His task, to find what had interfered with the safe passage of Weeman's samplers.

He'd found the answer and had barely escaped to bring news back to Primo. The repeated losses of automated sample craft were now attributed to a race of space-travelling creatures. Worse, it seemed the creatures had captured whole at least one for the lost samplers. If they managed to get that functioning, they would have a folddrive and could reach the Orion–Perseus junction at any moment, then move on to Primo in a matter of days.

Entering the control room, Steph was heartened to see it abuzz with dozens of scientists working at the rank of LPAs surrounding the mighty Goliath. It shimmered and flickered with billions of tiny lights shifting to form and reform patterns as countless calculations and displays cycled through its enormous processing volume. The familiar scene brought a small sense of relief, and she hurried toward the Goliath's corner steps.

Climbing them, she absently stretched out a hand, reaching into the open-sided Goliath, then smiled as the shimmering spots of light darted away from her approaching fingers. How the spots of light were kept constrained within the framework was unclear. One day she'd work it out; today, it was enough that they were. Reaching the top step, she paused, granting herself just a moment of quiet before preparing to tackle the weapons problem again.

Every new task was vital. Vital for the general and Primo. Vital too for Steph, helping her block out the dark thoughts that now always encroached on her private moments; keeping at bay the very personal pain she was feeling.

Jamie MacAulay was lost. It had been with him that she first encountered Weeman and Primo and all its opportunities for humanity, which Earth's leaders had so disastrously squandered. As commander of S-3, he had vanished with his Leviathan. If the craft was still functioning, it was lost in the far reaches of the Orion Arm. She knew how to search; she knew very roughly where to search. Roughly wasn't good enough, roughly meant an area of space so vast it might take the whole Leviathan fleet a lifetime to scour.

She needed to narrow down S-3's location, had some ideas how to, but the general had forbidden it. Primo's two mighty Goliath processors needed to be directed toward the biggest problems of the moment. One Goliath, here in the main control room, dedicated to resolving the armaments issue, to defending humanity and Primo, and to work on the scores of other supporting issues to enable them to understand the full extent of Primo and its secrets. The other Goliath was located in the reserve control room, buried deep in Primo's secret bowels. It was allocated for Celine when she returned from Earth. Her task was to calculate how to break Earth free of its debris field, to save any few who may have survived the virus.

The general had insisted that the crew of a single lost Leviathan could not come ahead of the bigger picture. All humanity's available assets needed to be focused on saving and protecting the rump. It hurt. Her relationship with Jamie had progressed well beyond friendship.

Stepping onto the hard transparent top of the Goliath, she peered down into the depths of the display and stroked the sleeve of her suit, watching ripples run through the lights below as they readied to respond to her instructions. For now, she followed General Dower's orders, sorting his problems. She knew the bigger picture came first. But if, as she had calculated, Jamie's Leviathan really had survived its terrorist attack, she would not give up on him.

She knelt down, pressed her palm to the surface. 'One day soon, you'll help me find him,' she said quietly.

Chapter 2

Earth Orbit

Celine frowned and looked up at the mighty Leviathan's bridge screen. There she could see the scattered flotilla of observer craft that had spent days supporting her and the team on O-2 in surveying and probing the atmosphere. Now, all those efforts had come down to this moment. As the project manager, the outcome rested on her shoulders.

They had identified a few gaps in the upper layers of the atmosphere's shrapnel-filled debris field, but these seemed to offer scant consolation. Until she and Lily could return to Base Primo and run a full analysis in the Goliath LPA, they couldn't tell for certain, but right now, it seemed there was no clean descent path to be found. From the atmosphere's uppermost layers where high-altitude geostationary satellites had once hovered, all the way down to the lower altitudes, everywhere was blocked.

Earth appeared to be completely cut off.

'Test craft launching. Stand by, everybody. Activate all sensors, descent in ten…' said Lily, as she crossed the bridge to join Celine. Acknowledgements sounded in her collar-phone as the scientists in O-2's workrooms and others stationed in the spread of surrounding observers all anxiously made their final checks.

'There it is,' said Lily, pointing up toward the screen as the newly launched observer emerged from the Leviathan's hangar to appear on-screen. It pulled a little ahead of O-2 before pausing to hold position relative to its mothership.

'Yes, I see it,' said Celine. 'All our observations point to this as the best spot to break through, but—'

'But *best spot*'s a relative term, I guess,' said Lily.

'Very relative. I think if it gets halfway down without taking a debris collision, it will be a good start.'

Lily glanced at her sleeve. 'Going down in five, four...'

The unmanned observer looked chunkier than the others of its class. Back at Primo, Professor Steph Simpson had struggled for several days to override the manufacturing system's pre-programmed construction design. Eventually, her success had resulted in production of the new and heavier version that now held station ahead of them. It was layered with extra coatings of protective metallic skin. Now was the moment as it hovered on the cusp of descent.

Even here, so far above the Southern Ocean, above the seas and sky that humanity had squabbled over least, even here, the atmosphere below was not clear. Every exploding missile and satellite and every physical collision had randomly scattered fields of debris up, down, to all sides. But here, at least, the wreckage was more thinly spread.

'... two, one! Descending now,' said Lily, keying the order on her sleeve controls then looking up to the screen.

The observer tilted and began to descend slowly, ensuring as much data would be collected as possible.

'Go on,' said Celine, almost under her breath. 'Go on.'

The two women stood together watching. Across the bridge, the Leviathan's captain and her first officer watched too. Behind them, the deadlight curtain twitched and shifted as several other crew members suddenly found reasons to be on the bridge. They shuffled in quietly.

'Entering debris field now,' said Lily.

The team watched in silence; this was not far from the location where Captain Kingston and Lily's sister Fay had seen an automated sample craft founder in the first days of the debris field's formation. How would this compare?

The observer dropped. Whispers in Lily's collar-phone confirmed data gathering was fully functional.

The descent continued; the craft dropped steadily for perhaps twenty seconds. Then all hell broke loose. One bright flash signalled a debris strike, then another and another. A succession of small artefacts collided with the craft, but it continued its descent. The thickened hull was holding, and both Lily and Celine almost dared to hope for just a moment.

Thirty seconds in, the tide began to turn. First, the craft took a heavy strike and shuddered, almost paused, before continuing down. Then in quick succession, multiple strike flashes glowed against the craft's hull. These were followed by another shudder and flaring as significant debris punched through the outer protective shell.

'Hell,' said Celine as the craft went from controlled descent to fireball.

'Hell,' said Lily.

The two scientists had been charged with getting the atmosphere open; to rescue any survivors on the ground. It wasn't' looking good.

'Let's get the data back to Primo; we need to process it quickly,' said Celine.

Chapter 3

Opsythia System: P-1 Beyond Base Secundo

Colonel MacMillan stood steady on the travelator that carried him aft along Leviathan P-1's broad central passageway. He gave informal nods or waves of acknowledgement to crew members who he passed; the commander of the Perseus Squadron was determinedly projecting an air of calm.

Reaching the hangar zone, he stepped off and made his way to the port side hangar's entrance. As with all sensitive access points, it was now guarded by a soldier. He was content that all P-1's crew had passed as loyal, but the recent terrorist attacks that had so devastated the Sagittarius Squadron meant no chances were being taken anywhere.

With an acknowledgement of the guard's salute, he stepped into the vast space; it was almost empty. At the far end were two hoppers and a single observer craft. An access door beyond was unguarded. It let into the big hangar that normally housed a small sample craft. It had been sacrificed to make space for more construction materials. Two days earlier, at the Secundo construction site, P-1 had dropped off all its earth-moving and construction machines, its stores of construction materials and most of its hoppers. The hoppers doubled up as both terrestrial-based patrol craft and local pickup trucks.

Nothing moved in the hangar. After a minute's contemplation, the colonel stepped back out. With a parting nod to the guard, he crossed the central passageway, dodging across the fore and aft moving travelators as he went. The guard at the starboard hangar door had watched his progress and stroked the hangar access door open before snapping to attention and throwing a salute.

'As you were,' said Colonel MacMillan.

'Sir,' said the guard, nonetheless maintaining his rigid stance.

Entering the hangar, MacMillan was struck by how equally empty this one felt. But first impressions were deceptive. At the far end were two more hoppers. Beside them were two warbirds. Matt black in colour, they had a far smaller footprint than the observer stowed in the port hangar. These were low slung, almost insignificant at first glance. The colonel knew otherwise.

As he crossed the hangar, the warbirds' features became quite distinct. Only fifteen feet high – including the three short legs each bird rested on – thirty feet wide from stubby wingtip to wingtip and fifty feet in length. The colonel allowed himself a smile. *There was no fat on these babies.* As a former fast-jet pilot, he appreciated exactly what the warbirds had been built for. He knew the protrusions beneath their wings and those jutting out from their nose cones were weapons systems.

Like each of the craft designs developed by Weeman and his kind, there was no halfway house. If a job needed doing, Weeman's people designed a craft to do that job without compromise. These were machines capable of extreme destruction.

The warbirds had been laid up for an age in Primo's hidden depths. Concealed until Weeman had reluctantly revealed them to Steph. Their original and unintelligible markings were now gone, replaced with contemporary signage. The nearest craft was marked P-1:C1, its neighbour P-1:C3. The common prefix P-1, their mothership identifier, the Leviathan P-1. The suffixes C1 and C3, designating them as combat craft with their individual flight numbers. The third craft, P-1:C2, was absent.

A voice called out an alert and several people emerged from a door set in the hangar wall beyond the warbirds.

Captain Breeze Ash saluted the colonel who waved her and the other pilots to stand at ease.

'Well, Captain Ash, how are things back here?'

'We're all set, sir. You say the word, we'll engage.'

'Good. I'm hoping there will be no engagement. But you must be ready. If these insects turn up, there will be trouble.'

'We'll be ready; be sure of it, sir.'

'Thank you, captain, I know you will. How's the rota working out?'

'Great, sir. We have two pilots to each craft, so we're able to fly extended missions. My co-pilot and I came in about half an hour ago on this one.' She reached out and rested a hand on C1's fuselage. 'C2's taken over on patrol, smooth as clockwork.'

'Excellent. If there's anything your team need, just call out.'

'We're good here, sir. Just wish I had a few more warbirds.'

'You and me both, captain. You know, I reckon you could fit ten in here.'

'A dozen, sir. We've been measuring it. Do you think Professor Simpson will be able to sort out how to get more?'

'That's the plan. Captain Kingston's training more pilots back at Primo. If… when, Steph Simpson sorts out warbird production, we'll get reinforcements, for sure.'

'Thank you, sir. We'll manage until then.'

***

Grainger, captain of P-1, peered down through the transparent top of the navigation-room LPA while touching and stroking her suit's sleeve controls.

Beside her was Eric Fritz, the Leviathan's recently appointed chief scientist. When Celine, his predecessor, had been transferred to new duties on Primo, Grainger had been very concerned. That anxiety had faded once Fritz got on board. During the passage from Primo to the proposed site of Base Secundo, it had become clear he had as good a grasp of the technology as anyone.

They looked again at the planetary system displayed in the LPA. At its heart, the sun, Opsythia A. While very similar to Sol, it had a retinue of just four planets. The inner most planet, Opsythia b. was rocky but quite inhospitable. The second planet, Opsythia c., was a gas giant. Beyond that lay two further rocky planets.

The third planet, Opsythia d., was hot and uninviting, on the inner edge of the habitable zone, just habitable but no more. Their track line through the LPA showed they were not far from that planet now.

'When we came here first time around, we checked this planet out, but established it would have been too uncomfortable to put our base station on. It's hot as hell,' said Grainger.

'It's odd isn't it. Opsythia e. is at the outer edge of the habitable zone and seems almost as uncomfortably cold as this one's hot,' said Fritz, his speech delivered in perfectly formed English that could not quite mask his German origin.

'Doubly odd – this is the only system we've found so far that has two planets included in the atmospheric sample-sharing scheme,' said Grainger.

'Hmm, I wonder why,' said Fritz. 'Though we've only scratched the surface so far. Perhaps it's more common than we think. You have to ask, why did they choose either of these? They are both so marginal for life. You know what I think? I reckon something might have disturbed the planets' orbits. Perhaps they were both better placed within the goldilocks zone and then each got bumped to either end of the zone.'

'What might do that?' said Captain Grainger.

'I don't know, it's just a thought. Perhaps a rogue star passing close by. Who knows? We're right at the end of the Orion Arm, on the very cusp of Perseus. Move any further beyond this and you edge directly into it. A wandering star from there perhaps? Whatever caused it, everything seems stable now.'

Sparks leaned round the comms control room's door, into the navigation room. 'Captain, I thought I heard your voice. Nothing to report. Just like our last visit here. No signals, nothing. Still all clear.'

'Thanks, Sparks. No news is good news. Send a message through to P-3, please. Let them know all's well with our patrol. We are now proceeding directly back to join them at Secundo. Then Colonel MacMillan will transfer down to join them and assume command,' said Grainger. She tapped her arm and called through to the first officer who was standing bridge watch. 'Number One, we're all clear here. Let's get back to Secundo.'

When the Perseus Squadron had arrived in the Opsythia system, her Leviathan had taken the duty of patrolling the system and had set out on a full initial sweep, just to be sure nothing nasty was lurking.

Meanwhile, P-3 had been detailed to support development of the base on chilly Opsythia e. and P-2 had slipped back into the Fold to maintain a careful watch in folded space.

With all the squadron's construction kit and materials deposited on Opsythia e., the building teams under P-3's protection should have been making good progress.

Grainger touched her sleeve. 'Colonel MacMillan, sir. Setting course for Secundo.'

MacMillan's voice sounded in her collar-phone. 'Very good, captain. What's our ETA?'

Chapter 4

Base Primo: Reserve Control Room

Lily caught her breath as a concealed access door manifested itself in the chamber wall as Steph approached it. Without pause she followed Steph and Celine through into the reserve-control-room complex. Experienced now in using the regular LPAs, being entrusted with a Goliath was a massive step up.

The small linguistics team who had cracked the locust-like aliens' language using this Goliath had now been shifted to a cluster of the surrounding regular LPAs. Today they were focusing on construction of a two-way communication process, should the locusts appear.

The Goliath was unattended. Countless tightly packed strings of lights stretched away into its depths. The array pulsed gently waiting to be put to work. Occasional light flickers shivered through the system as it underwent regular internal calibration. Otherwise, it was still.

'So, here we are,' said Steph. 'I'll upgrade each of your suits' access settings to enable you to enter and leave this secure area, same for the technicians who will be joining your team in the next day or two. I have not upgraded anyone's information access permissions yet. That's something the general will need to sanction, and with everything that's going on, we just haven't got around to it yet. Bear with me.'

'With dedicated access to this Goliath, we should be able to develop and test a range of theories pretty quickly,' said Celine, confidently. All three women paused a dozen paces from the Goliath. They took a moment to absorb the sense of latent processing power, so strong Lily felt it was almost reaching out toward them.

'Well, let's go for it. You know how urgent re-opening Earth's atmosphere is. Likewise, the general needs the weapons issue resolving just as quickly. Once I've got on top of that I'll help you as much as I can. But for now, you're on your own,' said Steph.

'No problem. I'll start by getting Lily up to speed on working a Goliath, then we'll be full steam ahead,' said Celine. She followed close behind as Steph led the way up the Goliath's side steps and out onto its hard top.

Steph crossed to the edge and looked down to where the linguists were busy working at a pair of the standard-sized LPAs that encircled the Goliath.

Beyond them, at the back of the room was an innocuous door. She shivered. Through that door was the sarcophagus room where Weeman had died. In there was an LPA even bigger than the Goliaths. Its sole purpose seemed to have been supporting the cloning works that Weeman and his ilk had relied on. They were all gone now, and the giant LPA lay redundant, cold and grey. Lifeless like Weeman's body that rested in the sarcophagus in the furthest corner of the room.

Steph closed her eyes, recalling her desperate efforts to save Weeman, to get him into the sarcophagus in time. All pointless – he was dead when the lid closed over him. His body still lay inside; she would need to do something about that, another day.

Sensing the arrival of Celine and Lily behind her, she turned to address them. 'You both know I estimate perhaps only fifty million people have survived the virus worldwide. Without power, even those survivors will struggle to survive, and that's before we even think about the hunger they'll have to face. That survivor number's going to drop and fast, so there's not a moment to lose.'

'I just want to say thanks for the opportunity to help, to show what I can do,' said Lily. 'I won't let you down. Won't let either of you down.'

'I know. Now let me introduce you both to the linguistics team down there. Then it's over to you – I have to get on top of other issues,' said Steph.

Chapter 5

Osarus c.

Looking up the side of the valley, Jamie felt a sense of satisfaction. He raised a hand and waved, noted the mirrored response of Major Baz Browning, the leader of his military detachment who stood high above him at the crest. He and Browning went way back, and each had complete faith in the other.

This was no military expedition, but the presence of the one hundred marines was reassuring. In the days since he had guided his Leviathan S-3 down to its landing place nothing had presented any direct threat. Indeed, much of what Jamie had seen so far suggested an almost Eden-like habitat: calm and green, not that there had been much time to select a good location. Nonetheless, most of the signs were positive. It seemed the hurried choice had been sound.

The whole crew was still shocked at the violent and complete destruction of their squadron's sister ship S-2. They understood, too, in the ensuing chaos, their squadron commander Brigadier Smith-Brown and his Leviathan S-1 could not have marked where S-3 had dropped from the Fold. The distances were so vast, S-1 could search forever and might never find them. All knew they were as good as lost.

That awful knowledge was tempered with relief that they had, at least, made a safe landing. Jamie had not been able to hide from his crew that their craft would never fly again. Yes, S-3 had weathered the explosion they suffered in folded space. However, that blast had damaged the hull above the Folddrive Power Unit rendering it inoperable. Flight stresses had exacerbated that hull crack, forcing S-3 out of folded space close to the nearest habitable planet – Osarus c.

In ordinary space, the split had continued to lengthen, eventually threatening to spread across the Gravdrive Power Unit, at which point they would have lost all routine power too. He couldn't have risked that happening in open space – the only choice had been to land fast. Happily, the clean touchdown had brought everyone down safe.

Once grounded, the extent of the hull damage was clear to all. Everyone recognised that S-3 could never take off again. Jamie turned his gaze to the crippled Leviathan. His eye traced the line of its hull, looked up to the ramp that let into a wide hangar. Higher still, he saw the hull gently curve away from him toward a summit ridge that ran the whole length of S-3. Up there, he could make out Chief Engineer Martha Solomon and Ossie the chief scientist, stooping together to inspect the hull damage. The wicked split that had altered the course of all their lives.

Jamie turned his attention back to ground level and S-3's landing site. They were settled firmly in a broad, high-sided river valley. It cut through a range of hills that formed an otherwise solid barrier between an inland high savannah and a narrow coastal plain.

S-3 rested on a level terrace at the mid-point in the valley's length. It had landed comfortably on the higher sided bank of the river, where they were safe from any threat of flooding. He looked out across the slow-flowing water to the much lower far bank and beyond that to an expanse of savannah that stretched smoothly away for half a mile to where the opposite valley side rose to mirror what was immediately behind him.

His first action on landing had been to order a combination of manned and drone surveys beyond the immediate landing site. Nothing had presented as a threat to his crew other than an isolated though frightening incident in the downstream thicket that grew where the valley's mouth let out on to the coastal plain. The thicket completely obstructed downstream access on their side of the river.

In that thicket, they had encountered a giant serpent-like beast. The team had escaped, and thereafter the beast had shown no inclination to leave its hide and approach S-3. The thicket was now off-limits, and automated cameras had been rigged to ensure no unwelcome visitor from the thicket could arrive unheralded at S-3. None had, so far.

The voice of a pilot sounded in his collar-phone. 'We're loaded, sir. Good to go.'

Jamie stepped toward a small sample craft that rested on the terrace just downstream of S-3. Having manoeuvred from its berth in the Leviathan's hangar, the sampler was being used to ferry construction equipment and materials, which it had been shuttling up the valley's side all morning. As he approached, the sampler's own hangar began to close and the two-man bipedal hoppers that had been loading it stepped away.

Clambering into the sampler's stern access port, he swiped it closed and hurried through the inner airlock door that slid closed behind him. 'I'm on board, let's get up there,' he called to the pilot.

By the time he'd reached the bridge, the craft had already risen to a position some fifty feet above the crest. On-screen he could see a dozen marines and technicians. Behind them, two hoppers stood motionless, waiting for work. A little further off he noted more marines in temporary defensive positions. There were hoppers there too. Those, however, were allocated to guard duties.

'You get a good view from above,' said the pilot, pointing at the screen. 'They've already marked out where we should drop this load. And see how the defensive position is right on the ridge edge overlooking S-3. It'll make a neat little redoubt.'

Jamie took in the scene. This was the most critical defensive location. Should a danger ever present, holding this high ground would prevent attacks on S-3 from above and simultaneously offer support to the terrace below. The river provided S-3 with a natural defensive screen to the other side, leaving only the narrow terrace upstream and down to be protected. Browning had already outlined his defensive plans for those. He proposed two barrier walls, each reaching across the narrow terrace from riverbank to valley side. One upstream and one downstream of the Leviathan.

Bringing his attention back to the redoubt construction site, Jamie saw white, spray-painted lines marked out a square shape on the ground. Each side was thirty paces in length. One line ran tight along the crest, the other lines traced back from it to form the box shape. Standing to one side was Baz Browning engaged in earnest conversation with a technician.

'Okay, pilot, thank you. Let's land. I'll go straight to the airlock now,' he said.

'Thank you, sir. I'll have her down before you reach the airlock.'

Back on the ground, Jamie joined Baz to watch as the machinery busied about the redoubt plot.

An excavator dug away swathes of earth, trenching out a foundation to the depth of a man's height and heaping the spoils beyond the boundary. There, another machine pushed and shaped the spoil into a rampart.

Beyond the foundation square, a machine was equipped with a long, articulated boom. Mounted on the boom was a broad pipe tipped by a spray nozzle. It swung out over the foundation and moved steadily from side to side, spreading a foundation construction mix. As soon as it touched ground the formulation began to expand, thickening to three feet in depth. In moments it began to harden.

'That stuff looks just about set already,' said Jamie.

'You're right, it is. Now see what's happening,' said Browning.

More booms had swung over the site and spraying resumed.

'It's starting the walls,' said Jamie. 'Seems this'll be finished later today.' He was surprised by the speed, yet when he thought how quickly the craft themselves had been made, he realised he shouldn't be. 'Baz, you've got this all under control. I'm going to have to leave you to it. Need to start thinking further afield. I'll get one of the hopper drivers to carry me down the hillside.'

Browning grinned at him. 'This is shaping up. Pray God it's never needed but the redoubt's in a perfect location to hold the ridge and protect S-3 from attack. Once the barrier walls are constructed down on the terrace at either end of the Leviathan, I'll be organised.'

'Just barriers?' said Jamie.

'Just about. They'll be simple, eight-foot-high and stretching the full width of the terrace, incorporating a three-foot-high firing step behind. We'll have a watchtower and gate at the riverbank end of each wall to allow people and hoppers in and out. Supported from up here, and with our firepower, we should have enough to hold back any threat.'

Jamie nodded in appreciation of the simplicity of the plan as they peered down into the valley to where other construction machines were already busy building the upstream and downstream barrier walls. 'They're making good progress down there too,' said Jamie.

'It looks like it,' said Browning.

Jamie headed toward the first of a pair of stationary hoppers and clambered up to the cabin. Sliding into the shotgun seat, he had the driver go directly over the edge and make his way down the steep slope to S-3. The journey was short but bumpy as the hopper stepped confidently down the slope. A sudden movement in the river caught Jamie's eye, and he focused intently on the spot. There was nothing there now, but he was sure he had seen a movement... It must just have been a swirl or eddy.

The hopper reached the valley floor and moved onto the level terrace where the ride became much smoother and quickly ended beside the Leviathan. With a thank you to the driver, Jamie clambered down, smiling to himself.

Perched on a bough of a nearby tree were two of the great black birds that had become a fixture since S-3 had first landed. Their beaks shifted as the pair watched him move toward the Leviathan's hangar. As he disappeared from view, the two birds turned their gaze back to the hopper, watching it begin to climb steadily back up the slope.

Chapter 6

Base Primo

The travelator continued its steady journey. The first part of the trip had taken Steph away from the familiar and frequently bustling areas around the central control room. Then it continued through ever quieter places. She passed the step-off point for the concealed access door leading to the reserve control room. There, Celine and Lily were busy trying to find a solution to accessing Earth. She stayed on the travelator, journeying yet deeper into the base.

Just the whispered whir of the travelator broke the silence. Nothing moved ahead of her where the passageway stretched out into the distance. She glanced at her sleeve display then promptly sat and crossed her legs; there was a way to go before she reached her goal.

A dozen paces behind Steph was an armed man. She turned, caught his eye and pointed in the direction of travel. 'You may as well sit, there's a while before we reach our destination.'

'Yes, thank you, ma'am,' said Borland. He remained standing.

Earth in conflict, then Weeman killed, terror attacks on Leviathans and, finally, an extremist's frustrated attempt to seize a warbird. Humanity had shown it could never be really trusted to behave – there was always one more threat, one more madman. Consequently, the general now insisted Steph was the most precious resource he had, and she must be guarded. Captain Besinski had appointed his best men, and Borland, Ahmad and Earl now spelled one another as her constant shadow.

Steph had been very unhappy about it, had argued the threat was past, but the general had insisted. So, to ensure the guards could always be with her or get to her, she had enhanced their suit access permissions and controls. She liked all three of her minders but insisted during work they kept well back. Space was essential for her to think and, sometimes, say out loud things nobody should hear. Come breaks and meals, they always sat together. This was not a break, and her focus was only on the information flow displayed on her suit's sleeve.

Her upgraded suit delivered so much information, so fast. The system had not been designed for a human user, and it had taken some time to appreciate how it could even be possible to exploit the enhanced interface efficiently.

A tip she had been given by Weeman was that knowledge was layered. Some information could not be accessed out of sequence – she had to walk before she could run. Right now, she was just a little bit above crawling. The regular site plans for Primo were displayed on the arms of all her various science and engineering teams and were perfectly adequate for their needs as they spread out and worked methodically through the base. Her sleeve's security-enhanced access displayed details of yet more plans, more base. Now they were journeying along a route that did not display on regular suits.

This secret route was carrying them deeper into the mountain. It seemed to run parallel to the Grand Canal and corresponded with a puzzle that had attracted her attention elsewhere. The Grand Canal, through which all Primo's space traffic flowed, was very much in the public domain. There were countless viewing ports ranged along it, and many people now spent off-duty time watching for the various craft that came and went, almost all with no human involvement.

Right now, it was the length of the Grand Canal that intrigued her. The regular site plans that her teams were using to explore Primo showed the base exactly as they might expect, located between four and five miles in from the Canal's entrance. However, an observer craft surveying the Canal had determined its length as nearer twelve miles. One craft had travelled to the deepest point and reported that, beyond the five-mile mark, the hangars and viewports gave way, for a distance, to solid rock walls.

Then, as it journeyed on, closer to the deepest end, more viewing ports appeared, all tight shut. They and a series of sealed hangar-access doors showed dark and forbidding. Immediately beyond them the Grand Canal finally ended in a broad, blank end wall. None of this distant habitat appeared on any known site plans – there were simply no records of this location, no clue as to its purpose.

Steph had to keep all the activities of Primo progressing, but her most pressing job was to fix the armaments shortfall. Her upgraded suit was mostly silent on the matter, it's only reference to military hardware being the operating instructions for warbirds and the ability to enable other suits to pilot them. She had passed all that on to Captain Kingston and his trainee pilots.

It was a growing frustration for her. She could print-manufacture observer craft and the like at will. But nowhere could she find instruction codes to print warbirds – not a sign, nothing.

The warbirds they were now using had been hidden in a secret hangar close to the reserve control room, itself a secret place with doors only accessible to the wearers of suits with high-security clearance. Such hidden doorways only became visible and functional when the wearer of a high-security suit was in close proximity.

Now she needed to see what was hidden in the depths of Grand Canal, hoped that there she would find the answer to the weapons shortfall. It was her best hope.

Primo needed the warbirds urgently, and only when she had solved the weapons shortage would General Dower allow her time to consider finding Jamie.

Chapter 7

OPSYTHIA E.: BASE SECUNDO

Colonel MacMillan's arms were outstretched, his hands braced against the side walls of the open airlock. Fixed in position, he looked out through the observer's stern access and down onto the building site that was Base Secundo. He was impressed.

The crew, troops and engineering teams of P-3 had done a great job, ably assisted by the military compliment transferred from P-2 before it had gone on patrol in the Fold. An extra cohort of disciplined and trained people made a difference to any project. Here more than most.

He was oblivious to the eddies of wind curling into the airlock to tug against him. At last, something was going to plan.

Spread out below, he could make out all the base's key components. In the centre, a square building two stories high and each side one hundred paces in length, its flat roof edged all around by a parapet. He could just make out an access door set at the roof's centre, through which several people had just emerged.

Behind the building, two smaller single-storey structures were under construction. He knew one was a mini Gravdrive Power Unit, to energise the base, the other contained water tanks and their feed inlets, accessed from bore-holes drilled deep to reach liquid water far below ground.

Bots were streaming in and out of the building, ferrying in the stocks and equipment needed to make Secundo the self-sufficient command centre it would soon be. In front of the building was a great levelled area. Its purpose, once complete, was to be a landing pad for as many as three Leviathans at any one time.

Beyond the landing pad, print constructors were busy forming a defensive compound by erecting a boundary wall. It was nearly as high as the building it protected and replete with a parapeted firing step from where defenders could safely engage any attacker. A reinforced gatehouse offered the only terrestrial access point to the whole compound. He let out a laugh – back on Earth, its layout might have formed a big version of the classic desert outpost fort.

'Take us down, pilot,' he said into his collar-phone.

'Yes, sir.' The observer began to turn, the pilot setting up his run-in to the building's roof. As it turned, MacMillan got a clear view of the surrounds. Behind the construction site, the land rose quickly to snow-topped hills. To one side, the land was scoured by a series of rib-like trenches; he had no idea what had formed them. Perhaps they were old stream beds from a time before the planet had begun its big chill.

At the front, beyond the gates, the land sloped very gently down and away toward a broad, level plain. At the foot of the slope rested P-3, serving as a crew base and living quarters during the construction. He'd be happier once the landing pads within the perimeter were finished – they were very nearly done.

A pair of heavy-laden hoppers stepped away from P-3, moving steadily up the slope toward the base to deliver yet more equipment. As the turn continued, he saw the other side of the base – what had once been a river was now frozen. He'd read the reports: a block of water up to thirty feet thick and a hundred yards wide. It would once have presented an impossible watery barrier, now it was as solid as the land that bounded it. Like every other feature, it was sprinkled with a dusting of fresh snow.

The observer gently settled on the roof, just yards from the access door. MacMillan flipped his helmet away and immediately felt the cold air, sharp against his face. In that moment he understood exactly why all the construction crews had expressed disquiet at his choice for a base. The climate here was cold and unforgiving. Hard for his people but manageable, and Opsythia e. was the system's outer planet, so a Leviathan could shift into folded space very quickly after leaving the planet – strategically it was the better choice.

He didn't follow the science completely but had accepted Steph's explanation that local travel using gravdrive was safe everywhere. On the other hand, there was a massive backward energy release when any Fold-capable craft entered or left the Fold. When leaving the Fold, the energy discharged backward and dissipated into the Fold creating only a minor disruption in regular space, so craft were able to enter ordinary space quite close to a planet. However, for a craft entering the Fold, it was very different – it needed to be both beyond the orbit of the outermost planet and above or below the system's orbital plane. Safety mechanisms prevented any craft from folding until that was so, otherwise folding risked disturbing planetary orbits.

'Thank you, pilot, I won't be flying again today.'

'Very good, sir,' sounded the reply in his collar-phone.

MacMillan stepped onto the rooftop and headed for the access door and the heart of his new command, strategically placed exactly at the Orion–Perseus junction: Base Secundo.

Chapter 8

Osarus c.

Standing quietly on the bridge, Jamie watched the screen. The split-display setting allowed him to see both downstream toward the coastal plain and upstream toward the high savannah. The defensive barriers were complete. Both walls had gateways flanked by stubby towers set close to their riverbank ends. The gates were open, a single marine standing guard at each. Everything seemed quiet. He looked round to see Ossie come through from the navigation room.

'Sir, we need to talk,' said Ossie.

'Go on, what's up?'

'Well, you know I'm not hopeful of our ever getting off this rock?' he said, closing on Jamie.

'I do. I'm still hoping you might come up with something though.'

'No chance with S-3 I'm afraid, sir. It will never fly again. If we even try to take off, I believe the hull will split open, end to end. The gravdrive would blow, and anyone on board would die.'

'You've said before. So where does that leave us, Ossie? What are our options?'

'Well, it leaves us stuck here on the ground. We talked earlier about getting food crops growing – the Leviathan's stores can't sustain us forever. The agriculture team's ready to go. I think you should allocate land for food production. I'd suggest the strip of land from here up to the head of the valley where it lets out onto the savannah.'

'Agreed. Leave downstream for now. Whatever's in the thicket down there is best left at arm's length. It stays off-limits until we've time to work out what it is and how to deal with it. What else have you got?'

'We recognise S-3 will never fly again, but Martha and her engineering team have been nosing about in the Folddrive Power Unit. She says it's actually not so badly damaged. She thinks it can be repaired, that the main problem's the hull.'

'Okay, so how does that help us?'

'It's just a theory, and I've a lot of numbers to crunch, but I might have something.'

'Go on, what?'

'This Leviathan carries a small sampler and two observers in its hangars. All are planetary-system vehicles with no folddrive capacity,' said Ossie, the slightest sense of thrill spilling among his words.

'Yes,' said Jamie. 'We know that already. How does it help us?'

'I'm going to need some time to work this through, but there's a slight chance I could shift S-3's folddrive into the small sample craft. It would be a jury rig, and not guaranteed to work, but maybe, just maybe, we could get it into the Fold.'

Jamie looked sharply at Ossie. 'You could? Maybe? But we couldn't transport four hundred and twenty people in that craft; it's far too small.'

'No, sir. I don't think we need to. In fact, I'm not sure how long the craft would hold together under the huge stress generated by travelling in the Fold – it's not built for that. A few minutes, maybe a few hours, a day... I've no idea.'

'Come on, Ossie, I need a plan with legs. Why wreck our biggest serviceable craft for no reason?'

'That's just it, sir. There is a reason. You know the Leviathans all report their positions to Primo by periodically releasing beacons that return to our home system and deliver a position report. I just might be able to set that up.'

'You can do that? Get a signal back to Primo?'

'In theory, maybe. But its fraught with problems, starting with: Can I shift S-3's folddrive? Even then, can we propel the small sample craft into the Fold? And will it hold together long enough to launch the position beacon?'

'If there's a chance, we have to go for it,' said Jamie. For just a moment the weight on his shoulders eased.

Ossie gave a little shrug. 'There's more. The sampler will need its existing Gravdrive Power Unit for its regular function and propulsion. So, I'll need to rig the folddrive up with another power source.'

'You have one?'

'Two. Well, it'll take two. I'm going to need to strip out both the observers' gravdrives, hook them in as a substitute power source to operate the folddrive. It's all we've got.'

'Seriously? That will leave us here with no aerial capability other than drones.' The elation of moments before drained from Jamie.

'That's not the end,' said Ossie. 'If all of those bits work, and we get it into the Fold, I have no idea how long the position beacon might take to reach its destination.'

'What do you mean?' said Jamie.

'Even if everything else works, it still might not be travelling relatively fast on entry to the Fold. That speed is significant, the beacon has its own mini folddrive and power source that's just sufficient to keep it in the Fold. But the starting speed and its acceleration thereafter will be determined by the speed of the launching craft. It may mean the difference between a beacon arriving back at Primo in a week or a year, or maybe much longer. I just don't know.'

'I see...' Jamie stared hard at the screen, as he weighed the risk. Finally, he turned to Ossie. 'If there's any chance of getting our position back to Primo, we have to take it, no question.'

Ossie's normally serious face broke into a broad smile. 'Thank you. Thank you. I'll get on it right away. I'm not even sure it will work yet, or how long it could take to execute.'

'Do your best. I want it to work, but you know what, Ossie? If you can just get it away, it will give the crew hope that one day, some day, whether in a month or a decade, a craft will come for us. What resources are you going to need?'

'Today, nothing. It's only a theoretical possibility at this stage. I'll get three or four of my science team working on it, and with your permission, I'll ask Martha Solomon to have engineering do a discreet appraisal of what would be involved in actually shifting S-3's folddrive. Even that's a massive task. It may be beyond us, so we'll keep the whole thing quiet for now.'

'Agreed. Let's see how it all stacks up before we go live. What's next?' said Jamie, suddenly enthused.

'Now we have the defensive structures in place and a grasp of our immediate surrounds, I'd like permission to send science teams out with your hopper exploration patrols. It will be useful to start analysing some of the geological anomalies to confirm the signs of resources picked up by the aerial scans we've been doing.'

'Of course. I'll tell Baz Browning to include your people on future field trips. It's Lieutenant Grieves who leads them out. Anywhere of particular interest?'

'Well, on the far side of the high savannah, where it meets the foothills beyond, there are some interesting readings, could be ores worth mining.'

'I think Baz has another patrol going in that direction pretty soon. Best warn your science teams the patrols will last two or three days, and they'll be roughing it all the way.'

Chapter 9

Base Primo

Steph watched the passageway's end wall get steadily closer as the travelator ran its course. She got to her feet moments before it stopped. Glancing over her shoulder, she saw Borland; he was still holding the wary protective stance he had maintained throughout.

The morning had been a long stretch, and it had been some time since they had last passed anything of note. This was the third long tunnel they had explored. So very remote, it must have been dug for a purpose; its travelator did not run for no reason. Now was the time to find its secret.

The previous tunnels had not been productive. She had hoped this one would be the one to lead to the end of the Grand Canal with its lonely hangars and sealed viewing ports. Instead, a blank wall. *Why?*

Stepping off the travelator, she approached the wall. With every step closer she hoped that her high-status suit would act as it did when she approached the reserve control room's entrance and trigger the revelation of an otherwise concealed access door. Nothing happened.

Her hands traced the wall's surface. Smooth, consistent, nothing to see, nothing to feel. She scanned about – still nothing. She tried one side wall then the other, even moving further back down the passage, always drawing a blank, completing the whole search several times, to no avail.

'Can I help, ma'am?' said Borland.

'Thanks, but I don't think so, I'm looking for an entrance. Maybe something like the one leading to the reserve control room. You know, the door outline that appears when an authorised suit approaches that spot in the wall.'

'I do, ma'am. But sorry, that's above my pay grade. I thought you had the top access. If not you, then who? Maybe there is no door.'

'Yes, I have high-access permissions. Weeman didn't say he'd held anything back. But you know, it's not that simple – some things can only be accessed once another thing has been done. It's frustrating when you don't know what that first thing is.'

'Like levels in some computer game?' said Borland.

'That's it. For ages, I bang my head against a brick wall, then there's a breakthrough, and suddenly it's obvious. Simple. One, two, three, and we're off again. Great, once solved, but frustrating initially.'

'I'll bet, ma'am.'

'So, how do we get to the next level?' said Steph, stepping across the width of the tunnel end while stroking her sleeve. She tutted in frustration. 'Weeman, what didn't you tell me? Come on. Where is it?' In frustration, she slapped the wall. Nothing.

Taking a step back toward the end of the travelator, she was brought to an abrupt halt by a shout.

'Stop, ma'am! Stop there!' Borland took a couple of paces toward her and pointed up toward the passageway roof. 'Look. Above you.'

Steph looked up to review a plain and uniform roof. 'There's nothing there. What do you see?'

'You've passed it. Take a step back, ma'am. Just a small one.'

Steph did as Borland advised, all the time staring up at the roof.

'There, ma'am! See it?'

'I do. I see it. Well spotted, Borland!'

'What is it for?' Involuntarily, Borland stepped closer to Steph, and together they stared up to where the faintest circle shimmered in the roof above them.

'That, my friend, is something most people never see. It's the focus-face of a gravlift. It'll take hold of you and lift you above it.'

'Ma'am?'

'Exactly the same as we have on the craft for lifting and lowering people and kit to and from the ground. It's the same principle but smaller and fixed in the building. Clever. Think of an elevator – activate it, and you can be pulled as high as it's calibrated to go.'

'You can't go through stone roof.'

'No, that's not roof. I'll bet it's an image projection, a holographic disguise. It's just been finished to look like the regular tunnel roof when inactive. Blends in perfectly.'

'Sure does,' said Borland.

Steph took a step to the side, and the light ring immediately faded away, gone, blended into the ceiling sameness.

'Now all I need to do is work out how to operate it.'

***

Looking down from the top of the reserve control room's Goliath, Lily could see the two linguists who had given up their own access to the Goliath to accommodate her and Celine. The pair were working quietly, dotting between the cluster of adjacent LPAs they had been allocated.

She saw them cast occasional furtive glances up to where she and Celine stood.

'Come on,' said Celine, guiding her away from the edge toward a central spot where they could not be seen. 'Let's check one more time.'

'I think we're stuck, aren't we?' said Lily.

They both consulted their sleeves and further information displayed below them in the Goliath. With every swirl of its lights, the magnitude of the problem they faced grew.

The Goliath had taken in all the information gathered during the recent test in Earth's atmosphere. It now displayed that data exactly as it might otherwise have displayed the galaxy. This time with Earth at the centre. Far off to one side, the moon. Surrounding Earth in layer upon layer of light spots were the countless signals that represented the detectable components of Earth's debris field.

'What you can see is only a fraction of the total. We have only the targets large enough to be detected at a distance. Goliath's own predictions suggest, close up, there will be a thousand scraps, golf-ball-sized or less, for each bigger one we can see here,' said Celine.

'I know, and I've had Goliath programme umpteen trial routes through the mess. It's given us nothing. There's no safe way through the big stuff, never mind the stuff we can't see.'

Celine knelt and tapped a finger on the clear surface. 'It's certain that we can't break through this barrier, but we must. What do you think, Lily? Any brain waves?'

Lily shrugged. 'I'm sorry, Celine, right now I've got nothing.'

'Me neither. We've got the biggest processor you can imagine, but this is one big problem. It's the random nature of each orbit in the debris field. Unless you know every single orbit, you can never be sure of not taking a hit, and you can't know every orbit because most objects are too small to observe.'

'All I've got right now is… maybe we could build a stronger hull shield of some sort. I don't know what material… Maybe Goliath could come up with that?'

'Well, let's try it. You put in the question, and meanwhile, I'll have to let the general know just how dark this problem is looking.' Celine stood and gazed down into the Goliath for a long moment. She sighed and left.

***

Borland packed the remains of lunch into his rucksack as Steph got to her feet and once again stepped beneath the gravlift portal. It glistened and shimmered in response to her proximity. Staring intently at the layers of information displaying on her sleeve, she stroked and tapped repeatedly. Eventually she made an exasperated tutting sound. Countless attempts had brought nothing.

'Is there a code of some sort?' said Borland.

She nodded. 'Probably, but I have no idea what it is. A complete blank. All I want it to do is lift me up and—' Her words vanished in a swirling column of fluorescence as she was carried up by the gravlift. Next moment, she found herself in a dark tunnel whose lighting flickered into action on her appearance.

Steph stood in silence, watching as the string of tunnel lights fired one after another. They ran off into the distance, illuminating another long passageway that sloped steadily down and away. Beneath the lights, the tunnel was empty and still.

'What the hell just happened?' she asked herself out loud. 'All I did was say—' A distant movement caught her attention. For just a moment she felt a surge of fear before laughing. She'd seen this show before, the day Weeman first took her to the reserve control room. Somewhere ahead, bots had stirred and were now emerging into the tunnel to resume a long-paused cleaning routine. She felt a slight movement in the air as ventilation kicked in, and Steph knew things were as they ought to be.

Borland's voice reached her through the portal that still glistened active. She shouted back down to him. 'I'm good, Borland. Everything's okay. I don't know what I did, but the gravlift just lifted me up.'

Borland rose through the portal and, holding his weapon at the ready, stepped clear and into the tunnel. For the slightest of moments, they looked at one another in surprise. Then Borland stepped beyond her, suspiciously eyeing the distant movements coming up the slope toward them.

'It's okay, they're bots, cleaning.'

Borland nodded while maintaining a wary watch. 'What happened, ma'am? How did you get it working?'

'I'm not sure I did anything.'

'Well, I sure as hell didn't... begging your pardon, ma'am.'

Steph laughed. 'Well, we must have a friend somewhere, something certainly got us up.' She stared intently at the gravlift interface as it shimmered again then stilled. 'Did you see that?'

'Ma'am?'

'The gravlift just activated. I think it's voice-activated. I said up, and it shimmered.' Both watched as the interface shimmered again.

'I wonder,' said Steph stepping onto the interface. 'Down.'

She dropped smoothly to the lower passage. Then with scarcely a pause, she issued an up order that swiftly returned her to the upper level and Borland.

'Definitely voice-activated. Clever system. It's learned our language and uses the easiest instructions for activation. Up and down. No code at all!'

Testing quickly revealed Borland's voice would not activate the gravlift. 'I see the security measure; only I, or more likely my suit grade, can operate the gravlift.'

'Whatever's here must be pretty important then,' said Borland.

'Must be. Let's go see.' Steph touched her sleeve and was pleased to find the routine instruction codes worked here. The travelator started up and travelled away down the incline. 'Shall we?' she said, looking at Borland.

'You're the boss, ma'am. But this time, I need to take point.'

Steph tried to object and for the first time found the soldier in Borland would not give way to her. She waved him on and stepped behind.

Within moments, they were beyond the first of a line of bots that whirred along uncaring of the passing humans, intent only on sucking up generations of dust.

Steph edged forward until she was close behind Borland, nudging at his broad frame to get an equal spot on the travelator. All the while, she studied her arm and the newly appeared layout plans – different plans.

Time passed. Twenty minutes into the journey and no features had broken the monotony of the tunnel ride.

'Up ahead, ma'am, the tunnel's opening out.'

'I see it.'

The roof level rose, and the walls widened as the travelator carried them into a chamber. Many doors and access arches branched off to either side, the space must once have been a bustling location. Today, it was still and empty, save a couple of distant bots.

'This'll do us,' said Steph, stepping off the travelator. Borland followed, and a moment later, the travelator stopped. In the stillness, they looked about. Through some doorways, Steph could make out a scattering of LPAs, all clouded grey and lifeless.

'It looks similar to the layout of our own hub,' said Borland.

'It seems so,' said Steph, while continuing to consult her sleeve display and its newly revealed layout plans. 'I'm thinking there should be a control room that way. Let's go see.' Steph set off.

Borland at once overtook her. 'I'll take point again, ma'am. Just keep behind me, please.'

Steph frowned slightly but didn't argue. Borland made for the doorway Steph had indicated. As the door slid open, he stepped in, weapon raised, sweeping it in an arc about the chamber.

'And there it is,' said Steph. Another Goliath, cold grey and deathly still. While Borland completed his search, she busied herself activating the Goliath. A few flickers told of success, but she knew it would take some time to format for action. They'd come back to it later.

'Let's look about while we wait for that to come to life.'

Borland gave up trying to lead as Steph hurried from the control room. He followed on, weapon still raised but now accepting that there was probably no imminent threat.

Steph headed in the direction of what she assumed would be great docking chambers and viewing ports overlooking the Grand Canal. The viewing ports were there but sealed tight shut. What lay beyond them was a mystery. The pair got on a travelator and journeyed deeper still. Everywhere, everything was sealed.

'It's like a total lockdown, ma'am.'

'It is. Strange.'

'Why would they have abandoned this?'

'No idea. Though once, Weeman told me that long ago the others of his people had gone away. Maybe they didn't need the space anymore, but that seems a bit lame.'

Borland was suddenly silent, staring ahead into the tunnel, focusing every faculty on something he wasn't even sure he'd heard.

'Borland, are you okay?'

He raised a finger to his lips before cupping an ear and pointing in their direction of travel. Then he waved her off the travelator. A few moments later, it stopped, and in the motionless silence, what Borland imagined he'd heard became sharp reality.

The distant sounds of a workshop were echoing up the tunnel.

'Someone's up ahead, ma'am.'

'Or *something*. We'd better go see.'

They stepped back onto the travelator, with Borland again on point. Journeying on, the noise grew steadily louder. Further ahead in the tunnel, flashes and sparks could be seen, accompanied by occasional crashes.

'I guess they're not worried about surprise visitors,' said Borland.

The trail of overhead tunnel lights continued to flicker into life ahead of them, marking their progress as the travelator moved them closer to the locus. As the noise grew, Steph and Borland again stepped off, and the travelator stopped. They walked on cautiously as the last of the tunnel's roof lights flickered on ahead.

At the tunnel's end, they peered out onto a nightmare scene. Great streaks of light and the glowing white of molten metal illuminated shadowing hulks and wrecked structures. Laser cutters, bright like the sun, carved away at sections of hull in what might have been some nightmare battlefield.

They edged forward into the vast chamber's mouth, and suddenly proper lights began to flash on.

'Hell, we've triggered the chamber's lighting system,' said Steph, backing into the tunnel. From there, they watched while organised lighting kicked in, bringing order to the scene.

'It's a breaker's yard,' said Borland.

'It's a big, big breaker's yard. And you know, I think, automated. Look, there's no one, nothing, here. It was functioning in the dark because machines don't need light. That's our medium,' said Steph.

'Why though? What's it for?'

'I'd guess it's reclaiming raw materials. Look, just look at it!' Steph stepped into the chamber and Borland hurried beside her.

Now properly lit, the sense of threat had evaporated, but the imposing activity remained. Stretching into the distance were the hulls of perhaps twenty giant sample craft. Huge constructions, second in size only to the Leviathans. Grounded here, they were out of their element, stranded in the biggest enclosed space either visitor had ever seen.

The laser-cutting arms swooped down from the roof to steadily slice away sections from the condemned samplers. The product of the slicing was then gathered and cleared by an army of bots scurrying back and forth across the floor.

'Helmets up, I think. Some molten metals and synthetics might produce noxious gases,' said Steph. She located the course of the travelator, and they stepped on. Running close to the side wall and well clear of the busying bots, it carried them the length of the chamber. There, the travelator continued into another tunnel. Steph decided to carry on.

After a few minutes, she eased her helmet back into its collar housing and looked excitedly at Borland. 'That was something.'

'It was, ma'am. But why? And where did all those craft come from?'

'It's clearly a recycling plant. Why? We've probably used up a lot of Primo's stored resources building the Leviathan fleet. There are automated mining craft out gathering fresh resources all the time, but you know, I think this is simple efficiency. Eventually, every craft will wear out. What better way to scrap something than recycle it into fresh construction materials? Our recent construction project has probably just triggered this process.'

'Up ahead, ma'am. Another chamber coming.'

They stepped off the travelator as more lighting kicked in to show a familiar scene. Smooth walls, more bots busying about after their long rest. And a row of viewing ports and hangar access doors; each one was sealed tight.

'I wonder what's behind them,' said Steph.

Like the ones they had encountered close to the dormant control room, these hangars appeared locked and showed no signs of opening. After a few attempts, it was clear to Steph she was not going to make progress.

'Look over here,' said Borland from beside an archway.

Steph joined him and almost cooed with joy. 'Borland, you're a star. A real star.' She hurried through the archway into the room beyond, stopping beside a regular-sized LPA; it was active and flashing happily away to itself. Steph circled the device, studying its display, then tentatively began to stroke her sleeve, interrogating the LPA.

She looked up and smiled to Borland. 'This has activated to control the breaker's yard process. Just like we thought, it's kicked in now to start replenishing Primo's stocks of materials that we've been running down. I can see there are many more old sample crafts sitting in docks just waiting to be scrapped. Scores of them. Hundreds! We're near the end of the Grand Canal now, all those sealed hangars we saw from the Canal, they're full of retired samplers. A whole fleet of them. Waiting there to be scrapped when needed!'

'Can you open the hangars?'

'I hope I can from here. But no need today. We know what's happening now. It's been a long day. I think we'd better get back,' she said, leaving the LPA and making for the travelator.

They retraced their journey, helmeting again to pass through the breaker's yard, before stepping off near the dormant Goliath.

'Let's just check if it's active yet,' she said.

One glance told her it was a long way from resetting. Disappointed, she accepted that probing its secrets would be the work of another day.

Chapter 10

Opsythia e.: Base Secundo

Colonel MacMillan stepped aside as two bots whirred into his square-shaped control room set at the very heart of the base. Between them, the bots were ferrying in an LPA, heading for the centre of the space where another LPA had already been installed. He was happy to see the first was displaying the myriad of confused buzzing lights that was their formatting sequence. Shortly, the LPAs would settle to show the repeating lines of suspended light spots of an LPA ready for action.

A row of regular workstations was already in place, and each wall was equipped with a screen that presented the corresponding external view. MacMillan was now quite used to an architecture that prioritised displays over external windows. He glanced up at the unsettling ceiling view where screens had been fitted to display a three-sixty-degree perspective of the rooftop. He couldn't see the central access door so guessed that doubled as the housing for the rooftop cameras.

Outside, it was morning and the sun shone bright but cold through the cloudless sky. He knew the cold was cruel, for all the brightness in the atmosphere, but he had to admit it was preferable to the bitter darkness that closed so quickly with the sunset. The night before, he had ventured onto the base's flat roof to experience the dark. Almost at once, he'd been forced to close his helmet against the cutting chill.

Most of the crew and work teams had opted to stay overnight down on the plain, comfortable within the warming environs of P-3. Each morning, they ferried up in a series of observer craft shuttle runs. A handful of hardier military types had opted for a jog up. He gave a little laugh to himself, hoping the athletes had made the most of it. Soon, P-3 would be moving up to the base's now ready landing pad. From tomorrow on, Secundo would be home to all.

Chapter 11

Primo Main Base

'So, there you have it,' said Steph. She crossed her legs, leaned back slightly in her chair, and gazed around the leadership team gathered in the general's office.

'Thank you, Steph. That's a huge discovery. The immediate question has to be: first impressions, do you think there may be more warbirds down there somewhere?'

'There was no obvious sign, general. On the other hand, once I got into this new complex, its mapping became available to my suit. It's vast, every bit as big as up here. I'm suggesting we now differentiate. Rebrand up here as Primo Main Base and the new-found complex at the inner end of the Grand Canal as Primo Deep. I've begun to study it, but who knows what I'll turn up. After all, even the warbirds' hangar we found up here was off-plan.'

'Getting in and out of this Primo Deep is going to be very hard if it's only your suit that will operate the gravlift access,' said Celine.

'I know. I've tried to locate an override but nothing yet. For now, it seems controls rest only in the upgraded suits Weeman issued to me, the general and Jamie…'

Celine frowned slightly, kicking herself for directing Steph's thoughts toward her lost friend.

'I don't understand what the Deep is actually for. Why is it separated from our section up here?' said Lily from where she stood behind Celine's seat.

Steph shrugged. 'We have no idea. Weeman did say that once there were many more of his people here. They went away for reasons he didn't share. His team was tasked with maintaining the system until the others returned.'

'But they never came back, and here we all are,' said Brigadier Smith-Brown.

'Well, Steph, I want exploration teams in Primo Deep now. I'll have Besinski detail soldiers to participate, and you'll need to allocate science teams,' said Dower.

'It's going to take up a lot of my time – I can't be a full-time gatekeeper at the gravlift,' said Steph.

'I know, we'll muster a full team, send everyone in as one, then leave them to it. Let's set a regular rendezvous time when you or I will turn up to operate the gravlift.'

'How big a team?'

'You know what, I know there's a lot of detail still to uncover up here at Main Base, but any big finds are going to be made in the Deep. If there are any more weapons, anything special, it'll likely be down there. I want you to recall all the search teams up here, shift everyone you can into the Deep. Let's give it a big push.'

'There's still a lot to learn up here,' said Steph.

'Yes, but we need the big finds now. If there are any left to discover, they'll be in the Deep. You have twenty-four hours to organise and then we'll be marching in.'

'How many of these retired sample craft do you think there are?' said Lily.

'I've no idea. It appears, once they have reached a certain age or level of wear and tear, they're retired. From what I've seen, most look perfectly operational, just you might not trust them to do a circuit around a spiral arm. They are simply held in storage until their materials need to be recycled, which is what has just started up because of our previous activities. Based on the number of sealed hangars our external survey found within the Grand Canal, there could be hundreds. But who knows what's in every hangar? As the general hopes, there may be more warbirds, or something else altogether.'

'And we'll find out soon enough. Steph, every effort now must be put toward exploring the Deep. Find me something, anything, to reinforce our defences.' Dower stood, drawing the meeting to an end.

Chapter 12

Primo Main Base

Steph sat cross-legged on the travelator, her eyes fixed on her sleeve display. Several days of routine link-ups at the Deep's gravlift had established a new working pattern. Now she cherished the journey time, filling it with undisturbed data analysis. Behind her stood Borland, ever watchful. Today's trip back from the gravlift had been interrupted by an excited call from the reserve control room. Could she meet with Celine and Lily ASAP?

Steph stood and stepped off the travelator just as it passed the hidden entrance to the reserve control room. Borland followed her. As they approached, sensors detected their suit permissions and the doorway appeared. They were quickly inside and at the Goliath.

'What's the problem?' said Steph, climbing the steps to join the two women on the Goliath's top.

Lily was almost bubbling with enthusiasm; Celine controlled.

'I think we, well actually, Lily, may have come up with a way of opening up the atmosphere. We need your opinion,' said Celine.

'Go on,' said Steph.

Celine glanced toward Lily. 'It was your idea – tell Steph.'

'Well, I've been thinking about something that happened yesterday. I went with my father to the Deep's gravlift. He was doing the scheduled link-up with the Deep teams and the travelator journey was a chance for us to have a catch-up.'

'I know, the general and I take turns on that duty.'

'Yes, well, while he was operating it, I couldn't get in.'

'Sorry, what do you mean?' Steph looked puzzled. 'It should have transported you with no problem.'

'Oh yes, it did. I mean, while it was active, I couldn't move things into the gravlift's beam. It just wouldn't let me. The vortex was like a solid barrier.'

'Yes, I know. Otherwise, if you were able to step into it you might end up with half a leg up and the rest of your body still down. What did you do? Why did you even try?'

'Oh, he wanted to see if we could speed things up. I was pushing a metal rod into the beam while he kept it active. I couldn't make a dent.'

'Of course not. The general didn't tell me you'd been trying that. Quite pointless. So, what's the big excitement about?'

Lily took a step closer to Steph. 'That's just it. Nothing can get through the beam. Just think if we could get a gravlift in Earth's atmosphere we might create a shielded channel right down. We could reopen access to Earth. We could get your craft down with the second virus to neutralise the first.'

'Come on, Lily, a gravlift's a tight beam. I've no idea how far one could reach, but at best it's likely to be miles, and there are thousands of miles to penetrate through Earth's atmosphere. That'll never work.'

Celine frowned slightly. 'You're right, Steph; I'm with you on that, but Lily's thinking big. At least hear her out. And frankly, we've got nothing else right now.'

'Lily?' said Steph.

Lily took a deep breath and marshalled her thoughts. 'Well, this is just a thought plan right now. We've still to crunch the numbers, and I think we'll need your contribution with some of it. But just imagine. Every sample craft has a gravlift. If we could increase the beam's power and modify the focus, broaden the beam, to something huge... wide enough for a craft to enter. I don't know, a quarter-mile, maybe a half-mile wide – a vast footprint. Direct all the craft's energy into its gravlift beam, and I'll bet we could create a wide tube many miles long.'

'Okay, I'll go along with your argument for now. How does that help us?'

'Imagine a stack of sample craft positioned in Earth's atmosphere. Each one precisely positioned miles beneath the next, creating a column that nothing could penetrate. It would open a narrow navigable passage to Earth.'

'I see. Clever idea, Lily… in theory. But it would need a lot of things to be just right. Can we reset the beam's power and focus? Can we position one craft above the other and keep them exactly stationary within a gravlift beam without that beam moving the craft below? The construct would be intrinsically unstable.'

'I thought about that. We'd need to adjust the beam's strength to get the extra breadth so the whole craft beneath was protected within the beam of the craft above, to shield it from space debris, but position that lower craft exactly at the base point of the above craft's gravlift. That way it wouldn't be subject to any downward pressure that might distort the tube. Think of it like a great virtual tower of building bricks. It could work. Couldn't it?'

Celine and Lily watched intently as Steph pursed her lips. There was an intense silence as she thought the idea through.

'Maybe. If we have enough sample craft in storage, and that's a big if. And maybe, if they're all functional and we can recalibrate their gravlifts, and we don't know if that's possible either. And maybe, if we can remotely control a fleet of hundreds of massive sample craft operating in close order, because we don't have nearly enough pilots. That's a lot of maybes.' She looked to Celine and Lily. 'A *lot* of maybes.'

The sparkle dropped from Lily's eyes. Celine put a consoling arm round her shoulder.

Steph smiled. 'But those "maybes" are a lot better than anything else we've got. A long shot, but right now, we've nothing to lose. We three might just make it work. Let's give it a try!' She reached out her arms and embraced Celine and Lily, and they all began to talk excitedly about the challenge ahead.

'So, forget sleep. You two, run the numbers now.

'Lily, I'm allocating you a sampler, pilot and tech team. Let's see what you can do – see how wide and how long you can set a gravlift beam? Find out how many craft you'd need to create the tube.

'Celine, I need you to create a program to control all the samplers as one.

'I'm going to start breaking out the mothballed sample craft from the Deep and move those that function properly into orbit above Nine, ready for you both. In two days, I want to be heading for Earth, no later. Any resources you need, just say.'

Chapter 13

Osarus c.: The High Savannah

From his vantage point on the slope above the campsite, Lieutenant Grieves looked down to the busying geologists who'd been seconded to his detail from Ossie's science team. Scanning further out across the savannah, he traced a meandering tree-line that charted the course of a river as it flowed out from the foothills near where he sat, past their encampment, and then ran away over the flatlands. About halfway across the savannah, that now distant tree-line merged with another, marking where two tributaries joined. Then as a single strand, the trees continued to trace the broader flow of water that trailed away beyond his sight toward the distant gap in the hills marking the valley where S-3 lay.

He'd carefully read Browning's reports from the various explorer drones that flew out across the savannah every day. They'd made no sightings of big fauna, but occasional life signs had been identified – from beaten tracks through scrubby undergrowth to pathways worn into riverbanks, though no actual sightings of big animals, yet.

The signs of bushfires were ubiquitous. Some small local affairs, and in other areas, broad expanses of the once dry browned grasses were reduced to char-blackened stubs. It seemed their immediate location had been lucky to have avoided a fire.

Dry as things were now, the savannah grasses hadn't grown up in dry ground. Ossie's scientists had speculated on the nature of the weather patterns. Earlier today, the meteorologists among them had passed on a message that rain was anticipated. Lots of rain, soon. As if on cue, he felt the slightest of breezes against his skin and turned his face into it. This was a change – what had been a distant cloud-line had suddenly puffed and filled. Black clouds were rolling in fast, and the wind was suddenly picking up – time to move.

Grieves stood. At the bottom of the slope, he could see Corporal Archer had almost finished packing away the camp. The two geologists, Fifi Russell and her assistant Pete, were loading the last of their samples into the two hoppers' storage holds. He opened his collar-phone channel. 'Okay, team, it's time to head back.' He jogged the short distance down to the waiting hoppers.

'All aboard, people. We must go now,' said Grieves. As if to emphasise his point a few heavy drops of rain fell about them.

Grieves climbed into the lead hopper followed by Fifi. Corporal Archer clambered into the second hopper with Pete. Hatches open, all four looked about the lonely site one last time. Then Grieves pulled his hatch shut, put in a call to S-3 announcing their departure and, with a wistful glance at the rolling savannah before them, set his hopper in motion.

Almost at once, they were stepping down the riverbank, at its steepest now with the dry season at its peak and the river at its lowest point. The trees lining both sides of the river around the fording point were similar to the ones he'd passed beneath on the day of S-3's landing. Occasionally at night, he would wake up sweating and fending off the gaping maw of the serpent that had attacked that day. Its fangs and drool so real he fancied he could still almost touch it, even once he'd awakened.

Today, Grieves felt no concerns; several times in the past couple of days, while the geologists had gathered their samples, he'd paused above the fording point to scan the adjacent treetops for signs of undesirable residents, but there were none. Here, at least, there were no serpents.

Once down the bank, he struck out across the river. At no point was it deeper than a man's knee. Both hoppers crossed and climbed the far bank without incident.

With the river crossing behind them, he set an autopilot course across the savannah, eased back in his seat and smiled at Fifi.

'It's a straight-line journey now. A bit over four hours, and we'll reach the other tributary, just above its confluence with the one we just crossed. Once over that, we follow the river downstream to base. Home before dark.'

'It sounds easy. Why didn't we just cross the river once, downstream of the tributaries' confluence? Surely crossing only once would have been quicker.'

'The main river is deeper, and the only safe crossing point is way downstream at the entrance to the valley where all the rocks are gathered. As the rain gets going, the level will rise, and we don't know by how much or how quickly. Easier to cross the two tributaries as quickly as possible. Then be safe home for sure.'

They settled down to discuss the findings of their trip. As the hoppers moved steadily across the savannah, the initial drops of falling rain increased by stages to become a constant deluge.

Chapter 14

Osarus c.: S-3

Ossie let out a long sigh, and at last dared to believe his plan could really work. He looked out from the Leviathan's open hangar, peering through the rain toward their small sample craft. It was surrounded by scientists and engineers, all oblivious to the falling rain. They were clapping each other on the back, and a ragged cheer rose when they spotted Ossie. Martha Solomon detached from the crowd and joined him.

'Two down, one to go,' said Martha. 'It's all looking good.' She slipped an arm around Ossie's shoulder and hugged him in tight. 'All looking good!'

Ossie couldn't deny it. A sense of cautious optimism was definitely spreading. It had taken a lot of planning and much more sweat and tears, but it was shaping up.

First, Martha's engineers had disconnected the folddrive from its charred housing and wrecked power source deep inside the Leviathan's Folddrive Power Unit. The bots had objected, frequently trying to reassemble the engineers' disassembly efforts. Once he'd had the bots excluded, things had gone better.

The team used hoppers to transport the folddrive from the bowels of the Leviathan to the sampler's starboard hangar – it had been a tight squeeze, but they'd got in every part they needed, eventually. They'd left the greater part behind – the huge encasement shielding that protected life on board from the deadly emissions of an active folddrive. This was to be an unmanned venture, no need for any excess load, no need for shielding.

He'd tried to interact with the excluded bots, tried to engage their programming. Whether it had worked or not he didn't know. What he did know was, once one of the sampler's own bots had chanced on the disassembled folddrive in its hangar, it had gone to work and was quickly joined by others from the Leviathan.

Suddenly, the bots were assembling the folddrive, faster than the hoppers could deliver the sections. Nudging and shuffling, welding and connecting sections of the whole back into the one that it had been, then waiting impatiently for hoppers to move heavier pieces into place before resuming their labours. Man and machine working with a single goal that was reached more quickly than any had dared hope.

Elsewhere, set tightly into the corner of the portside hangar was the gravdrive unit they'd extracted from one of the observer craft – that powerless hulk now rested a little distance downstream.

He'd calculated, at the very least, two gravdrive units would be required to power the Leviathan's folddrive, even for a little while. All that was needed now was for Jamie to berth the second observer in the port hangar. There was just enough room left there for a good pilot to manoeuvre it in beside the gravdrive they'd just positioned. The team would hook them together and link them to the folddrive in the starboard hangar and then, in theory, there would be enough power to activate the newly installed folddrive. In theory…

'I'm happy as I can be that the folddrive is functional. We can't test it, but it is reassembled as it was originally,' said Ossie.

'And the bots finally stopped tweaking and fiddling. They must have decided it's functional too. Now, come on, you,' said Martha, letting her arm slide from Ossie's shoulder to hook through his arm, and with a broad smile, she led him through the rain toward the craft. They pushed past the little throng that had gathered round the craft's rear passenger airlock door.

Inside the airlock was a piston-like ram. It had been constructed from materials harvested from S-3. In front of the piston rested a position beacon. The size of a camper van, square, squat and, today, quite benign. The beacon had been taken from a store deep in the Leviathan's bowels. Now it lay ready to be launched into the Fold through the outer airlock door – a very tight fit.

When it launched into the Fold, its own in-built mini folddrive would activate to sustain the beacon in the Fold – such miniaturisation was for unmanned journeys only. Its use entailed the release of raw power, and the absence of the enormous layers of dense shielding found around a regular folddrive installation was an impossible threat. Any lifeforms that had the misfortune to be in the vicinity would be shredded from the inside out.

Ossie gave an involuntary shiver – he had engineered a device that was at once life-saving messenger and inescapable killer.

'It's all set,' said Martha. 'Just as you planned. Once the small sample craft is travelling in the Fold, the airlock door will open automatically and the ram will launch the beacon. Not very dignified but certainly effective.'

'Effective's all we need,' said Ossie, with a last look at the beacon. He led Martha back out while activating his collar-phone and glancing warily at the pouring rain, now accompanied by distant rolls of thunder and flashes of lightning.

'Hello, Jamie. We're ready for you now. We should pick up the pace. Let's get it finished before the rain comes on any harder,' said Ossie.

'Coming in now,' said Jamie, eyeing the open hangar as he gingerly edged the observer to its final resting place beside the other observer's gravdrive unit. At once, engineers and scientists swarmed about, running power cables and control lines in a carefully planned sequence. Jamie abandoned the craft and joined Ossie outside.

'No going back now,' said Ossie. 'Let's pray we can go forward. The calculations all indicate it's feasible, but we'll only know for sure when we try.'

The rain came on harder, and Jamie retired to S-3's bridge, leaving the scientists and engineers to hook up and secure the various power units. There was nothing he could do to help, so better out of the way. Ossie had calculated two gravdrive power units in a small sample craft would provide enough extra energy to power the folddrive for a little while, until the huge power demands of maintaining a craft in the Fold burned out both gravdrives. Jamie prayed it would function for long enough.

On the way to the bridge, he stopped off at the comms control room. Sparks looked up and greeted him with a slightly concerned expression.

'What's up, Sparks?' said Jamie.

'Glad you're back, sir. The hoppers have reported that they're falling well behind schedule. The rain is turning the savannah into a quagmire. Streams are forming everywhere as water drains toward the river system. Lieutenant Grieves is concerned they won't get back until after sunset.'

'I see, tell him to report in, every fifteen minutes. If things deteriorate further, I want to know at once.'

'Yes, sir... And sir, there's more.'

'Well?'

'The weather forecast is bad, very bad. There's a powerful wind getting up now. And... the marines have just reported one of their long-range drones has picked up life forms moving along behind the rain.'

'What? Any details?'

'No, sir. Word just came to me as you arrived. More information to follow.'

'Thanks, Sparks.' Jamie left comms control and crossed to the bridge where the screens displayed the watery scene outside. He touched his sleeve.

'Baz, what's the news on these life forms?'

'Jamie, I've just had to land the long-distance drone. Weather out on the savannah is just getting too rough,' said Browning. 'There is a huge herd coming along behind the rain. Still a good way off. At the speed they're travelling, we estimate around four or five days before they get here.'

'Okay. How far is "a good way off", and what are they?'

'The leaders are over a hundred miles off, but the animals stretch back a long way behind – it's a mega herd. They're big quadrupeds. Drone footage suggests hair rather than scales or feathers, so I'm guessing mammal. And there appear to be several different body shapes, so looks like different animal species moving together. The way they travel some way behind the rains suggests they're feeding on new sprouting grass. I'll be passing the data over to Ossie and his science team now.'

'All right, knowing Ossie he'll want to take control of your drone once the weather improves – science first.'

'We'll share, but now we've seen big animals, my team are going to want to monitor for any other threats that might come with that herd.'

'Are all your drones grounded?'

'We normally have three out at all times. The long-range one had to land way off in the coastal hills. It'll stay down for the duration. The second had been patrolling along the course of the river. We've called it back before it's embroiled in the heart of the storm. Should be arriving soon. It overflew the two hoppers as it came in. They seem to be struggling a bit – the savannah is turning to a mud bath. At least they should be crossing the second tributary soon.'

'The sooner the better, the water levels will be rising upstream.' Jamie glanced at the screen; the normally slow brown of the river was changing. There was a perceptible rise in water levels with white bubbling in places, and swirls and eddies all speaking of a faster flow. 'It's rising here already. How are things looking down on the coastal plain?'

'Wet. Wet but quieter. As a precaution, we've landed the drone over that way too.'

'Okay, let's pick this up later.' Jamie ended the call and immediately keyed in another, opening a link to Lieutenant Grieves in the hoppers.

'Sir?'

'Grieves, just to let you know the drones are all grounded now. This weather is getting worse.'

'Yes, sir. It's very bad here. Strong wind, driving rain. Sky's dark with cloud and the sun's just about set.'

'The key objective is to get across the river safely. Then it's only a steady walk back to base. Take care now; we'll see you soon.'

'Thank you, sir. We're approaching the river. We'll commence our crossing immediately on arrival.'

Jamie looked intently at the screen, watching the worsening weather. A sudden movement in the river revealed a tree trunk floating quickly downstream. The waterflow was increasing rapidly.

Chapter 15

Orion–Perseus Junction: P-2 in the Fold

Alone in the Fold, P-2 had maintained careful lookout for any traffic while the other Leviathans supported the construction of Secundo. From their first moment in the Fold, everything had been calm. Now Captain Hogan hurried onto the bridge. In front of him, the first officer stood staring up at the screen, his lean frame silhouetted by the familiar streaks of rushing starlight.

'Well, Number One, what have you got?' said Hogan.

'Top right of the screen, coming our way. I don't know what it is, but it's a solid image, no tail streak. So, whatever it is, it's moving in the Fold.' A jabbing arm directed the captain's attention.

'I see it, thank you. Have Science got any readings for us yet?'

'Nothing, it's running silent, sir. I've got the second officer maintaining a watch in the LPA. He's calling out its movements; it's come straight out of Perseus and will cross the boundary into Orion in minutes.'

'How long before we have to change direction?'

'About the same, sir.'

'Damn… Sound quarters. This is about as bad timing as we could get.'

'Yes, sir,' said the first officer. Stroking his sleeve, he addressed the whole crew. 'Stand to! Stand to! All crew to stations and stand by for further orders.' He turned to look intently at the captain. 'Sir?'

P-2 had been making short runs back and forth across the Orion–Perseus boundary. It was not possible to remain motionless in the Fold, doing so would result in immediately falling out. Equally, since speed increased exponentially with duration while travelling in any one direction within the Fold, P-2 could not spend more than fifteen minutes heading in any particular direction before it began to race beyond the intersection it was monitoring.

They had devised a technique of flying in a diamond circuit centred on the boundary. The frequent course alterations putting the brakes on their acceleration with every change. It kept them within reaching distance of Secundo at all times while ensuring they could maintain constant monitoring for any traffic in the Fold that might reach the Orion–Perseus junction. And now, they had traffic.

'Can you magnify that image? Could it be a remote sample craft on the milk run, returning to Primo?'

'I don't think it's a sample craft, sir. We've registered no auto-signals declaring its identity. I'll try to boost the image, but it's coming in at a hell of a speed, growing almost as we watch,' said the first officer.

Have they seen us?'

'I don't think so, sir. If it's who we think it is, would they even know to be looking?'

'Who else would it be? If they haven't noticed us, altering course will likely draw their attention. But if we don't, we'll be off-station and out of the loop... We need to maintain station. Number One, make your next course alteration now. Have every channel monitored – at least let's know straightaway if we've been noticed.'

'Yes, sir.' The first officer stroked his sleeve, issued monitoring instructions and began the course change.

The chief science officer entered the bridge. 'Captain, I've got all my people on this. If we pick anything up, you'll have it at once.'

'Thanks,' said the captain. 'We're still stuck with the question we haven't managed to find an answer to. If needs be, how do you fight in the Fold? Anything that's detached from its means of propulsion will drop out into regular space in under a minute, so missiles are useless except at the very shortest of ranges.'

The scientist remained silent. He had no answer, either. Then their star-streaked screen began to shift.

'Altering course now, sir.'

'I see it on-screen,' said the captain. 'Have a warbird ready for launch. If we get involved in a chase through the Fold, I want something to drop into normal space and alert Colonel MacMillan at Secundo.'

'Settled on new heading, sir,' said the first officer.

From his post at the LPA, the second officer's voice sounded with a note of concern in all their collar-phones. 'This course is going to bring us very close to the object. Our nearest point of approach is going to be very tight, almost a collision risk.'

The captain and first officer glanced at one another. 'Ease our heading a little, Number One. I think it best if we avoid bumping that beast. Let's pass clear behind it.'

'Very good, sir,' said the first officer making a further course adjustment. This will take us somewhat off our regular circuit and further away from the Opsythia system.'

'Yes, but better safe than sorry. What do you make of that now?' The captain pointed up at the screen. The course change was bringing them quickly toward what had previously been an unidentifiable on-screen blob, so that it now came into focus. 'It's the cone shape Colonel MacMillan saw during his reconnaissance into the Perseus Arm, isn't it? The one that contained dozens of attack vessels that went straight for him, no questions asked. Got out by the skin of his teeth.'

'It is, sir.'

'Number One, get this information to a warbird and have it launch right now. It will drop out of the Fold immediately and contact Colonel MacMillan without delay. Then it will have to make its way back to Secundo. We'll rendezvous with it there, when events allow.'

'Very good, sir.' While issuing the instructions, the first officer kept his eyes firmly on the screen. With every moment, the cone grew in size.'

The second officer reported from the LPA. 'Settled on new course. We'll pass well astern of the target, sir.'

'No signals traffic at all, sir. It's radio silent. Not a sound,' Sparks said, calling out a report from comms control.

The chief scientist stepped closer to Captain Hogan. 'My team are detecting nothing either. It's like a ghost ship. Interesting that it's so silent. I wonder what's going on over there. They must see us now, surely?'

All three men stood in silence, watching the screen as P-2 moved steadily along its closing course with the cone. Nothing wavered in the cone's direction of travel.

'If only we had something to hit it with,' said the captain. 'Number One, let it pull ahead slightly then alter course again – let's follow this bad boy. See where it takes us.'

A voice sounded from the distant hangar. 'Warbird launching in three, two, one. Warbird away. Warbird away.'

'I have it in the LPA, sir,' said the second officer.

Captain Hogan watched on the screen as the tiny warbird showed, running ahead on their starboard side. It began to pull away with the added impetus of its own gravdrive. However, now separated from the Leviathan's folddrive, a milky disc formed in front of the warbird, and it quickly slipped through.

'I've lost the warbird from the LPA,' reported the second officer. 'It's dropped into normal space.'

'Now altering course to trail the cone, sir,' said the first officer.

'Good. Second officer, can you make any predictions as to where they're heading?'

'Wait one, please, sir.'

A few moments passed in silence on the bridge while they waited for the second officer's calculations.

'Sir, their course will take then directly past the solar system.'

'Past or to?' said the captain.

'We have to assume *to* and not past,' said the chief scientist. 'Remember, when Steph's team broke their language, she worked out that these monsters are essentially swarm creatures. They arrive at a planet, eat everything – everything. Strip it bare and move on. If you're looking for a feast, Earth is packed with food.'

'But it's sealed off,' said the first officer.

'They can't know that. Plus, you've seen the surveillance footage Colonel MacMillan brought back from his first encounter. These aliens are clever. Heaven's sake! Look, for them to be here, they have to have converted that captured sample craft into a fleet transporter. Could we do that on our own? I don't think so. Perhaps, as well as harvesting a planet's life as food resources, they somehow gather the knowledge too – learn.'

'How the hell do you harvest knowledge?' said the captain.

The chief scientist shrugged. 'I don't know. But it seems they might have a way. And they must learn to apply that knowledge fast.'

The first officer tilted his head slightly then glanced at the display on his sleeve. 'Something's happening ahead.'

'I'm picking up signals traffic.' Sparks' voice sounded in everyone's collar-phones. 'Increasing intensity.'

'That tallies with what my team's just begun reporting. They must have seen us,' said the chief scientist.

'What's that?' said the captain, pointing toward the screen. 'What am I seeing?'

'Something's breaking away from the rear. A vessel is detaching from the cone,' called out the first officer.

'I have a signal in the LPA. Definitely a vessel separating from the cone. We're closing on it fast, but now it's detached it will fall out of the Fold at any moment,' the second officer's voice narrated what they could all see on the screen.

In a swift and seamless motion, the solitary alien vessel reversed direction and fired its rockets, accelerated toward P-2 and launched a second salvo. The missiles showed clearly on the screen as P-2 closed.

'Targeted, sir. Missiles incoming, contact imminent.'

'All crew, brace for impact. Brace! Brace!' The captain called his orders but, even as he spoke, milky pools appeared in front of the missiles and the alien vessel, and all vanished harmlessly into normal space.

'They've gone, sir. They can't touch us in the Fold!'

'Steady, man. Not so fast. What's this?' The captain cut short his first officer's cry of triumph.

On the screen, the cone was suddenly substantially nearer.

'It's slowing right down. Cut its speed dramatically,' reported the second officer.

The chief science officer gripped the captain's shoulder. 'I know what it's doing, Captain – they're damned sharp. Get away from it quick. Pull away. Do it now!'

The captain paused for just a moment then looked toward his first officer. 'Hard to starboard, Number One. And push the speed up as quick as you can.'

'Too late, captain!' The chief scientist pointed up at the screen. Three more vessels were detaching as P-2 closed on the suddenly slowed cone. The Leviathan struggled to change its course, to escape contact with the three alien vessels that were rapidly filling the screen.

'They've released a missile salvo into the Fold, sir!' The second officer's voice could not mask rising concern.

His warning came too late. Even before an alert could be broadcast, the missiles showed on the screen only to explode almost simultaneously, splitting open P-2's bow. A shockwave rippled through the hull. Milky pools formed immediately ahead of P-2 where the attacking vessels and exploded missile debris began slipping away. The captain was certain the Leviathan could cope with the missile damage. A moment later, his confidence was shattered. The third alien vessel to launch was just sliding into its cloudy exit pool as P-2 rammed into it.

The part of the alien vessel that had not yet passed into normal space was enveloped, caught and channelled directly into the Leviathan's gaping bow wound. From there, the thrust of the accelerating Leviathan forced the remains of the vessel further into the Leviathan's body. The captain felt a life-sapping shudder in his craft as the alien was driven yet deeper, burrowing beneath the bridge deck clearing everything as it went. Disembowelling the Leviathan.

The rump vessel smashed through into the Leviathan's central passageway where it was suddenly free of resistance and accelerated for just a moment. In that flash of time, it raced the length of the open promenade and crashed into the engine room access where it finally stopped, just as the Leviathan lost all power. Then a milky disc formed to drop the broken Leviathan out of folded space.

As the Leviathan hulk slipped away into normal space, a disc formed ahead of the cone, and it followed the dying Leviathan through.

Chapter 16

Orion–Perseus Junction: Normal Space

Dazed, the nurse forced open her aching eyes; Susie Perue had no idea what had happened.

Only minutes before, she had been alone in her cabin when an alert was called. She remembered having taken the precaution of flicking her helmet up as she hurried to her station at the sickbay. Once there, some of her team had mocked her for taking such excessive precautions. Before the teasing had ended, they were all dead.

Susie peered about, then clamped her eyes shut. No joy in surviving. No gravity. She was in freefall, drifting slowly away from what remained of P-2, floating toward an infinity of darkness. Her home was a hulk, burning and flashing wherever pockets of oxygen flared against the dying sparks. She was alone, her despairing eyes closed, and she slipped back into unconsciousness.

The nurse opened her eyes again. Daring a glance, her worst fears were confirmed. More distant now but just as broken. P-2 was dead, and so too was she. Tears slipped down her cheeks. She wished her suit didn't have so much oxygen, knew the scrubbers would keep her supplied for a long time. She screwed her eyes tight shut and prayed. *Could she open her helmet? No, the safety programs prevented that.*

Time passed; she didn't know how long. Every moment a misery for lost friends and a longing for her own end. But then, in a flash, her despair vanished. Susie felt strong arms grip her, guiding her backward to safety. She laughed and cried at the same time. Craning her neck, she turned to thank her saviour. And every euphoric emotion careered headlong into the buffers of reality.

She wriggled, struggled, but was no match for the arms that held her. The strange, tall, dome-shaped helmet was too big, and a dark visor hid what lay beneath. The suit was not Primo issue. She kicked out, and immediately, her legs were pinned by a long limb wrapping round hers. Susie was held fast as her saviour carried her back to its vessel. She closed her eyes again.

On board, the environment was still weightless, no gravity control here. One brave peak was enough to confirm what deep-down she already knew. Different suits, different technology. No saviour. It was them.

The nurse's suit was expertly sliced and stripped from her body. She felt cool hard limbs press against her flesh, restraining her as the helmet was prised from her head. An involuntary breath confirmed a breathable atmosphere, and she cried out in natural relief and her heart's bitter disappointment.

Held tight in the strong grip of arms that crushed her flesh at the slightest sign of resistance, Susie Perue struggled once again. The grip tightened like a crab's claws, squeezing, cutting. Finally, in the face of ever mounting pain, she screwed her eyes tight shut and went limp, surrendered to the detailed analysis.

Later, what seemed an age of heartless prying and probing ended. The cruel indignities may have stopped, but any faint sense of relief vanished as quickly as it formed. The lightest of touches stroked back and forth across her face, traced and wove through her hair. She finally opened her eyes and screamed. Close in front of her was the monster. Locust-like, bigger than her, its antennae long and waving were sweeping across and around her. She shook her head, pulled back.

A clacking and hissing sound from the monster triggered a response from the one behind that already restrained her. Its grip shifted and her head was locked in place.

The antennae wafted, paused over her eyes and stroked across her cheeks before gently nestling against her temples. Then they traced toward her eyes.

She closed her blue eyes again, shook her head and moaned. 'No, no please...'

More arms swept from behind her, neat little digits firmly and irresistibly manoeuvring her eyelids open.

All she could see were waving antennae and bulging black eyes as big as fists.

The antennae hovered, poised. Suddenly their slender tips pressed forward, delivering excruciating discomfort as they slipped in behind her eyes. In a convulsion of distress her eyes rolled and flashed. The feelers pressed on, followed the curve of her eye sockets back and round to finally curl about the optic nerves, searching for a point of engagement. Nerves damaged, she squealed in fear as her eyesight blacked. Blind and defenceless, she felt the probing strands withdraw, sliding out to the sound of rapid clicking – impatience.

Her senses were so overwhelmed, for just a moment she did not feel the tips of the antennae tracing the shape of her ears, circling. Then they moved, sliding into her auditory canals. In deep, reaching, touching, tracing the surface of her eardrum. The tips of the antennae pressed, pressed then pierced. She screamed again. The antennae continued in just a little further and the monster began very gradually to sense her brain rhythms playing faintly through her pulsing pain signals. It felt the thought patterns and slowly, very slowly, it learned.

The locust looked over Suzie's shoulder to clack and hiss at its companion. Suzie saw nothing, heard nothing. Her brain only registering endless waves of pain.

Wanting more, the monster pressed its antennae in deeper. For Suzie, it was a blessing. The deep penetration induced a brain fit that her body couldn't hope to contain. She convulsed and mercifully her conscious mind closed down.

Withdrawing its antennae, the locust hissed at its companions. Content with this first learning. It would certainly take more intrusions to learn how to read these minds without breaking them completely. More still to harvest their race's full knowledge. It was a good start. Already they understood how to open the book. And they understood this new race's frailty – its fear of death. The locust clicked again – death would come for this one now, and there were so many of its kind, so many; they could feast for a long time on this prey. A very long time.

Now, the taste test. The locust reached out its short arms and began to press and squeeze again. Finally settling on a sample spot, it leaned forward, the great mouth opened, and it bit into bare, fleshy belly, pulled back with its mouth full and chewed.

A screech and rattle of carapace delivered a positive taste verdict. As it leaned in for more, the restraining monster behind her bit too. Others closed in to feast amidst a chorus of clicking and hissing.

Chapter 17

Osarus c.: Retreat

Fifi's easy chatter of earlier had faded with the continuing rain. Now she was staring directly ahead. Grieves traced her gaze. In the fading light, he could see the break in the riverbank where it led down to the fording point. A thicket of trees grew tightly around and the only space between the closely gathered trunks formed a natural avenue leading down to the water. Boughs reached out to link overhead, enclosing the route beneath in deep shadow.

Beyond the avenue, the river flowed. From their vantage point, it was clearly fast-flowing, very fast.

'Is it safe to cross?' said Fifi.

'We'll be fine,' said Grieves. Then he opened a channel to Corporal Archer, following in the second hopper. 'It's been a long journey, corporal, but let's go straight down. The water is only going to get higher. We'll rest on the other side.'

Everyone was exhausted after hours bouncing about in the hoppers. A short break was desperately needed.

'Very good, sir. I'll follow you down to the water. How should we cross?'

'I'll assess it when we reach the bank.' This was the only accessible crossing point they could reach in what remained of the daylight. They'd have to cross here, no matter what. He slowed the hopper as it reached the tree-shaded slope down to the river. Entering the avenue, Grieves instinctively glanced up to the interlocking lattice of tree boughs, searching for unwanted residents, seeing none. Dark was coming, so he flicked on the hopper's external lights. Unconsciously, he sped up, eager to reach the bank and move out from beneath the tree canopy. A backward glance told him the corporal was tight behind and matching his pace.

At the bank, the atmosphere was perceptibly lighter than beneath the tight woven tree canopy, but twilight was closing fast as rays from the setting sun steadily diminished. Filtered through the heavy cloud, little light reached between the dark, shadowed riverbanks.

Tips of bankside ferns and bushes were just visible above water level as they tugged and strained against the rising water's flow.

'Corporal, see those plant tops bobbing in the water? I'm reckoning they were dry a couple of hours ago – the water's rising fast, up more than a man's height already.'

'I see them, sir. That water's really going some.'

They all watched a tree branch float swiftly past.

'Are you sure it's safe to cross?' said Fifi.

'Hmm, it's our only way back to base, and we have no idea how long this flooding will last. We could be stuck here for days, weeks even, and we've no rations beyond today. It looks a bit sticky, but we must go on—'

'Holy cow! We're under attack!' The corporal's voice sounded in Grieves' collar-phone while his hopper was nudged from behind by the corporal's. 'Forward, sir. It's the serpents. Above me in the trees!' Grieves could make out the sound of blows raining on the second hopper's canopy, transmitted through the corporal's collar-phone. 'Advance, sir. I must get clear of the tree canopy now or they'll have us over.'

As Grieves got his hopper stepping into the water, the hopper behind barged into his, almost toppling him. 'Steady, corporal!'

'Sorry, sir. Can't help it – they're like battering rams coming from above. I'm following tight behind you.'

A little beyond the bank's edge, they moved clear of the attacking serpents, and Grieves paused, testing the hopper's resilience against the water flow. It seemed all right. He turned to look back; the second hopper was tight behind his. The corporal stony-faced. Pete had adopted the foetal position in the shotgun seat. Their hopper was intact, but through the rain, Grieves could see heavy dents in the bodywork, and thick trails of what he knew to be venom tracing slowly over the canopy.

'It was your serpents again, sir. Came in from the tree canopy. More than one. I don't think the hopper would have taken another blow.'

Grieve peered into the trees behind them. 'I don't see anything back there, corporal.'

'No, sir. Came out of nowhere, then just vanished when we cleared the bank. Thank God, they didn't follow us; they just about had my hopper broken open.'

'All right, let's move on. The water's getting faster. To be safe, let's support each other. Cross as one, double the weight – it'll be safer. Grip these with your arms,' said Grieves while swinging his hopper's mechanical arms back as far as they would go.

'I'm on you, sir,' said the corporal, making his own hopper's arms reach forward to link. All four limbs locked together.

'Right, let's go ahead while we still can. Slow, steady, match my step, pace for pace.'

Locked together as one, the two hoppers edged out across the river. With every step, the water deepened. At midstream the river level was up to the entrance hatchway. Fifi looked anxiously to Grieves.

'Don't worry, we're waterproof,' he said.

'Look out!' said Fifi. 'Tree trunk!'

Grieves didn't have time to turn his head before they were struck, knocked over and settling toward the bottom while the current rushed them downstream. Strapped in his seat, Grieves felt the spin and tumble increase as they were washed into the turbulence of the merging tributaries. Now on the bottom, and on their sides, the hoppers carried along in a water-powered tumble.

'Corporal, report!'

'Still with you, sir.'

Grieves looked over his shoulder and could just make out the second hopper, still armlock-gripped to his own.

'Are you watertight? How's your passenger?'

'All good here. Pete's shook up, didn't have his safety belt on. He'll live... What now, sir?'

'We've lost the fording point, it's way back upstream. Even in a quieter water flow, there's nowhere to get out of the river between here and the valley mouth. And that's the way we're heading.' Grieves stopped talking for a moment as the eddies within the powerful current combined to flick them over again. He was suddenly facing back upstream as the water propelled them on.

'These hoppers are damned heavy, how is the water moving us?' said the corporal.

'Flowing water is very strong. Just think about the great rocks you see in and around rivers,' said Fifi, suddenly pleased to contribute. 'And I'd guess the air cavity in a hopper reduces the average density, making it even easier to shift in the current than a solid boulder.' She caught her breath as a bump and grind signalled their passing over rocks in the riverbed.

'Quiet, everyone, just hold on tight. We have to contact S-3. I'm going to try now,' said Grieves. He activated the hopper's comms system without success. Broadcasting through his collar-phone was equally ineffective.

'What will we do?' said Fifi.

'Keep trying. The river's deep here, and I expect the water turbulence might be causing some interference. We'll get a signal through, just need to keep trying. Could even be interference from electrical storms.'

'This is one hell of a current to be washing two hoppers along like they were soap boxes,' said the corporal. His voice sounded distorted in Grieves' collar-phone despite their close proximity.

Grieves and Fifi both twisted round to look out of the rear-view window. Through the murk and swirl of the rushing water, they could make out their two grim-faced companions in the second hopper.

'At the rate we're moving, I reckon it won't be long until we're at the valley entrance. We need to figure out how to stop ourselves being rolled over the rocks and rapids. Never mind your serpents back there, the rocks will break us for sure. Any thoughts?' said Grieves.

An extended silence gave its own answer.

'Right, listen up, everyone. Seems even the combined mass of the two hoppers can't prevent us being carried forward. Yet the way we're presently linked together doesn't help. We need more drag, more catching points. We should release one of the hoppers' arm grips. We'll still be locked together with our second arms, but we'll also have two arms free to grab and drag.'

'Won't opening our profile up turn us into a sail? We'll be propelled faster in the current. The risk will rise?' said Pete.

Grieves turned again to look toward the blurry shapes of the second hopper's crew. He raised a hand to acknowledge the comment. 'You're right, Pete. Can't argue with that, but as we are, we can't stop ourselves. With two mechanical arms free, we can use them to grasp any riverbed objects that aren't moving, get a chance to tether ourselves, slow us down.'

'And what then?' said Pete.

'I'll be happy enough to worry about *what then* once we've got control of our forward movement.'

'How will we do it, sir?' said the corporal. 'We're left arm to left arm, right to right. Releasing one arm grip will mean one of us will always be facing the wrong way and will never be able to see and grip any likely anchor points before they're past.'

'Okay, five steps. Step one, we'll each release our left grip at the same time. Step two, corporal, with your freed left arm, immediately take a lock-grip on my hopper's leg to keep us clamped tight together. Step three, I'll bring my left arm round to where the two right arms are still locked. Then step four's the tricky bit, we release the right-hand grips and immediately my left and your right grip one another. Let things settle for a moment, test the new grip and then you release my leg. We can extend the newly gripped arms to separate the two hoppers a little. We'll end up with two free hopper arms to act as lockdown grips. Are we good?'

'On your word, sir,' said the corporal.

'Hold on, hold on. What happens if your new grip fails? We'll be swept apart!' said Pete.

'That won't happen,' said Grieves. 'Stand by on my word, corporal.'

'Standing by, sir.'

Suddenly everyone shook as the hoppers bumped against more rocks on the riverbed. They were bounced into the upper water flow then began to drop again before hitting yet another rock and rising once more.

'There's a lot more rocks now; we must be nearly at the valley entrance,' said Fifi, her tone betraying deep concern. 'The current must have carried us far faster than we thought. What will we do?'

The hoppers again bounced up into the main waterflow. 'Switch arm grips while we can. Corporal, on my word... Now.'

As the two hoppers turned in the flow, both released their left arms and followed Grieves plan to the letter. It took only moments to complete the sequence. Then, side by side, linked by the single locked arm grip, the two hoppers seemed to hover, suspended in the water column for just a moment, like giant spacemen.

'Rocks! Rocks ahead!' said Fifi.

'Got them,' said Grieves. 'Steady everyone, this is going to get bumpy.'

Ahead, the water column was turning cloudy white, bubbling where it rose and tumbled through a rocky barrier. The general flow of water up and over the rocks lifted them too. For just a moment, they broke surface before submerging. Then the legs caught briefly among a cluster of riverbed rocks, tilting the hoppers forward and down, propelling them cab-first, like a brace of torpedoes.

The hoppers' floodlights shone down onto the jumbled rocky mess of riverbed rushing past below. Feeling almost detached from the fear and jeopardy, Grieves noticed that Fifi had covered her eyes. He tilted his head up to look through the cabin-top's viewing port that was now leading their direction of travel. Nothing. Throwing a switch kicked on a sky light, and at once he saw the scale of the problem ahead. A wall of rocks was looming: the main rapids.

'Corporal! Drop the legs, get some traction, slow us down.'

Both hoppers dropped legs, trying to drag across the jumble of riverbed rocks. A leg caught and dragged, slowing the hoppers but slewing them round. The leg broke free and the hoppers washed on. Again, fleetingly breaking the surface, the hoppers' headlights picked out the tops of rocks. Together the hoppers bumped and crashed as the torrent washed them along a maze-like course. No matter how they tried, the current was too strong to allow the legs to hold fast. Nor could occasional arm grabs make a firm connection.

Grieves' heart suddenly sank. Directly ahead was a boulder the size of a house. They could not avoid it, had no defence. He didn't have time to call a warning, just reached out a hand and squeezed Fifi's.

With a crash, their forward movement banged to an instant halt. Shaken in their seats, the party shared a common moment of dread as a sickening, grinding sound filled the cabs, filled their worlds. Then nothing.

Grieves could not see the other hopper. In front of his cab was a sheet of rock, eerily lit by the hopper's floodlights whose beams were mostly pressed against stone. Water pressure trapped the hopper hard against rock.

'Corporal, report!' said Grieves.

'Sir, we're pinned tight. Can't see your hopper, it's vanished.'

'Us too.' Grieves glanced at his controls, and he understood. They showed his hopper's arm still gripped the other hopper's. But the enormous load of thousands of tonnes of water pressed them hard against opposing faces of a wedge-faced rock. The weight of water was far too much for even a hopper to resist. Now they were linked only by the hoppers' gripping hands that joined about the leading edge of the boulder. How long could they maintain a joining grip against such force?

While repeatedly transmitting radio calls to S-3, he twisted in his seat to look back upstream, the rear-facing floodlamp beams shining uninterrupted, picking out a jumble of rocks behind them; they had travelled further into the rapids than he had judged.

'Lieutenant, what next?' said Fifi. She still held his hand, and now doubled down, adding her other, compressing his in a hand sandwich.

Grieves opened up a collar-phone channel. 'Right, listen up, everyone. We're pinned to either side of this bolder. We can't raise S-3 and we're stuck. There's only one way we're getting out of this. We have to let the hopper arms release their grip on one another, separate and go with the flow. Each hopper will just have to make a fix where it can. Use its arms to climb above water. From there, we should be able to get a much cleaner signal, call for help.'

'That sounds hellish dangerous,' said Pete. 'Wouldn't we be better to hold tight together? Wait for the waters to ease back a bit.'

Grieves shook his head. 'Maybe, but who knows how much rain's still to fall? I'm thinking there's way more to come. We're pinned here for now. Look at the stuff rushing past in the water. Any of those tree trunks hit and they could punch right through a hopper canopy. We're sitting ducks here...'

The silence told him everyone recognised their position was unsustainable.

'Brace yourselves. On my word, corporal, we release the hopper arm grips—'

'Wait, please, I'm not ready yet,' shouted Pete into his collar-phone. 'Just give me a few minutes to prepare.'

Chapter 18

Osarus c.: S-3

'Any sign of them?' said Jamie as he stepped back onto the bridge.

Browning looked round, and grimaced. 'They were at the river when both hopper signals just vanished. Bad atmospherics could be having an effect, but we had clean positioning signals. Then, bang – nothing.'

'What do you think?'

'I'm thinking they might have been caught in the waterflow while fording the river. Washed downstream.'

'You'd still have a signal though.'

'You'd think that. But ahead of the rapids, the riverbanks are really steep. Maybe that creates a shadow, and if the hoppers are under water that won't help signals get through. The air–water interface can really mess up radio signals.'

'So, what precisely do we know?'

'The hoppers have gone. My team have just put a drone back up, but it's struggling to stay airborne in this weather. As soon as we get a fix, I'll let you know.'

'Okay, if you need any of the science team to help get a lock on them, just say. Ossie will give you somebody.'

'No need. Military drones, my lot are using them all the time.'

'Right, keep me posted,' said Jamie, turning his attention back to the screen.

Looking upstream, he could just make out the defensive wall through the falling rain; a marine was hunched in the guard tower trying to avoid the downpour as best he could. Beyond the wall, everything was lost in a blur.

Running close by, the river was raging. The lower far bank was burst, its edge submerged beneath the spread of rising flood-waters. At the higher near bank, brown water rushed past and was topped everywhere by swirls and crests of foam. Organic debris, branches, even whole trees, everything moved unstoppably on, propelled like crazy things in the growing flood.

'Jamie, we're ready.' Ossie's voice sounded, and Jamie switched his attention to the terrace immediately downstream of S-3. There, Ossie and Martha Solomon stood in the small sample craft's portside hangar entrance. Streaming out of the hangar was a line of bots, all making their way back to S-3 through the rain. Engineers and scientists joined the exodus, hurrying past the bots to get into the dry.

'I see you,' said Jamie. 'Looks like you've come in ahead of schedule.'

'We have. And now it's ready, I think we should get it launched ASAP. Storm conditions shouldn't normally affect a craft's flight abilities, but I've been watching some of the weather patterns – along with this rain, there are some massive electrical storms coming in. Having added the folddrive and other bits of kit, we've massively increased the payload. It might affect stability and control responses to some degree – we can't tell for sure. I don't think we should wait a moment longer than we need to.'

'Okay. You and Martha close up down there and get back here. We'll auto-launch it together from the bridge. I want to feed the news to all the crew simultaneously... Oh, hold on, Ossie, I've got something else coming in.' Jamie turned toward Browning. 'Go ahead. What news?'

'We've found them, Jamie. It's not good. The hoppers are trapped underwater in the rapids. That's why we've been having signal problems but the drone's close enough now to pick up their signal from underwater.'

'Any casualties?'

'Not yet. But I don't know how we'll get them out. They report trees and all sorts of debris flowing past. Any direct contact with a tree will likely breach a cabin. They're trapped below water and no way out. I'll run the drone feed to the screen now.'

'Right... Ossie, did you hear that?'

'We did. On our way up now.'

Jamie looked up to the screen as images from the drone began to display in one section. The image borders were all black as night. The middle part flickered under the illumination of the hovering drone's search beam. It revealed a seething mass of water churning over and between the tops of great rocks that only a day before had dominated a gentle river. Now they were diminished to little more than splash plates, when they could be seen at all.

Martha and Ossie joined Jamie on the bridge. They stood in silence watching the torrent break over the boulder tops.

'What are we going to do, Jamie? I've got a live link with Lieutenant Grieves via the drone. What should I tell him?' said Browning.

'No one will get out through those hatches. Even if they did, they'd be swept away at once. It's a death-trap,' said Martha.

'It is,' said Jamie. 'But I can't leave them to die.'

'There's nothing anyone can do,' said Ossie.

Jamie stared intently at the cruel waters displayed on the screen. 'There must be something I can do. Suggestions?'

'Jamie, what are your orders? The hopper crews are desperate.'

'I'll have to use the small sample craft to mount a rescue before we launch it into the Fold. It's the only option.'

'That won't do you any good,' said Martha. The chief engineer shook her head and looked down at the deck. 'The hoppers are underwater. There's nothing you can do even with the sampler.'

'She's right. And besides, that craft is carrying a massive extra payload – that folddrive we've added is a huge burden. Once it's up, we can't risk bringing it down again. If the stresses are too much, we may not get it airborne a second time. In fact, I'm not sure the load isn't too much for a safe landing anyway. It's a one-launch opportunity.'

'Okay… So, what are the odds of launching it twice?' said Jamie.

'I have no idea. It's a miracle we got everything to fit in. The whole thing has been guesswork and inspiration. All our calculations were based on one launch and away. Having got this far, to risk not getting the position beacon into the Fold is pure madness. What are four lives compared to the rescue of four hundred? Let me launch the craft now, before the storm gets any worse. Please!' said Ossie.

Jamie looked again at the screen. Beneath the raging waters were four of his people. Their lives entirely in his hands.

Martha stepped closer to Jamie. 'Ossie's right, sir. With all the extra load we've added and the structural modifications, we can't be sure the craft will maintain its integrity through the stresses of two launch sequences. If you take the craft up and somehow manage to rescue our people, you can't bring them back down. You'll all be stuck on board; you'll have to go all the way. This is a one-way trip into the Fold. A death sentence for anyone on board...'

The bridge was suddenly illuminated by a searing light that blazed across the screen. It flashed, flickered, then flashed again before subsiding.

'Lightning,' said Ossie. 'Big lightning. And look at the rain – it's almost horizontal. The weather's going to hell. We need to get the sampler away now, while we still can.'

'Jamie, what do I tell the hopper crews?' said Browning.

'Tell them I'm coming for them, right now.'

'You can't; you mustn't,' said Ossie. 'Please, the risk's too great. What can you do?'

'Ossie, enough! I'll tell you how we're doing this, and that's final.'

Ossie made to argue then stopped himself, throwing his arms up in exasperation, before letting them fall against his sides in a resigned protest. 'You're the boss.'

'I am. Now listen, we need to move fast. From here on, just do as I say, no more questions. This is my area of expertise.' Jamie jabbed a pointing finger at the screen's ominous display.

Martha and Ossie looked slightly puzzled.

'He's a military helicopter pilot, done plenty of rescues. If anyone here can pull this off, it's Jamie MacAulay,' said Browning. 'I'm with you, Jamie.'

'Thank you, Baz. Tell Lieutenant Grieves to stand by for instructions.' He put an arm out to turn Martha toward Ossie. 'Now you both need to do exactly as I say. There's no practice session. We get it right or they die.'

'And what about the craft?' said Ossie, still unhappy. 'I don't see how we can save these people and get into the Fold.'

'That's because you're a brilliant scientist. Leave the practical day-to-day stuff to me.'

'I'm not seeing anything day-to-day or routine about this,' said Martha.

'Not for you two, maybe. All I need to know is, can I override the autopilot course you've pre-programmed the craft with?'

'Of course, but—'

'That's all I need to know. You two stay here and do anything that's required on my order.'

Before they could ask another question, Jamie was sprinting for the bridge's deadlight curtain and on toward the sampler.

***

Half a minute's exposure to pouring rain had soaked Jamie in his dash from S-3 to the sampler. Staring into its LPA, he was oblivious to the little pool of rainwater forming at his feet. He caught his breath after the barrage of orders he had fired out in the course of his sprint. Now he was focused entirely on the streaming lights and flickering responses as he keyed in override instructions.

Satisfied he had manual control, Jamie moved forward to the bridge and its screen. Directly ahead was the towering shape of S-3, its image blurred in the heavy rain. He could just make out the river rolling past to one hand, to the other – a hint of the steep rising valley side. He took a deep breath, checked his sleeve controls were set exactly as he wanted and readied to take off.

'We're on our way, sir.' Sergeant Grant's voice sounded in Jamie's collar-phone.

'Thank you, sergeant. Move ahead fast as you like.' He watched a column of hoppers parade out of the Leviathan's hangar and move smartly off upstream, quickly disappearing into the falling rain as they hurried toward the rapids. 'Baz, how are things up there?'

'Our drone has the trapped hoppers pinpointed exactly. No change, the current is still holding them tight against the boulder. We've moved the drone a little clear of the zone, off to the far side of the river. It has a laser beam locked on our target,' said Browning.

'Approaching rapids, sir. We'll be on station shortly,' said Grant.

'Thank you, sergeant. Stand by everyone. Radio silence, wait on my word… And here we go.' Jamie stroked his sleeve then tapped, and the sampler began to rise very slowly. He frowned, touched his sleeve and tapped again. The craft's response to his instructions was sluggish. Ossie's concerns about the weight overload were well founded.

As it continued to rise, he began to gently work the craft, testing its reactions while recalibrating his expectations and response timings. Scarcely above the height of S-3, he propelled the craft slowly upstream, following the riverbank and executing further handling tests as he went.

'I see you sergeant,' said Jamie, as the hoppers came into view.

'We see you too, sir. Standing by.' The hoppers stood in a well-spaced row a little back from the riverbank. All faced out over the water, their floodlights framing lonely snapshots of the raging torrent that only a day before had been a rocky crossing point.

Jamie moved the craft out over the water, where he paused for a moment to adjust the screen display, splitting it in two: half showed upstream, half directly below. Unwavering, he stared steadily into the screen. Focusing on the drone's laser beam where it played on the water to paint the target, Jamie edged ahead. As he moved above the spot highlighted by the laser, he continued to struggle with the unresponsive craft. This was so much bigger than his favoured observer craft, and certainly not ideal for the task in hand. Immediately below, a green beam of light reached in to touch the water surface.

'I'm over the target,' said Jamie. Maintaining manual control of the craft was straining his intuitive flying skills to the utmost, but he couldn't trust anything to autopilot. Every dip and kick of wind, even the changing volume of rain hitting the craft, everything needed to be felt and responded to as it happened. No automated system could be so intuitive.

He stood unwavering, eyes always on the screen, and all the time touching and tweaking the flying controls to maintain a perfect position.

'Lieutenant Grieves, can you hear me?'

'We hear you, sir.'

'Good, listen carefully. I'm going to pull you all out with the gravlift.'

'Yes, sir. We're ready, thank you.'

'I knew he'd think of something! I said he would,' said Pete.

'Quiet! Listen up, all of you. My craft is completely overloaded, there is no way I can lift two hoppers in the gravlift without jeopardising the craft. And anyway, with all the extra kit on board there is insufficient space to accommodate one, never mind two hoppers. I can't lift the hoppers up.'

'Well, what the hell are you going to do? You've got to get us out,' said Pete, his voice wavering.

'Corporal, I am directly over your hopper. I have a lock on you. Can you patch through a video feed from your body cam? I need to see what's happening from your angle.'

'Patching it through now, sir.'

A third image appeared on the screen and Jamie saw what the marine corporal saw. It didn't look good.

'Got you corporal. I'm locked on. Helmets up. I want you to release your seatbelts, and on my count, open the hopper's top hatch.'

'What? Are you mad? He will *not* open it!' Jamie saw Pete's arms reach around the corporal's shoulders trying to restrain him.

Jamie watched events in the hopper play through. His screen showed the corporal loosing his safety belt, showed Pete struggle in vain to prevent the burly corporal reach up to release the geologist's own safety belt before stretching a hand up toward the hatch-release.

'Three, two—'

'No! No! Please God, can't you see—'

'One. Open.'

'Opening now, sir.'

As the corporal triggered the hatch-release, Jamie activated the gravlift. The hatch was swept open by the torrent exactly as the gravlift's swirling funnel plunged down and surrounded the two men, lifting them up and away from the hopper.

For a couple of seconds, the screen distorted as the corporal's bodycam travelled up the gravlift. Then Jamie was content to see the two men and a spread of water appear safe on board the deck. It had worked.

'Move clear of the gravlift now!' said Jamie. His barked order triggered a military response from the corporal who acted at once, pulling Pete clear too. He released the corporal's bodycam feed.

'Lieutenant Grieves, it worked. I'm coming for you now. Give me your cam feed.'

Jamie repeated the procedure. This time there was no drama or resistance, but he could see that Fifi was holding tight to the lieutenant. It took only a moment to lift the pair up into the craft. Immediately, he veered off toward the bank.

'Sergeant, stand by. I'm gravlifting four down to your location. Recover and return them to S-3. Gravlifting down, on my word.'

'We have you, sir. Standing by to recover.'

Jamie watched the four crew members gravlift down onto the saturated earth, saw the hoppers closing in. Content, he began to reprogramme the LPA. Its familiar glow and flash confirmed his instruction was received, and at once he felt the craft begin to rise. The automated program was in play.

He sprinted across the bridge as the screen showed the craft had already climbed into the lowering cloud bank. Swiping open a locker hatch, he squeezed himself in and it shut behind him. Scrunched up in the tight confines, he struggled to reach one hand across to the other. With a final desperate effort, he managed and pressed against the sleeve to trigger release. The life pod slid rapidly along the ejection tube and parted from the craft. It plunged toward the ground as the craft accelerated up and away into the cloud-obscured sky.

***

Jamie came to in S-3's medical bay. A dim figure loomed over him, and he registered distant voices making unintelligible sounds, then lapsed back into unconsciousness.

'How is he?' said Browning.

'Blacked out again, but he's physically fine,' said the nurse, looking at Baz then to Ossie. 'He took quite a bump.'

'Not half,' said Browning. 'When Sergeant Grant found his life pod, it was half buried in the mud.'

'Hmm. The pod is fitted with a gravitational dampener, but it can't absorb the full shock of impact. The rain softened the ground, which helped. Otherwise...' Ossie ended with a shrug of his shoulders.

'Otherwise, I'm not sure he would have survived at all,' said the doctor, stepping over to join the bedside vigil. 'The commander's body has suffered a huge shock, but he's strong and fit, and nothing physical is actually broken. Several times he's begun to regain consciousness, albeit briefly. I'm hopeful he will regain full consciousness soon. But you'll not be getting him on the bridge today, that's for sure.'

Chapter 19

Opsythia e.: Base Secundo

'Sir! Colonel MacMillan!' An anxious voice sounded in the colonel's collar-phone.

'What's up, man? Identify yourself, whose calling?' said MacMillan from the base's rooftop parapet, where he'd been watching the bustle in the compound below. There, equipment and stores were being unloaded from P-3 where it was newly settled on the landing pad, safe within the walled compound.

'It's Barrington, sir. I'm running comms in the control room. Something's happening, sir. I don't understand.'

'I'm on my way down to you now. Speak to me...' MacMillan turned and hurried across the flat roof, passing an observer craft while making for the rooftop entrance. 'Don't leave me hanging, man. What's the problem?' said MacMillan as he stepped through the doorway and started down two flights of steps.

'We've received a warning signal from one of P-2's warbirds. It's dropped out of the Fold, to warn us the cone has been spotted heading into the Orion Arm...'

MacMillan entered the control room to see Barrington standing at the comms console. The technician's face, wrought with worry, lifted slightly at the sight of MacMillan.

'What's the message exactly? Has there been direct contact with the cone?'

'Yes, sir. P-2:C1 dropped out of the Fold at the far end of P-2's patrol route. The warbird's heading back here, but it's a way, way off.'

'Okay, and what of P-2?'

'Nothing, sir. No sign.'

Chapter 20

Opsythia e.: Base Secundo

MacMillan looked across the control room to where a technician was frantically beckoning him toward an LPA.

'Well? What have you got?' said MacMillan.

'I'm displaying the planet's atmosphere and the immediate space beyond. There are signals above us, signals everywhere. Everywhere, sir,' said the technician waving his hand toward the LPA.

'What signals?'

'It's the cone. It's coming in directly toward the planet, and it's started launching vessels.'

'Sound general alert! Tell P-3 to launch its warbirds immediately, get them up and intercept that lot right now. P-3 needs to get airborne too, it's a sitting duck out there. How many of them are there? Where are they heading?'

The control room's four screens displayed real-time action outside. He could see soldiers abandoning their tasks, some heading for P-3 where their weapons and combat kit were stored. Others who had already shifted kit to their new billets ran for the base building.

'The cone has shed around twenty vessels, sir. They are entering the atmosphere, coming right for us. First contact in five minutes, maybe less.

'Where are the warbirds?'

They're launching now, sir.'

MacMillan glanced up to the screen as the three warbirds manoeuvred smoothly out of an open hangar in P-3's side. They rose gently while jockeying into formation before soaring away. Flying directly up, they were quickly out of sight. They hurried to meet the incoming attack fleet, providing a shield for the grounded Leviathan as it readied for launch. Behind them, P-3's hangar door was already closing.

In the LPA, he saw the warbirds' blue signature lights climbing into the high atmosphere even as the host of red enemy lights entered. *Outnumbered six or seven to one, at least*, he thought.

'How far off is P-1? Can it get back here?' MacMillan looked toward Delacroix. The French Canadian had travelled with the squadron to assume the duties of base commander and MacMillan's second-in-command of the Perseus Squadron. If the shock attack had rattled him, it didn't show.

Barrington called out from his LPA. 'It's on the far side of the system, Colonel. A day's flight by gravdrive. I've sent an alert message, but P-1's behind the sun right now, in its signal shadow. I'll keep broadcasting until we get a response.'

MacMillan nodded. 'Delacroix, get your defensive squads in place. Now they're here, I doubt those monsters are going to hold off and just admire the view. And Barrington, why isn't P-3 airborne yet?'

'It's just about ready to move now, sir. The captain had to wait for the troops to get well clear before taking off. She's going through the take-off sequence this instant.'

'Good,' MacMillan turned back to the screen to watch P-3 launch while he tapped on his sleeve to activate his collar-phone. 'Major Sarsen, I want an immediate update on the base's defensive status.'

'P-3's taking off now, colonel.' Barrington's tone was steadier.

'They're coming. Coming now!' said the technician monitoring the traffic LPA.

'Facts, man, facts. Report!' MacMillan's gaze remained fixed on the screen displaying P-3 and its gradual upward motion.

'The warbirds have engaged the incoming vessels in a dogfight, sir.' The technician's voice waivered. 'But some of the attackers have bypassed them. They're coming right at us. They're almost here!'

MacMillan watched the screens as fine vapour trails formed in the high atmosphere and traced a route down toward the base. 'Sarsen, have you got anything ready that can provide ground-to-air defence yet? Anything?'

'Nothing ready, sir. Sorry, I have a team breaking out kit now. The main system's still in its transport packaging. It's going to take thirty minutes, maybe more.'

'We don't have thirty minutes, major. Get me something, anything, right now!' MacMillan returned his focus to the closing vapour trails. Black shapes now showed at the head of each.

Delacroix appeared at MacMillan's side and both men stood and watched: a slow-motion event in a fast-evolving crisis. For just an instant, nothing else mattered. The Leviathan was rising smoothly from the landing pad. First to the height of a man, then a hopper, it rose on above the height of the perimeter walls, and still upward.

'Get up, get up,' urged MacMillan.

'Too late, sir. The enemy's here. P-3 won't get away in time,' said the technician monitoring the traffic LPA.

The distant black dots had grown into tangible vessels, four abreast, closing on Secundo and the labouring Leviathan as it steadily raised its great bulk higher.

One vessel in the attacking flight launched two missiles.

'God, no,' said MacMillan.

***

Major Sarsen ran out into the compound from the base's main doorway; hurrying behind him were four soldiers, each humping a shoulder-launched surface-to-air missile. He pointed toward the line of attacking vessels that were closing on the base. 'One each, left to right, take them out. Move it now. Move!'

As the soldiers began readying the shoulder-launchers, bright flashes bloomed overhead, P-3 had taken two direct hits. The Leviathan rocked, paused then dropped back to the pad sending out a shuddering shockwave that bowled Sarsen and his men over.

The attacking vessels held off, began flying in a circuit beyond the perimeter wall, observing a moment of caution. Then one peeled away from the circuit and advanced slowly, passing high over the perimeter wall and across the compound.

Small arms fire from troops on the perimeter was ineffectual against the heavy metalled hull. The vessel continued, unabated, crossing the pad to hover some fifty metres above the beleaguered P-3. There it stopped, watching. A second craft flew over the perimeter wall to join its leader.

Sarsen rolled onto his side and glanced about. His men were downed too and dazed, like him. He turned his attention to the pad where P-3 sprawled broken. Flames and smoke plumed from two separate wounds in its hull. Otherwise, it seemed intact, but it had come down without its stabiliser legs deployed and had rolled half to one side.

Beyond the perimeter, he counted two vessels still circling while above P-3 two ugly hulls hovered. Unlike the near-silent craft from their own fleet, these attack vessels roared and growled to dominate the soundscape. Sarsen looked back again toward his stunned men. From their place tight in the shadow of the building they were, he hoped, unnoticed for the moment. He knew they had to act at once. Even as he framed orders to shout over the roaring engines, his eyes began to close, and shock reclaimed him.

***

MacMillan stared in horror at the broken Leviathan. The plumes of black smoke were being dissipated by the alien vessels' thrusters as they hovered overhead.

'Barrington, I need to speak with P-3's captain. Now!'

'Sorry, sir, their comms are down, and there's too much interference.'

'Have you been able to raise Major Sarsen again?'

'No, sir, there's been no response to his collar-phone since P-3 went down.'

'Right, send a runner, I need to know where the major is and what people we've got at our disposal.'

'There's movement! Look, the hangar's opening in P-3's side,' said Delacroix. 'There are survivors! They're getting out through the hangar.'

MacMillan returned his attention to the screen as members of the crew emerged from the steadily opening hangar door to scramble out onto the lopsided hull. Swirling smoke surrounded them, and in the background, a red glow told of flames deep within. Some struggled with the injured, others scrambled ahead, ready to lend a hand when it came to the final drop to the ground. With their helmets up and suits intact, they were all protected from the developing inferno, for now.

'God bless those suits. They're going to make it. Ready the medics; we've got casualties coming in.' MacMillan turned toward Barrington again. 'Has that runner caught up with Major Sarsen?'

'Not yet, sir. She's searching now.'

'What the hell is this?' said Delacroix, drawing MacMillan's attention back to the screen. While survivors struggled away from their broken craft, a dozen monsters dropped from one hovering vessel. The great locust-like creatures landed effortlessly, their jointed legs folding and absorbing the shock of the drop. Half of the attackers mustered in an extended line ahead of the escapees. The others jumped up and forward, landing amidst the fleeing crew, then jumped again, carrying them beyond all but a solitary straggler. There, they formed a second line behind the crew.

'Get me some firepower. Take those locusts out!' said MacMillan. 'Where the hell is Sarsen?'

'Still no word, sir,' said Barrington 'The runner's on her way.'

'None of the soldiers on the perimeter can bring their weapons to bear, P-3's blocking the line of sight for some, others will have to guess as they'd be firing through the smoke. They could hit our crew as easily as the enemy, sir,' said Delacroix, slapping a clenched fist into his open palm. 'Damn it!'

'There are plenty of soldiers still inside the base. Delacroix, I want you to form them into three teams. I want a strike party – get them out there and engage those locusts. I want a rescue party to bring in the crew survivors and a third party standing by to defend this building,' said MacMillan.

'Yes, sir,' said Delacroix, hurrying for the exit.

'Barrington, is that air-defence system ready yet?'

'No, sir. They're working flat out, but it will be at least another twenty minutes.'

'Hell, press them. We can't wait.'

MacMillan turned his attention back to the screens, just in time to see one locust at the far end of the line ranged behind the retreating crew raise something in its hand. A second later, there was a swirl across the screen as a fine mesh flew from the device, spreading out and above the fleeing crew.

It descended onto them, and for a moment, arms and legs struggled against the unexpected hinderance.

'Get me a close-up – what the hell is that?'

Focusing on one crewman in the melee, MacMillan saw it was a net. The figure he was watching struggled against it to no avail. Then, as if triggered by the struggle, tendrils sprung out from the fabric of the net to entwine struggling limbs. With each coiling tendril the struggling body was constrained, wrapped. Tied into the covering net.

The locusts in the forward rank had captured the few stunned crew who had passed beyond the reach of the net. They carried them back, throwing them onto the net where more tendrils entwined around them.

'Delacroix, where are you? I need you on that landing pad now! Engage! Engage those devils!' MacMillan could not hide the frustration in his voice. His people were being rolled up, and it seemed there was nothing he could do. The enemy had come at the worst possible moment – an hour later, even half an hour, and the defensive setup would have been very different.

'Just reaching the exit now, sir. We'll be engaging imminently.'

'Go for it.'

MacMillan returned his attention to the main screen just as the locust that had fired the net raised its device again and fired. This time no net. A fine cable soared high and beyond the downed Leviathan toward one of the hovering vessels where it homed in and locked against the hull.

For a moment, nothing more happened. Then MacMillan was horrified to see the cable and fine net shimmer and flicker as a power surge channelled down from the vessel and through the net. The net rippled as trapped bodies arched and shook in response to the power. Then, stunned, the catch stilled.

***

Emerging from the building, Delacroix squinted against the brilliant sheen of blue light that flickered across the netting. A squad of soldiers followed him out, blinking and pausing for just a moment in shock. Drawn from deep in the base, they had not seen the control-room screens. This was their first encounter with events, and from their angle at the building's entrance, there was little smoke to obstruct their view. They took it all in:

the crashed Leviathan's billowing smoke and flames, the locusts on the ground, the trapped crew and, above, the hovering vessels – hell.

A few paces ahead of Delacroix was Sarsen and his squad. The runner was frantically working her way from one to the next, checking.

Delacroix crossed the distance in a moment and knelt. 'Sarsen, how are you?'

'I'll be fine, sir. We took the full shockwave when P-3 went down.' Sarsen began to sit up. 'What's happening now?'

'The locusts are on the ground. Crew were getting out of P-3, but they've been caught in some kind of net. I'm taking my squad in to rescue them. Join us as soon as you're ready. Hell...' The cable attached to the hovering vessel had begun to tighten. Both men struggled to understand want was happening.

'They're hauling in our people,' said the runner who had stopped to watch.

'Not if I have anything to do with it. Listen up! All of you, form up, stand by to advance.' Delacroix rose, then paused as Sarsen reached up to grip his arm.

'Shoulder-launched missiles. My team were coming out to have a go at those vessels when we got caught in the shockwave.' Sarsen waved back toward the wall of the building where a heap of shoulder-mounted ground-to-air missile tubes had been blown by the blast.

'Beautiful. Old-school but effective. Good work, Sarsen.

'Sergeant, take a section, get those missiles armed and bring down those vessels. Launch as soon as you're ready.'

'Yes, sir.'

'The rest of you, on me. We're going in now.'

Sarsen forced himself to his feet, readying to follow Delacroix as the sergeant's section prepared the shoulder-launched missiles. Ahead, Sarsen could see the cable continuing to draw on the net, gathering in its edges before hauling it up and away. He began to shuffle forward, trailing after Delacroix's strike force as it closed rapidly on the enemy.

Delacroix's voice carried across the compound from his place in the middle of the extended line of soldiers. 'Halt! Let's thin this lot out. Single shots, aim high and careful, we have people on the ground. Three rounds each, choose your targets. Aim. Fire... Fire... Fire.'

The reports of volley-fire faded quickly beneath the continuing roar of the hovering vessels.

'Damn.' Delacroix scowled. Their bullets had dug into the locusts' thick exoskeletons, and their crocodile-like toughness had slowed the rounds to a harmless halt. The attention of the locusts turned from the tightening net to the soldiers, Delacroix took two steps forward. He turned to face his men. 'Close ranks. Fix bayonets!'

It took only a moment for the squad to respond. Even so, as Delacroix turned to face forward again, the furthermost line of locusts had already leapt across the net to join the nearer group. A dozen locusts lined against them. The net continued to drag slowly away across the ground – soon it would be airborne, the crew lost to whatever fate the locusts intended.

Before he could call an order, the locusts struck. The monsters jumped, landed at the line of soldiers and commenced grappling. Two soldiers had been floored by locusts landing directly on top of them. Sprawled, they had no defence as the monsters continued the attack. Huge back legs rose and fell, one man's chest caving under a crushing heel. The second soldier was disembowelled by a stamping foot loaded with talons sharp as box cutters, tough enough to cut through the man's protective uniform as though it were tissue paper.

All along the line, hand-to-hand fights were playing through, and everywhere the locusts were winning. Some soldiers had managed to thrust their rifles at their opponents, but the bayonets' sharp points had deflected off hardened exoskeletons, leaving the men face-to-face with a nightmare. Strong, muscular, human arms locked with the smaller upper arms of the locusts. Here, at least, the soldiers had an advantage but could not make it count.

While winning the arm wrestle, everything else was against them. Each moment demanded they constantly flex and turn their bodies to avoid the locusts' thrusting mouths and their great hind legs that kicked out, trying to tear the soldiers' bodies open.

A scream beside Delacroix told him the soldier to his left was in trouble, immediately confirmed by arterial blood spray that soaked the side of Delacroix's face. There was no time to dwell as Delacroix faced his own attacker. He twisted his body to avoid a locust's rising leg and then pulled back his head as the closing locust's mouth snapped shut exactly where his throat had been. He jerked his body again, furious inside that nothing touched these monsters, nothing – neither bullets nor blades. They had nothing to fight with. Already he knew it was only a matter of time.

He lunged in close, gripped the locust's arms and swung his legs in to wrap them round the monster's thorax. He tightened his legs to pull himself in, too close for the striking legs to make contact. His arms kept a tight grip on the monster's little arms, which proved problematic, preventing his own arms from going on the offensive. He heard the frustrated hiss and clack as the locust snapped for his throat, each time failing to make contact, as the rigid exoskeleton that protected it from bullets prevented it flexing enough to deliver the close-in killing bite.

More screams along the line told Delacroix not all the men had been able to resist. Any moment, the balance of numbers would enable the locusts to double-up, and then it would be over.

Whooshing sounds close overhead distracted him for a moment just as it did the locusts. Instinctively, all the combatants glanced up, and Delacroix felt a moment of elation. He sensed the slightest waver through the arms of his opponent. He couldn't see the targets, but he could see the exhaust trails stretching overhead. The sergeant's squad had managed to fire their shoulder-launched missiles.

The detonations were almost instant, targets engaged close by. They'd hit home. *Had they done damage?*

Whatever had happened, the locust had seen and now returned its attention with renewed vigour. Wherever that extra energy came from, Delacroix knew he couldn't match it. The monster's hard, thumping knee was suddenly getting up just a little higher, each blow beating a little harder into the small of his back. Each blow bumped his body higher, his neck getting closer to the snapping maw. With every last ounce of energy, he resisted, hating the great black eyes that got nearer with every forward thrust. Above him, the antennae slashed and cut the air, whipping his face.

Suddenly a man leapt on the locust's back, one arm tight around its neck, joining the fight. It was Sarsen. The locust seemed unconcerned, as though it knew a man could not harm it. The knee banged Delacroix's back again forcing him up and the mouth snapped so close his cheek was opened, and blood began to flow.

Then it happened.

Sarsen had been stabbing with his knife, going for the eyes, but whatever coated them was tough and the blade just slid off. In desperation, he'd changed focus, slashing at the wafting antennae. His blade cut the tip and the locust quivered, straightening up to its full hight. In fury, it shook Delacroix off and stretched its short forearms back and up, in an effort to dislodge Sarsen.

Sarsen didn't wait. Even as hard little claw hands reached round to grip his underarms, he slashed out at the base of the antennae. Connecting perfectly, severing one to its stump. The monster clacked and hissed in protest. Its carapace folded back to unfurl wings as Sarsen struck again. The blow chopped off the second antenna, and the monster dropped to its knees. It appeared to have lost all awareness of its surroundings, suffering pain so great it could concentrate on nothing else.

'The antennae are their weak spot. Cut them off,' said Delacroix into his collar-phone as he stooped to remove a bayonet from a fallen rifle then jumped onto the back of the nearest locust. He climbed up to cut away its antennae as it tried to kill the man it grappled with. Sarsen did the same with another locust. In just a minute, the tide had turned. Half a dozen locusts crawled around, agonised, directionless. Then, with the arrival of the sergeant and his squad, the remaining locusts abandoned the fight, leaping high and far in a swift retreat before opening their carapaces to unfurl their wings and glide off beyond the perimeter wall.

Delacroix looked about. The two vessels that had hovered above the base were downed. One had dropped beyond the perimeter wall, a plume of smoke rising to mark its location. The other had come down within the compound and was already a burning wreck. A long cable reached from behind it, at the end of which was the net – not shimmering now. Power cut off, it lay dull grey and inert. Even from this distance, he could see slight movement. The crew were still alive.

Delacroix touched his sleeve. 'Rescue party, forward. Get the crew out of that net.' He slapped a hand on Sarsen's shoulder. 'Well done. I thought we were losing it for a moment.'

'Thank you, sir. I got lucky. But don't you think you'd better see the medics? Your face is badly cut.'

'Yes, I'll see someone once they've dealt with the others.' Delacroix waved his arm across to where many of the soldiers were down. Several were dead with gaping belly wounds or opened throats. More again had slashes and bites that would keep them out of action for some time. 'Though I tell you what, Sarsen. I'll take lucky, every day. But for you, we'd be done for.'

He turned aside to listen to a message in his collar-phone. 'Yes, sir. We have it under control here. I'll have the site secured and get back to the control room.'

Two shots in rapid succession were followed by a hissing squeal. Delacroix spun round, ready for action. Instead, he relaxed and gave a nod of approval. 'That's a good idea, sergeant, has it worked?'

'Yes, sir. Dead as a doornail,' said the sergeant kicking at the stilled locust.

'Right, finish off the others too. Let's clear the decks, shall we?'

'Very good, sir.' The sergeant stepped over to the next locust that clicked in confusion and rolled from side to side with no balance or coordination, its carapace open, wings fluttering aimlessly. Moving behind the locust, he fired two rounds into the soft, exposed back.

'And good shooting with those shoulder-launchers too,' said Delacroix as the sergeant moved on to dispatch the next meandering locust.

Chapter 21

Opsythia e.: Base Secundo

MacMillan looked up from the LPA he'd been studying as Delacroix entered the control room. He beckoned his second-in-command to him. 'Good work out there; that was going against us for a while.'

'Yes, sir. Close run for sure. Those locusts have tough shells, virtually bullet-proof.'

'So I saw. But you cracked it.'

Delacroix glanced quizzically at MacMillan. *Was he making a joke? Perhaps, perhaps not.* He decided to play safe and ignore it. 'It was Sarsen. Took some courage to jump on the back of that monster. If he hadn't, I'd be finished.'

'I saw it on-screen. Saw your boys bring down those combat vessels too. It shows everyone these monsters can be stopped,' said MacMillan.

'Yes, sir. But what exactly happened? I was hand-to-claw with a locust so missed it.'

'I've just been reviewing it all, and I think we got lucky… or they got overconfident.' MacMillan looked toward a technician and nodded. 'Re-run the sequence but speed it up – we don't have much time.'

Both men watched the replay as MacMillan pointed out the four vessels circling the base. 'See, they start cautiously. Holding off beyond the perimeter. I think they're testing our air defences, trying to draw our fire. We have nothing to offer other than small arms, so they quickly decide it's going to be a walkover. Those two close in, while the other two remain circling beyond the perimeter.'

Delacroix pointed. 'I see that, and look at those shoulder-launched missiles fly in. Bang, bang. Bang, bang. Take out both vessels in short order.'

'Yes. I'm sure they have anti-missile defences, but they had relaxed their guard, weren't expecting it, and they were too close. No time to react. See how the remaining two vessels veered away as soon as we brought down the first two. They'll be more careful now, for sure. They've landed down on the plain where P-3 used to be.'

'What now, sir?'

'I don't think they'll risk flying directly overhead again. They'll try something else.'

'A ground assault?'

'I think so. But if they do try to fly in again, we'll have the main air-defence missile batteries dialled in and ready. Now, you need to go and get your face stitched. I've got every available person preparing. Military personnel armed and reinforcing the perimeter and roof. Support staff breaking open more weapons stores—'

'Colonel, you need to see this now,' said the traffic-monitoring technician from her LPA. There, Professor Baillie, the base's chief scientist, was already peering into the display.

The two men hurried across to join them. 'What have you got?' said MacMillan.

The LPA told the story. High in the atmosphere, coloured lights signed an aerial conflict that raged unseen from the ground.

Professor Baillie pointed into the LPA. 'The three blue signals are our warbirds. They've managed to hold the main attack force at bay so far. We're clearly more manoeuvrable, have better fire power. Several of the locust vessels have been downed. I think our technology really is miles ahead.'

'That's good,' said Delacroix, recalling the wave of twenty vessels that had first approached. Four had reached Secundo. There were now only eight red signal lights showing in the LPA. 'Looks like our warbirds can hold that lot off all day…'

Delacroix fell silent as the chief scientist frowned slightly and stroked her sleeve, changing the scale to display the whole atmosphere and beyond. The distant cone had shed more vessels. Ranks of red lights signalled a second wave of twenty more attackers that was just cresting the planetary horizon and would engage the warbirds imminently. A third wave was following behind that.

The scientist looked hesitantly at MacMillan. 'Colonel?'

MacMillan spun around and shouted across the control room. 'Barrington, raise the warbirds now! Tell them to break off immediately. There's a whole armada coming at them; they'll have no chance!'

Chapter 22

Opsythia e.: High Atmosphere

With just the slightest touch of finger on joystick, Ches turned P-3:C1 hard to starboard while simultaneously pulling the warbird's head up, powering it onward into a tightening spiral climb – a manoeuvre that would have been impossible in a regular craft. Here, the gravdrive maintained a perfectly steady environment inside the cockpit, neutralising the G-force even as it powered on at breathtaking speed.

The warbird's tightening circle rapidly brought its heading to bear on the enemy vessel that was closing behind P-3:C3. The vessel realised the danger it was in and suddenly began to turn, backing away from the closing warbird.

Ches whooped as his eyeline focused on the locust. He triggered a short-range laser that flashed out to burr against the locust's hull. The beam carved a hole in the enemy, and it fell away, crashing down through the atmosphere.

He heard words of thanks through the collar-phone as the pilot of P-3:C3 acknowledged his help. All three warbirds came together forming up in a line abreast and prepared to give chase to the remnant of the locust attacking force.

'Ches, message from Secundo. We're ordered to break off. Withdraw now,' said Nessie, his co-pilot.

'What? We'll have this lot mopped up in minutes. It must be a mistake. Double-check that order,' said Ches, his focus on the retreating locusts.

Nessie was half-turned in her seat, looking into the neat little LPA located directly behind their seats. 'We've got to go, Ches. Break off pursuit; the locusts are leading us into a trap. Look!'

Ches leaned round to see, as a babble in his collar-phone told him the other warbirds had spotted the problem. The LPA displayed a block of red light directly ahead, representing a tightly packed attack formation emerging from behind the curve of the planet and on collision course. He turned forward to see the new wave of twenty vessels join the remnant of the first wave, all deployed in a grid formation and closing fast.

'Everyone, let's get out of here. Fall back and regroup.' He touched the joystick and the warbird's head began to rise, arcing up and away from the oncoming locusts. Glancing to either side, he was reassured to see the other warbirds were with him.

The gravdrive's speed soon had them clear of the enemy, and as Nessie reported back to Secundo, Ches considered his next move.

'Big odds, but let's slow down a little, see if we can tempt them after us, draw them away from Secundo.'

A chorus of acknowledgement sounded, and the three warbirds slowed, allowing the following locusts to close the gap. For a few moments it seemed the ploy was working. Then, as one, the armada altered course, making for Secundo.

'Hell, we can't let that lot go in unchallenged. Come on, guys, on me, we're going back in.' As he turned the warbird, Ches glanced toward Nessie. 'What are the odds?'

'Not good, Ches. Back to where we started, I reckon, worse maybe.'

'No, not good. But we have to give it a go. We're Secundo's only cover. And hell, they've got to pay for P-3. Hopefully, MacMillan's got the air defences rigged now, so we can hit them from above and below simultaneously.'

Nessie nodded then spoke to the control room while closely watching the gap between warbirds and locusts close, in the LPA. She acknowledged a message from Secundo control room and quickly increased the range displayed in the LPA. She paled.

'Ches,' she said, in almost a whisper. 'Ches, there's a third wave.'

Ches turned to look into the LPA. 'Hell,' he said. The third wave had breached the horizon and was closing in behind the warbirds; they were caught between the waves. Turning forward again, he whistled. The leading wave of enemy vessels that they had begun to chase was turning in a great upward loop, bringing them above the warbirds. They were caught: a wave above, a wave behind.

Their best bet was to dive into the atmosphere but that would draw the whole fleet onto Secundo. Air defences or not, numbers like this would overwhelm the base.

'What's the plan, Ches?' came a worried pilot's voice. 'We're getting boxed in.' The newly arrived third wave was splitting into two parts, some peeling off to create the third side of a shooting box with the warbirds in the middle – suddenly they were the targets and would shortly be brought under fire from three sides at once.

'Incoming missiles! The second wave has launched a full salvo,' said Nessie, turning from the LPA to her pilot. 'Ches?'

His moment of indecision passed, and Ches kicked into action. The two parts of the third wave were closing, but they were yet still too distant to engage the warbirds.

'Lasers to auto-defence, evasive manoeuvres and forward, fast. Let's punch a hole through the second wave and take some of them out as we go,' said Ches, his voice calm. He powered his warbird ahead making directly for the locust second wave. He didn't have time to look but knew the other pilots were with him.

From the nose of his warbird a shaft of laser light burst forward and destroyed an oncoming missile, then another. Destroy, rinse, repeat; destroy, rinse, repeat. Flashes of light seen in the corner of his eyes told him the other warbirds were doing the same. Those missiles that weren't destroyed flashed past and on into oblivion.

Too late, the second wave realised that their missiles had failed; the warbirds were on them.

'Fire at will, take them out! Break through their line. On the other side, reform and we'll come straight back at them before they can turn; strafe them from the rear and fall back. We'll see how the odds look then.'

He looked toward a locust vessel, touched his trigger to loose a missile then turned his focus to another vessel, knowing the first missile would deliver a kill. He fired again, and again. Then he was through, turning hard, sensing the presence of the other warbirds lining up on him. As the turn completed, he heard Nessie catch her breath at the devastation they had caused. Nine of the enemy vessels were shattered, some burned, others left as hulks without power.

'On me,' ordered Ches. He led the three warbirds back toward the rear of the second wave where the remaining vessels were struggling to make a turn tight enough to bring their weapons systems to bear. No time, they failed, and the warbirds swept along the rear of the line, loosing six more missiles, six more kills. The gravdrive gave them an impressive technological edge.

Nessie reached out a hand and touched Ches' arm. She looked out and he followed her gaze beyond the shattered line of the second wave to see half the third wave closing in at maximum speed.

'They're coming through the line of their own ships; they can't fire on us from that angle,' said Ches.

A moment later they both watched in horror as the third wave loosed a salvo of missiles which streaked through the line of the second wave. Three vessels were hit by friendly fire and immediately exploded while other missiles streaked past, homing on the warbirds.

'Helmets up, Nessie. This is getting a bit tight!' called Ches as the warbirds' lasers began cutting down approaching missiles.

Ches looked on in disbelief as the locust vessels of the third wave ploughed through what was left of the second. Two further collisions took out four enemy vessels, but still they came. He looked at the onrushing line of vessels and released a missile at the nearest, fired at the next and the next.

'Ches. Above us! Above!' cried Nessie.

Ches looked up. Despairing, he realised he'd got the timing wrong as the other half of the third wave swept down on them preceded by a salvo of missiles. The auto-laser was committed to the front, there was nothing he could do except take Nessie's offered hand. They both squeezed even as a proximity-blast missile exploded, peppering the craft with shrapnel. The cabin fuselage shattered and vacuum immediately sucked out the air. The warbird was dead. In shock, the pair watched a second missile rushing inward. It ploughed into the cabin, exploding the warbird and its crew into particles of nothing.

Chapter 23

Opsythia e.: Base Secundo

'It's over,' said Baillie. The chief scientist looked toward MacMillan in despair as the last blue light flashed out. The atmosphere was left awash with red. One moment, the warbirds had been holding their own; the next, a tactical error had destroyed them all.

'Details?' said MacMillan, crossing to join her at the LPA.

'They're all downed, sir. We have nothing left. When this phase of the engagement started, our warbirds faced about forty-five active enemy attack vessels. Now, they have a little more than twenty active vessels in theatre. We have none.'

MacMillan turned back to the screens where he could see Sarsen on the perimeter wall briefing some soldiers. He touched his sleeve. 'Sarsen, are the air defences deployed and fully operational yet?'

'Yes, sir. Four batteries, deployed and ready around the site.' Sarsen's reply sounded clear and calm in MacMillan's collar-phone.

'Good, stand by now. We've just lost our air cover, and there are twenty and more locust vessels poised to come in on us.'

'Very good, sir. And you should know, we're observing the two vessels that touched down on the plain; the only movement has been a few locusts spreading around their vessels in defensive positions. No aggressive movement from them.'

MacMillan turned to Professor Baillie. 'I want you to catch up with Delacroix. He's beefing up the building's defences. Help him understand what we've got here and get your people working on how we stop those locusts. Facing a bullet-proof enemy is not good.'

'Yes, colonel,' she said. 'But before I go, there's something odd.'

'Go on.'

She pointed into the LPA. 'The remaining locust vessels are not making any attempt to attack. Quite the opposite, they have spread out and seem to be making a slow pass around the atmosphere.'

MacMillan joined her. 'Suits me, every minute counts right now. What are they up to?'

'I wasn't sure at first,' said Baillie. Playing with the LPA's scale display she closed in on one tight section of sky. 'Now you can see better. Look here, colonel. There are many more of these tiny red signals. At first, we attributed them to debris from destroyed vessels. But comms has reported many are emitting live signals. Too small for a vessel of any sort but, nonetheless, all emitting signals. And it looks like the locusts are attracted to them...'

'And?'

'I wonder if they are survivors from the vessels our warbirds put down. That could make sense.'

'Could do. Whatever they're doing, it's buying us time, so let's make the most of it. Now, Baillie, I'd like you to get along and link up with Delacroix.'

'Yes, on my way, colonel.'

'Colonel MacMillan, sir, I've got contact with P-1. She's just emerged from the sun's shadow,' said Barrington from his comms console.

'Great, patch me through now.'

Chapter 24

O-1 Above Earth's Atmosphere

Steph stood on the bridge of O-1 staring intently into the screen. All the calculations had been done. Everything checked, checked a dozen times. It was now or never. Celine and Lily stood ready beside her. It felt an eternity since any of them had slept. Now, all the thinking, all the Goliath's processing power, everyone's labours, everything, was all coming together, but would it be enough to reopen Earth's atmosphere?

'Right, you know the plan,' said Steph. 'It's time to begin. Be careful, I want only good news today.' The general had insisted she attend to oversee Celine's team in action; today's exercise was too important to leave to anyone else. Urgent as the weapons hunt was, it had been set aside for now.

Celine nodded an acknowledgement and activated her collar-phone. 'All stations, stand by.' She glanced at Steph who nodded permission. 'Commencing project now. Positioning the first sample craft in… three, two, one.' She stroked her sleeve and transmitted the start order.

The little group on the bridge watched as an observer flitted across their bow, leading a great sampler down toward Earth's atmosphere. The observer stopped, holding station as the sampler slowly continued its descent to the uppermost edge of the atmosphere… there it paused.

'There's the gravlift activated now,' said Lily, concern clear in her voice as she watched the broad iridescent tube project and widen from beneath the sampler.

'We see it,' said Steph. 'Now's the moment of truth. It works or it doesn't. All we can do is wait.'

'And pray,' said Celine.

'And pray,' echoed Steph.

Instinctively, the three women closed together.

'There's a flash,' said Lily. 'And another.'

At the outer edge of the atmosphere the sampler's modified gravlift was directed down to form a protective tube, against which debris was crashing. Some debris vapourised or burned in the energy release caused by abrupt collision. Other scrap was deflected and dropped, knocked out of their wild orbits.

'Integrity?' said Steph.

'Solid. Nothing is getting through the tube. We're good so far,' said Celine. 'Observers, what are you seeing?'

'All good from here, ma'am,' came a flurry of replies.

'Broaden the tube diameter to the maximum and extend the reach of the gravlift. I want the effective maximum tube length confirmed,' said Celine.

Acknowledgements returned through the collar-phones, and they watched as the power increased and the tube's reach extended below the sample craft. More incidental flares and flashes signalled repeated debris contacts. Utilising the sample craft's full power, the length of the tube had reached far below. Its extension was halted only when technicians reported the lower end was losing its resistance powers.

'Hold it there,' said Steph. 'Lock it, geostationary. Send in the second sampler.'

Celine implemented the orders and a second sample craft ventured ahead of O-1, where it manoeuvred to a position above the first. Then it began a slow descent. Passing close by the first craft, it entered the protective tube of the active gravlift. The downward transporter force kicked in, and the second craft suddenly accelerated down.

On O-1's bridge, everyone held their breath.

'Compensate! Compensate for that downward pressure,' said Steph.

A voice in the collar-phones provided acknowledgement that the science team was on the job. They watched as the craft's speed of descent reduced to a modest drop, coming to a halt at the bottom of the visible gravlift tube.

'In position,' said Celine. She glanced at Steph then broadcasted the command. 'Activate the second sampler's gravlift.' They watched the glistening tube project down, extending the combined tube further. 'That's good. Extend to the max, please.'

The tube extended beneath the second craft, again it maintained integrity; random flashes highlighted debris collisions to confirm success.

'Bring in the third sampler,' said Steph.

When the process completed for a third time without incident, she turned to Celine. 'Looking good. Now let's keep the process going, smooth and steady... and carefully – I don't want any bumps.'

Celine immediately began to issue orders, calling forward a fourth sample craft.

Steph walked from the bridge to the navigation room and joined a cluster of scientists around the LPA, its light display illuminating excited faces. At last, something was going their way.

The LPA was set to display Earth and the immediate space. The strings of lights made Steph's heart leap with joy and near disbelief. How had they managed to pull this off? And so quickly. She loved her team, every one of them.

Steph didn't need to count the lights. She knew exactly how many there were. Stretched out in a tight line astern were four hundred and ninety-seven lights. Each one an unmanned sample craft functioning under Celine's auto-program. The foremost light began moving slowly away from the formation, manoeuvring to take its place as number four in the column. If this one went smoothly, they could have confidence in the process and build the virtual shielded tube all the way down to the surface.

'Looking good,' she said as the craft slipped past the three in the column and continued downward, halting at the appropriate spot. 'Looking very good, but there's still a long way to go.'

Chapter 25

Osarus c.

The heavy rains finally broke as the wind carried much of the cloud beyond the mouth of the valley, and between sporadic showers, the sun shone again.

Baz Browning sat in the hopper's shotgun seat as it reached the top end of the valley. He scanned across the rolling savannah beyond. The river was in full flood, higher even than when Jamie had rescued the two hopper crews. There was no sign of the once familiar rocky river crossing, now completely submerged as water poured from the savannah into the valley.

Across the wide flat savannah, a fine morning haze limited their visibility to two miles at most.

'Hello S-3, Are you getting this on-camera?' said Browning.

'We are, it's amazing. Stunning,' said Jamie from S-3's bridge.

'You should see it here, for real.'

As far as the eye could see, the once dried browns and burnt blacks of sun-withered savannah had turned vibrant green. Fast-growing grasses had emerged, reaching up toward the sunlight. They raced for height against a multitude of wildflowers, every one of which seemed to boast a different colour, all combining into brilliant kaleidoscopic contrasts. The hopper's open hatch allowed in a heady floral perfume. They could see swarms of insects gathered at flower heads, flitting to and fro in a frantic rush for the best of everything, anything.

'Still no sign of the herd,' said Browning.

'The drone's showing them clearly, just over twenty miles out. Still very slow moving,' said Jamie, eyeing a drone video feed displayed on the screen adjacent to the hopper's feed.

'We'll move into the savannah; see if we can meet up with them.'

'Okay. But be careful, Baz – some of these beasts look pretty big.'

'Will do,' said Browning, tapping the driver on the shoulder and pointing him forward. The hopper moved away from the valley onto the savannah, then turned to follow the line of hills, heading toward the approaching herd.

As morning drew on, the sun steadily burned away the mist.

'Driver, I see them.' Baz pointed out across the plain. Then his arm swung in an arc. 'There. There. Everywhere.'

'Yes, sir, what now?'

'Let's get closer. Slowly, though.'

The hopper moved forward. With every passing moment, more animals were appearing, the fresh greenery nearly obscured by the mass of moving bodies. Hairy mammalian bodies – blacks and browns, whites and stripes, a variety of different species. Mostly heads down and grazing, but frequently the leaders looked up and scanned for danger.

One larger breed stood out. Elephant-like, males sported long mouth tusks complemented by a pair of horns. The shorter-tusked females had no horns but were almost all accompanied by young who stayed close to their grazing mothers.

The giants moved in harmonious procession with the smaller animals. Some heavy-set and thick-shouldered, others slight of build and fleet of foot.

'Sir, it's like something out of the African plains,' said the driver.

'It is. Perhaps this is how nature is everywhere when man's not around to mess things up. Stop here for a minute. Let's not cause them any anxiety. Let them come to us.'

The hopper stopped and both men watched in rapt silence as the herd approached. The animals, though displaying natural caution, were largely unconcerned by their presence and continued to advance. The first animal to near the hopper was a large, male elephantine beast; its trunk reached up toward the top of the hopper, exploring. Baz quickly shut the hatch, and both men watched the end of the trunk snuffle and feel, testing the clear surface. Huge tusks brushed against the hopper's side in the passing but applied no pressure. Ears flapped, listening for danger. Then, content, the beast moved on, followed by its family who all continued to graze as they wandered beyond the hopper.

'That was a big boy,' said Browning. He flipped open the hatch again, and now the air was filled with the sounds of unfamiliar calls, strange familial rallying cries and the bleated replies of lost young responding to searching mothers.

'These breeds all appear to be herbivores,' came Ossie's voice in the collar-phones. 'You'll have noticed the animals are always alert, even the biggest. Where there's lots of meat, there's invariably predators. Can you see anything?'

'No, it's all peaceful here. No obvious threats,' said Browning.

'Okay, but be on the lookout.'

'No problem.' Baz leaned forward to the driver. 'Let's try moving a little, see how they react. Slowly.'

The driver nodded and had the hopper edge forward, causing animals in the immediate area to start before returning to their grazing. The driver moved again, and this time the hopper continued forward. After an initial stir, the animals ignored it. Whatever they thought of the hopper, they did not perceive it as a danger.

An hour of rapt observation passed, and then Baz had the driver turn and head back for S-3. They reached the head of the slow-moving herd and quickly left them behind. 'At the speed the herd's moving now, they'll be at the river in another day, maybe two,' said Browning.

Chapter 26

Opsythia e.: Base Secundo

Sarsen stood behind the perimeter wall's parapet, looking down the gentle slope to where the first two locust vessels had been joined by others. Four neat ranks of five. Twenty loads of lethal locusts. There had been more, but two smouldering wrecks to the side showed the air-defence batteries were tuned in tight; anything flying in toward the perimeter wall was going down, hard.

The locusts had learned the lesson, and no further sorties had come toward the base. The flights that did go up were careful to take off away from the base. The control room had let him know these flights were following a pattern, steadily scouring the planet.

He raised his binoculars and again scanned the vessels on the plain below.

'Sergeant, there's a lot of them out and about now, and who knows how many are still on board their vessels.'

'Yes, sir, what do you think they'll do?'

'They'll come straight up that slope. Have to.'

'That's going to be tough. Our bullets don't scratch them, and we're outnumbered. Our own company from P-3 has only eighty fighting fit. Even with the troops we took off P-1 and P-2 to help with building the base, we're little more than two hundred and fifty strong, all in.'

'I know, said Sarsen, turning to look down into the base where groups of his men were practising paired assaults. Closer to the building, the soldiers of P-1 were reinforcing the base entrance; he knew another group was doing the same at the rear. Troops from P-2 were on the base roof, putting up a makeshift barricade to defend the roof and access door.

'What I'd give for some artillery right now, sir,' said the sergeant. 'Hit those vessels on the ground. Arrogant devils, they think we can't touch them from here.'

'They seem to have that right, sergeant.'

'Yes, sir. But I don't care how thick their locust shells are, a close proximity blast would do the trick.'

'Damned shame about our mortars.'

Both men turned to look ruefully at the hulk of P-3, broken on the pad where it had fallen. Smoke still billowed out of the two hull breaches and the open hatch. Occasional rumbles and flashes of orange told of explosions within.

'Looks like more hand-to-hand then.'

'Yes, sir.'

The men turned to look again at the locust vessels.

Chapter 27

Opsythia System: P-1

Captain Grainger stood considering the LPA. It presently displayed the whole system. Immediately behind P-1's marker light was the system's sun, Opsythia A. Distributed out beyond were the four planets, a course line projected from P-1 to the most distant planet, Opsythia e.

Beside her stood her chief scientist Eric Fritz. 'It's going to take a day to get back to Secundo. I've no military experience, captain. Do you think they can hold out?'

'I hope so. But be certain, our getting back does not automatically save anyone. Christ! They've already managed to down one Leviathan. Apparently P3's completely wrecked, and God knows what's happened to P-2. It should have been following that cone out of the Fold. We'll have to be damned careful; I'm not handing them this one too.' She turned to stare intently at Fritz.

'What can we do, captain?'

'We can fight. Colonel MacMillan has ordered us to forget about him and the ground crew for now. Our only concern is to get to the cone, do whatever it takes to destroy the sample ship they've incorporated into the construction. Destroy that, and no matter what else happens, these monsters will lose the folddrive capability they've pirated – then they won't be getting out of this system in a hurry. At best, we'll win. At worst, the locusts will be stuck here until General Dower and the Primo people come up with a force that can roll this lot up for good.'

Fritz tweaked the LPA settings, and the scale changed as lights rearranged to display the local Secundo data they'd received earlier. The situation at Opsythia e. and its nearby space flickered into focus, displaying the situation as it was in the moment when the last of the warbirds had been downed. The cone was clearly visible circling above the planet.

'What do you think?' said Grainger.

'I've passed the aerial conflict section directly on to Captain Ash as you instructed. She and her pilots are studying the data now. I'm not military so not about to start briefing anyone on strategy and tactics. I did have a look though and three things stand out to my untrained eye. Our warbirds are far more manoeuvrable, can pretty well dance around the locust attack vessels all day long. The warbirds are much better armed too, both our defensive and offensive weapons are infinitely superior… and the locusts so vastly outnumber our warbirds that any individual advantage is swamped by sheer weight of numbers.'

Fritz turned away from the LPA. 'Hell, Captain Ash has only three warbirds, what can she really do? Is there any chance?'

'Steady, Fritz,' said Grainger. 'Let Ash do the analysis and see what she comes up with. The colonel's given us a job, so we'll do it, come what may. Now tell me what else you've picked out of the data.'

'From our present distance, we can't see anything about the cone other than it's there and it's way too far off to detect the individual vessels. But picking through the data captured by Secundo, and the warbirds before they went down, we can make some deductions.'

'Go on,' said Grainger.

'The cone launched three waves of attack, around sixty vessels in total. It seems about twenty of those attack vessels survived—'

'Around forty taken out. Our warbirds put up a real fight.'

'Yes, ma'am. They did.'

'Hell, if we could have put all our warbirds up together, we'd have wiped the floor with them.'

'Perhaps. I've tried to calculate exactly how many attack vessels might still be on the cone, but it's hard to gauge. I think there could be eighty vessels, maybe as many as a hundred. We need clean readings to calculate that properly, and Secundo can't deliver sufficient detail from the planet's surface. It'll have to wait until we're closer.'

'That's more than we'd estimated initially.'

'Yes, it is.'

'We need to hurry. What's our soonest ETA?'

'Engineering has us running flat out, but Opsythia e. is the outermost planet. A full day on present progress.'

'Right, I want you and the whole science team on this, analyse all the data we've received. If these locusts have any weaknesses, I want to know. Meantime, I'm going down to speak with Captain Ash, see what she's thinking,' said Grainger.

Chapter 28

Opsythia e.: Base Secundo

MacMillan sat ramrod straight in his command chair. He listened to Delacroix listing progress in securing the base while he continued to watch events play out on the control-room screens. A little distance beyond the perimeter, he could see a squad of soldiers surrounding the first downed locust vessel. After taking a hit from shoulder-launched missiles, it had veered away as if starting a run for safety only to drop directly beyond the perimeter wall. Unlike the vessel that came down inside the perimeter, this one had retained its structural integrity – an opportunity to gather intelligence.

MacMillan touched his sleeve. 'Major Sarsen, be very careful. Any doubt, get out.'

'Yes, sir.'

MacMillan turned to Delacroix who was watching as one of the technicians channelled Sarsen's body-camera feed direct onto the screen. 'Big moment, Delacroix. Now we'll find out the true nature of what we're up against.'

***

Sarsen circled around the vessel. The fuselage was tilted to one side, marking its violent and undignified end. Perhaps eighty paces in length, its fuselage had a roughly square cross-section ten paces a side. At the rear were two exhaust outlets, indicating a burning fuel propulsion system. They were broken and twisted, showing exactly where one of the missiles had hit home. A dorsal fin emerged at the mid-point of the fuselage and stretched

117

back to the tail, rising in height all the way, ending, he guessed, at twice the height of a man. It was mirrored by identical fins to either side of the fuselage.

One wing was broken off and lay a little behind where the vessel had finally stopped, marking the point of first impact. The other wing, heavy-duty, and still in situ, protruded from about the mid-point of the fuselage, a manoeuvring thruster set near its wing tip. The whole wing reached up at an angle, signing the vessel's unbalanced end. The wing's underside bared the vessel's teeth – a row of missiles.

It seemed every surface was angular, no aesthetics; everything was functional.

'Right, sergeant, that's our way in,' said Sarsen, pointing to the gaping hole in the fuselage where the starboard wing had been ripped away. Close to the ground, the hole offered easy access. A few paces in front was a second hole, less inviting, its jagged metal edges all twisted and blackened where the second missile had hit home. Judging by the mess, Sarsen guessed it had been a direct hit into the vessel's fuel compartment – a vulnerability it was good to know about.

'I'll go in first. Once I know it's safe, you follow me in with the professor.'

'Yes, sir.' The sergeant took a brief moment to grin toward Baillie who was crouched close beside him and clearly out of her comfort zone. As she framed a question for him, the sergeant looked away, checking his men were exactly where he wanted. Three squads. One formed an inward facing perimeter – just in case something nasty had survived the crash. The second watched for any movement from the locusts down on the plain. The third gathered immediately around him, ready to do his bidding.

Sarsen flipped his helmet up as a precaution against the unknown and signalled two soldiers to follow him, then sprinted the short distance to the broken fuselage. There, they paused, alert for danger. Nothing happened.

Gingerly, he leaned into the hole and shone his torch about. There was nothing there. The space was empty like a cargo hold. The void stretched forward from the vessel's tail, ending at a bulkhead immediately forward of the hull breach he was peering through. He pulled himself inside and straightened up. Not much headroom with the helmet up but enough.

Swinging his torch beam around, he inspected the space more closely then took a couple of steps in from the hull breach. He paused beside the only object in the whole space. It was a large winch, its drum heavy with coiled cable. The cable's free end fed from the winch drum, up to the deckhead and around a cable fairlead that redirected the cable away aft. He beckoned his escorting soldiers in, and the three men spread out to search the space.

No signs of life. A flat and empty deck, clear bulkheads either side. The men worked their way to the aft end; the whole space was empty save for three more fairleads, each set tight to the deckhead and evenly spaced in a line, guiding the cable toward the aft bulkhead. From the rearmost fairlead the cable's end hung down, still.

He spotted what appeared to be hinging where the deck met the aft bulkhead but if it were a doorway, it was sealed tight.

Puzzled, Sarsen was about to report a blank when one of the soldiers called him forward to the winch and pointed upward. He hurried to join the man and was pleased to see what appeared to be a flap set into the deckhead.

'Well spotted, soldier, it's something – a hatch, but no handle. Does it tilt up, maybe? Come on, let's push together.'

In only a moment, they had the hatch swinging up. With a boost up from the soldiers, Sarsen rose too. Shining his torch about revealed a hellish tableau – a frozen scene of carnage. Almost reluctantly, he levered himself up. He knew nothing was alive up here.

'Hello, sergeant, bring in the professor and your boys. It's messy, but I don't think we're facing a live threat.'

'Roger that, sir. Coming in now.'

Within minutes, the sergeant clambered up through the hatch then leaned back down and offered a helping hand to Professor Baillie. She was up in a flash, and as more of the sergeant's men climbed up behind her, she stepped across the passageway to join Sarsen. The appalled look on her face was hidden behind her raised helmet.

Sarsen kicked at the blackened shell of a dead locust. 'This one's no threat. Burned to a crisp. Them too,' he said, pointing his torch forward to where several more locusts lay dead.

'It's brutal,' said Baillie. 'They're all dead. What happened?'

Sarsen looked beyond her to where the soldiers were mustering. 'Sergeant, form two squads, one move forward, one aft. Let's get a body count, find out how many monsters these vessels carry. Photograph everything. Any loose objects, gather them up. Let's be quick and let's be careful. Any sign of life, end it.'

'Yes, sir,' said the sergeant turning his attention to the soldiers.

Sarsen reached out to swipe his hand across a surface, then turned to face Baillie, showing the blackened fingers. He pointed forward to where the equally blackened deck was ruptured. 'It's soot. Residue from wild burning fuel. I think this is the other end of that charred hull breach we saw outside. Our missile punched through the hull, breached their fuel tanks and carried on into the accommodation, bringing a fireball with it.'

'Well, now we know they don't like fire,' said Baillie. 'It's a vulnerability to think about.' She knelt down beside the burnt insect to get a better look.

'All clear aft, sir. We count seventeen dead. All fried. The fireball must have spread the whole length of the vessel.'

'Thank you, soldier,' said Sarsen into his collar-phone. Can you make out what the rear areas are used for?'

'Not sure, sir. Everywhere is covered in soot, but we're thinking living quarters. There are rows of recesses, the same size as locust bodies. Maybe personal pods or some such.'

'Okay, remember, photograph everything. Gather what you can then fall back to the hatch.' Sarsen stepped over the dead locust then paused, waiting for Baillie who had remained kneeling to look more closely at the carcass.

'Look, major, it's the antennae again. They've curled and shrivelled in the flame. The antennae certainly seem to be their Achilles heel.'

Sarsen peered at the locust's wizened sensors then turned to look forward again; the leading soldiers had just about reached what he assumed would be the bridge or cockpit. 'Yes, just a pity we have to get so close to harm them. Come on let's see what the cockpit looks like.'

The squad searching forward had identified cabins off the passageway; some were storerooms, others: workshops and tech spaces. An open hatch like the one they had used to climb up into the passageway let down to what was an engine room of sorts. Down there, trails of smoke hung in the atmosphere, and Sarsen called back the two men who were starting a descent into the murk. He slammed the hatch shut – it was clearly still a hostile environment below and he had no intention of risking men needlessly.

The bridge was compact, at a pinch offering space for half a dozen of the locusts to work. They counted four dead. One of the soldiers pulled a soot-smeared object from the clutching claws of a dead locust and held it out for inspection. Dome-shaped, as high as a man's arm is long and half as wide. The soldiers reported finding other similar artefacts in the aft accommodation area, more lay scattered about elsewhere.

Baillie looked at it closely, rubbed the back of her suited hand across it to reveal the surface was transparent.

'It's very light, ma'am,' said the soldier, 'like a feather. What do you think it is?'

She took it, weighed it in her hands and expressed surprise at just how light it was. Then she turned it round. 'It's like an urn, only deeper. The locust was doing something with it when it was overcome by the fireball, but what?' She let her hands slide over the object, felt a lip or edging around the rim. Holding it at arm's length, she considered it carefully. Then she glanced at the dead locust and back to the object.

She knelt beside the carcass and felt around its neck. 'Yes, see here? It's carapace has ridging that I'll bet it could tense to clamp about the edge of this – it's not an urn, it's a dome. Actually, it's a helmet. I'm guessing a survival helmet, a space helmet maybe?'

Sarsen gave a nod. 'Makes sense. Space vessel… space helmet.'

Baillie pressed a gloved finger against the locust's body. 'This carapace is so thick and strong, when closed it'll be impermeable like a spacesuit. In fact, it's exactly a spacesuit. Their heads are the weak spot; had any managed to get their helmets on, I think they might have survived.'

'Lucky us,' said Sarsen. 'Why didn't they have their helmets on?'

'They were flying within a breathable atmosphere. Overconfidence, maybe? They had probably decided they had an edge over us, and your shoulder-launched missiles took them completely by surprise.'

In the absence of any onboard power, all the equipment was dead, and the systems could not be accessed. With no more immediate gains on offer, the team began their withdrawal.

Sarsen dropped through the hatch from the charred passageway into the relatively pristine hangar. He paused and took a final look around. 'This space is different from the rest. What do you think it's for?' he said to Baillie who had dropped down behind him.

'I've no idea. Storage maybe?' She shrugged and headed for the breach in the hull. Sarsen followed close behind.

Chapter 29

O-1 Above Earth's Atmosphere

'Send it in,' said Steph.

At once, a small sample craft peeled off from what remained of the hovering flotilla and headed toward the uppermost of the extended column of giant samplers that now formed the complete gravlift tube. The shimmering tube stretched down and away toward the Earth's surface, vanishing from human eyes long before reaching the safety of debris free surface air. Though far off and out of sight, they all knew the tube reached safely down – the steady flow of readings said so, and the regular flashes they were seeing stood witness to its existence as debris continued to collide and vaporise against the outer sides of the tube.

Steph chanced the briefest of glances away from the manoeuvring test craft toward another identical one that held station a little way off. It was laden with the second virus that weeks before should have been distributed through Earth's atmosphere to mix with, and naturally modify, the previously released first virus.

The intended product of that mixing was a more benign virus, which in turn should have been harvested for circulation back among all the life planets.

She looked back toward the test craft just as it paused above the giant gravlift tube. Everyone waited with bated breath. If this automated test flight made it down, Steph could send in the craft carrying the second virus. They could begin the rescue of Earth and its survivors.

The descent seemed to take an age, but care was needed to ensure the descending craft slipped safely past each of the samplers maintaining the tube. Then, a signal passed up the column from craft to craft, repeated and boosted by each in turn to overcome the signal resistance of the tube and the debris field. And finally, word sounded in Steph's collar-phone, she looked at her team and cheered. The whole bridge erupted in excitement. They were through the debris field.

As calm restored, Steph stepped to one side, and using her sleeve controls, personally initiated the key stage. She watched the delivery craft head for the tube with its precious load. Blinking away a tear, she looked off into the darkness of space. *I promised you I'd do it, Weeman… and I have.*

'There it goes,' said Lily. Steph looked back just in time to see the craft containing the viral antidote entering the tube.

'God speed. God bless,' whispered Steph.

After a long moment of contemplation, Steph turned to her team just as a second round of cheering greeted the news that it was through, and distribution could begin.

'Captain, I need to get back to Primo superfast. What's your best time?' said Steph.

'I'll have you there within the day, professor.'

Chapter 30

Osarus c.: The Animals

Standing on the redoubt's roof, Jamie took in the morning vista. Overnight, the river level had stopped rising, though it was still impossibly high. Like everywhere else, the sides of the valley were richly greened. Even the terrace below, always verdant due to its close proximity to the river, had managed to put on an extra spurt of growth.

Upstream, he could make out three or four of the agriculture team inspecting the land allocated for farming. Further on, just a few rocky tips broke through the water's surface to mark the location of the rapids. There was no sign of the abandoned hoppers – they had already been marked down as lost to the rains. Beyond, far out into the savannah, he could make out little dark smudges. The herd's trail-blazers coming toward the swollen river they'd need to cross to reach the new plant growth beyond.

High in the sky little dots had begun to appear that morning, marking the return of the birds that had vanished before the rains came.

Baz Browning emerged from the redoubt and joined Jamie; they rested their arms against the parapet and shared a moment of tranquillity.

'The herd is nearly here,' said Jamie. 'It'll be interesting to see what happens at the river.'

Baz turned, letting his back rest against the parapet, and gazed up absently into the sky. 'They'll have to swim – rather them than me. I wouldn't fancy my chances, getting across that water.'

Jamie clapped his friend's shoulder and pointed out across the valley. 'It could be worse. We're in a good location, and Ossie's plan to launch a position beacon worked – all we have to do now is wait and stay alive.'

'Yes, but for how long?'

'Who knows? We just have to have faith. Come on, I need to go down to the terrace.' The pair crossed to a rank of hoppers behind the redoubt.

'Hold tight!' Baz directed the hopper over the crest and down the steep slope. A zigzag track had been worn into the slope by successive hopper journeys. It had just been reinforced with a quick-set surface. Now Baz had the hopper hurrying down it in a rolling lilt.

The hopper stopped beside S-3, and Jamie climbed down to set off on foot for the upstream perimeter while Baz steered the hopper into the open hangar.

***

'Hello, commander, can you hear me? It's Ossie.'

'Go ahead, what's up?' said Jamie into his collar-phone as he stood looking at the fast-flowing river.

'The drone is showing the herd stretching away into the distance. The lead animals are at the river now. Most are diverting upstream toward the fording points above the confluence. Those closer to the valley mouth have paused at the stony crossing. They clearly recognise that using the rapids to cross is now impossible. The leading animals have just started to turn and are following the valley, heading directly for S-3.'

'Stand by...' said Jamie. He hurried from the riverbank to the low defensive wall that stretched across the terrace. Clambering up, he scanned upstream.

'I see nothing yet, how far off are they?'

'The front-runners are in the valley, but it's just a trickle for now. You should see some soon.'

'I've got one of our drones stationed at the entrance to the valley. We'll be able to estimate numbers quite accurately,' said Browning, joining the conversation from the marines' control room.

'Well, they won't get beyond this wall,' Jamie stamped his foot on the solid structure. 'But I see some of the agricultural team are out checking their plots again. Will you call them back in, to be on the safe side.'

Jamie scanned upstream, still no sign. He was pleased to note the agrics heading quickly back toward the gateway where a marine sentry stood watching their unscheduled return. Jamie hurried along the top of the wall to brief the sentry.

'Once those people are through, I want the gates shut and secured. There are some animals coming down the valley. They'll turn around once they realise it's a dead end.'

'Yes, sir.' The marine waved the agric team through and then began to swing the gates shut.

The team clambered up the steps to join Jamie. 'Are they here yet, sir?' said the senior.

'Over there, see!' said one of the team.

The sentry joined them, and they all watched as the exotic herbivores made their way downstream, oblivious of the barrier ahead of them.

'Well, it's all very peaceful out there, so I'd better get back to S-3,' said Jamie.

He turned toward the steps and was stopped in his tracks by a horrified shriek from the youngest agric. 'Oh my God! Look in the water. What's happened?'

The strong current and flood-dirtied water still raced past as it had done for days, and the water was still dense with plant debris. But now, among the broken boughs, there were bodies, many broken by their passage over the rock-strewn riverbed at the head of the valley. And the bodies were covered in brutal slashes and bites too, killing wounds dealt long before any beasts had reached the rapids.

'The herd must be fording the river upstream, at the crossings we've mapped. Strange though, we assumed some might struggle in the current and drown, but those wounds…' said Jamie.

The group looked down on the stream of bodies as they swirled past. Most of the carcasses displayed attack wounds – bites sunk deep into shoulders, backs and necks. Some were virtually decapitated. Floating miles downstream had washed the blood away, so now the wounds were laid bare for inspection.

'What could have done this, sir? So many killed,' said the young agric. 'So many.'

'Baz, where's your drone right now?'

'Still over the river, near the rapids. We're seeing the animal bodies passing by too.'

'I'd like you to send the drone upstream, find out where they're coming from. It's not drowning that killed them; they have attack wounds. Let's get up to speed.'

'Sending the drone now. You can watch from the bridge. By the way, the number of animals coming your way is rising significantly.'

'That's right,' said Ossie. 'Our science drone is watching too. The animal numbers heading into the valley are definitely rising quickly.'

'What does that mean? How many?' said Jamie, turning his attention from the river back to the land and beyond the wall. The herd was still thin on the ground close by. Further off, the ground was now thick with animals. Gentle gusts of wind carried the animals' cries and calls toward the watchers.

'Right, Baz. I'm on my way up to the bridge now.' He turned to the sentry, 'Nobody goes out through the gates, for any reason.'

'Yes, sir.'

Ossie met with Jamie in the navigation room, and they entered the bridge together, just in time to see Martha turn to first officer Casper Wills' and gasp. 'They're going to die,' she said.

One side of the split screen displayed the river from their drone's-eye view as it flew slowly upstream, the flow of dead animals continuing unabated. The other part of the display was the cause of Martha's concern. The feed from S-3's upstream-facing cameras showed the animals were now much closer. The space beyond the wall was full, and still they came. Pressing ever tighter against the wall.

Many of the leading animals were becoming crushed. There was no audio feed accompanying the pictures, it wasn't needed. Every watcher could imagine the cries of fear and pain, the bleating of lost young and the despairing calls of the injured.

'Sir, they're dying.' The sentry's voice sounded in Jamie's collar-phone.

Jamie looked to Ossie. 'Will opening the gate help?'

'Not now.' Ossie pointed at the screen as Martha turned away in despair.

'Hell,' said Jamie. At the middle point of the defensive wall, the leading ranks of animals had succumbed to the press of bodies behind them. Dead or dying, they dropped. The next wave of animals stepped up and over the downed. Some slipped and fell, breaking limbs and becoming trapped in the ever-rising, ever-widening ramp of bodies. The third wave followed, more stumbled and fell amidst the twitching pile. Some of the lighter, fleeter-footed creatures jumped over the dying for the parapet. From there, they jumped again or were bumped and tumbled into the compound. Some bodies broke on reaching the ground, lying as pillows to break the fall of the next. Others landed safely and resumed their steady progress, leaving the screams and distress behind them.

The flesh-built access and exit ramps grew steadily to either side of the wall. Elephantine males led their families over the bodies of the dying, their monstrous feet crushing down on the remaining sparks of life among the fallen. The herd would stop for nothing.

'Sir, what should we do?' said the sentry. The distressing sounds behind his voice carried the reality of the nightmare directly into Jamie's collar-phone; a cacophony of anguished cries, underscored by the rallying calls sounding from the raised trunks of the elephantines. Immediate family responses were followed by more distant calls, signing the approach of other family groups closing from the rear.

'Marine, who's still with you?'

'All the agriculture team, sir.'

'Okay. Leave the gate. It's already half-buried by the dead. Get those agrics down off the wall and running for the hangar. We'll close it as soon as you are all on board. Stop for nothing. Get them back here at the double. Move right now.'

'Sir!'

Jamie watched the screen. The marine hurried the agricultural team down the steps and herded them across the compound toward the hangar, always keeping distance between them and the leading animals. The animal numbers within the compound were rising but still mostly lighter antelope-like creatures who were equally as keen to avoid the running humans.

Jamie ordered the marine guarding the downstream wall to open that gate and retire to S-3. The man reached the hangar ramp only moments after the agric team. As the hangar swung shut, Jamie allowed himself a breath of relief. Everyone was safe, the craft was sealed.

The herd continued forward. Now, for all that had died, thousands more were crossing over the walls and continuing past S-3 to the downstream perimeter wall. Its open gate was of little use in saving lives as the grizzly pile-up of bodies repeated. Finally, as the second bloody ramp was formed, animals began to break out, crossing the downstream wall to reach safety. With each bite of vegetation and every step away from the compound they steadily settled down.

'How many have died?' said Martha in a hushed voice, while they watched in awe as the herd continued to move through.

'Thousands. God knows how many, and we caused it!' said Ossie. 'It was our boundary walls that did it.'

Jamie was ashen-faced at the suffering. 'We couldn't have known.'

'No, but we caused it all the same,' said Ossie.

'I don't understand what brought them on so fast. Something suddenly changed out there,' said Martha.

They lapsed into silence while Jamie did a department call-round. Once finished, he joined them. 'Is the flow of animals easing now?' he said.

'Seems to be. Most are through the compound and heading downstream,' said Ossie.

Jamie looked up at the screen for a moment, watching the stragglers passing through the compound. Then he touched his sleeve to open a channel. 'Hi, Baz. Can you have one of your marines take me out in a hopper right now. I want to get a closer look.'

'No problem. Make your way down to the hangar – it'll be waiting for you.'

Jamie glanced at Martha and Ossie. 'This is a good chance to observe the wildlife close-up, maybe find out what's driving them on all the time.' He left, raising a hand to acknowledge Ossie's request for a video feed to his science team.

Chapter 31

Osarus c.: Downstream

Sergeant Grant had the hopper move slowly downstream. Many animals were still moving through the compound, but there were no family groups now, just stragglers: the old, the separated young and, judging by their gait, those with limbs damaged in clambering over the trapped and dead bodies in the ramps.

As the hopper approached the open gate in the downstream wall, Jamie shuddered at the scale of carnage. The flesh-built ramp was not motionless. Now close up, Jamie could see it moved perceptibly with quivering bodies, broken and trapped among the dead, struggling in vain to escape or waiting helplessly for death. The air was full of the low moan of the buried-living crying out, calling their distress to an indifferent world.

'Move on, sergeant. Let's leave this behind us.'

Grant needed no second telling, and he immediately moved the hopper swiftly through the open gate. Beyond it, they looked to the side, ranged along the outer side of the wall was an equally distressing down-ramp. Some two hundred paces further downstream, he paused the hopper and turned to look at Jamie. 'Sir?'

'I see it, sergeant. Get us a bit closer. Nudge us into the herd a little if you can. Ossie, are you getting this? Directly ahead.'

'We're seeing it.'

Gingerly, the hopper edged on, working into the rear of the herd that was once again bunching up. None of the animals was unduly concerned by the presence of the great machine, and Grant was able to move it deep into the throng. In the middle, the herd was tighter packed, and Grant stopped. Any forward movement now would simply push the animals ahead of them into danger.

'Can't we stop it, sir?'

'I don't see how.' Jamie reached up and pulled the hatch shut, excluding the growing sounds of terrifying death. He heard Grant muttering a string of oaths under his breath and understood the sentiment exactly.

Directly in front of them was the thicket of trees that barred the way downstream. In response to the rains, what had been a dark, interwoven network of top branches now sprouted tiny leaves, with more growth yet to come. The green bunting fluttered and quivered while the branches moved in a godforsaken dance.

The thicket's original fringe of ferns had been trampled down by the leaders of the herd, and the animals had begun to pick their way between the trunks. Those first-rank animals had almost reached the other side before anything had occurred. Then in an instant, the thicket had become a slaughterhouse, screams and cries filling the air.

'Is it Lieutenant Grieves' serpent?' said Ossie. 'Can you make out what's happening in there?'

'We can see. Hold on, I'll pass you control of all the cameras.'

Jamie flinched. He knew now what the serpents were. The interlocking branches had loosened and straightened, allowing more light beneath the canopy, presenting them with a clear view of what was happening.

The herd leaders had made their way through the thicket. At first, they had moved steadily and comfortably, propelled on by the remorseless pressure of the following herd. Well past the halfway point, the front rank was almost clear of the thicket. By then, the trunks, freed from the bindings of their branch weave, had perceptibly straightened. The crown of every trunk was suddenly a gaping maw and the trunks swept down again and again. Each strike delivered a biting wound into the back or shoulder of its victim. The powerful blows grounded animals and lacerated their bodies.

Instinct and fear forced those that could to rise again. They struggled on a few more steps through the thicket, all the while draining their lifeblood into the earth beneath them. Returning to the ground eventually, either a victim of that first biting wound or downed beneath the slaughtering bite of a second strike.

Behind the dying, the main herd continued to push past the hopper, pressing those ahead into the thicket. Forced forward, they were compelled once again to begin a frightening climb over the dead and dying, where they too succumbed to the killing bites, adding their bodies to the slaughter heap. Nothing stopped the herd's advance. More and more entered the carnage, and the slaughter continued.

Not all died. Sheer weight of numbers meant some lucky animals emerged unscathed. Others, the victims of only flesh-wound bites, bolted clear to run from the thicket toward safety. Sadly, their venom-filled wounds would not stop bleeding, and their chances of survival looked despairingly slim. Other victims stumbled from the thicket and into the river. There, the water turned red as they bled out, and their bodies carried on toward the sea.

The butchery lasted for nearly an hour. By the end, the layer of bodies throughout the thicket was higher than a man.

The herd still advanced, struggling over dead companions. The earlier frantic drive was gone now, even the serpents had stopped killing. Sated or exhausted, the trees mostly straightened up, their crowns drooping slightly, dripping blood, their trunks stained dark red. Outstretched branches flicked and twitched in response to their neighbours' touch. Slowly, they began to weave and tighten. Jamie sensed this would eventually draw the trunks down again, bending them to re-form the thicket's tight overhead cover.

Jamie and Grant were profoundly unsettled by the senseless slaughter they had witnessed. Frequently during the horror show, both men had succumbed to an irresistible need to close their eyes. The scene would stay with them for a lifetime.

Chapter 32

Opsythia e.: Base Secundo

MacMillan turned his back on the rooftop parapet from where he had been watching the neatly aligned rows of locust vessels on the plain below. He looked back across the flat roof to the access doorway in the middle. The sun was rising, just cresting the icy hills that ranged behind the base. He squinted and turned again to look toward the locusts.

'Well, they didn't come during the night,' said Delacroix, mirroring MacMillan's gaze.

'Thank God. It's given us more time to prepare. But they'll come now; I'm sure of it.'

'Yes, sir. Why the delay though? It doesn't make sense; they've let us consolidate. Sarsen's got the perimeter wall under control. We have the base's main entrance fortified – if needs be he and his men can fall back toward the doors. I'll be up here, to hold the rooftop entrance.'

'Okay, but I'm not happy. It seems our only combat option is to go hand-to-hand and cut off their antennae. We managed it before, but we won't catch them off-guard so easily a second time.'

The sound of light steps hurrying toward them had both men turning as Professor Baillie reached them.

'Morning, gentlemen.'

'Morning, professor. Delacroix and I are considering how we might tackle these locusts. Have your boffins had any ideas?'

'So, colonel, we know the locusts' exoskeletons are too thick and tough for bullets to penetrate. In fact, based on how it seems their helmets can be sealed against the carapace we're now quite convinced their shell doubles as spacesuit.'

"What about air? They must need that,' said Delacroix.

'Yes, we're thinking there is some limited air-storage capacity within the carapace. Like our suits,' she said.

MacMillan pointed toward the locust position. 'If they attack wearing those helmets today, we won't be able to get at their antennae. Come on, professor. You'll need to give us something to fight back with. Yesterday, our gunfire was nothing more than a nuisance to them.'

'Well, we've had a couple of ideas,' said Baillie.'

'Go on, what have you got?'

'I think the first's a bit of a jury rig but worth a try. The carapace can stop a bullet, but the explosive force of a grenade is something else altogether. May break the carapace, even dismember limbs.'

'Surely that would rely on very close proximity explosions, if it even works. How do we achieve that against a fast-moving, high-jumping monster?' said Delacroix.

Baillie pointed across the parapet. 'My team are doing an experiment right now.'

All three looked down to where a little group of scientists and soldiers had approached the pile of dead locusts. The scientists busied themselves in directing the soldiers where grenades should be strategically positioned among the dead insects.

One of the scientists broadcast an all-staff alert through his collar-phone. Then, as one, the soldiers pulled the grenade safety pins and sprinted away. Immediately after the last soldier reached cover, the grenades exploded, throwing up plumes of smoke and disrupting the carcass pile. For a minute, guards on the perimeter wall turned inward to watch the show. As the smoke cleared, the scientists hurried forward to inspect the damage.

'Bingo! It's a winner. Limbs off, splits in the exoskeleton, holes in carapace. The grenades do real damage!' The voice of Baillie's assistant sounded in every collar-phone and was greeted by a ragged cheer echoing in from all corners of the compound.

Baillie turned to MacMillan and Delacroix. 'The explosive force at close proximity is too much even for their tough shells. We've got something that can stop them, for sure.'

'Yes, but how do we get the grenades to stick? Those beasts move fast. Throw a grenade and they'll be away from it long before it detonates,' said Delacroix.

'Well, my team came up with an idea we think might deliver. It's based on the locusts' own technology,' said Baillie, turning to beckon forward an assistant who approached carrying a sturdy shoulder bag that he placed on the ground beside them.

'We've snipped off some of those tendril-like wires from the netting they used to ensnare the crew yesterday. Fixed a grenade to one end and a counterweight to the other. It's very interesting.'

The assistant pulled out a tightly coiled tendril and determinedly uncoiled it. The tendril straightened to nearly twice the length of an arm. Once uncoiled it remained straight and still. To either end was attached a weight. Before MacMillan or Delacroix could intervene, the assistant swung his arm and hurled the weighted wire at Baillie. It flashed through the air and connected with her arm. She cried out in pain at the impact, dropping to her knees. As she did, the initial contact triggered the tendril's response. It coiled and twisted round her arm and body. Fixing itself tightly.

'And bang!' said Baillie, looking up from the ground, grinning through the pain, even as she struggled to disentangle herself. Her assistant hurried over and began to carefully uncoil it.

Freed from the tendril, she stood and rejoined the two men. 'Now we know for sure grenades can do damage, and we can attach them to tendrils. That's one throwing weapon that will stick.'

'Excellent work. How many can you make?' said MacMillan.

'We're limited to the number of tendrils we can take from the net. For various reasons, I don't want to remove too many. But it's a very big net, I'd think a few hundred. Excuse me, sir.' Baillie broke off to issue instructions to her team below.

'We're good to start, guys. Get as many grenades prepared and distributed to the perimeter as you can… and some up here too.' She turned back to MacMillan.

'Well done, Baillie. You said there were two ideas. I hope the second is as positive as the first.'

'I hope, better, sir. It's informed by intuition initially. Then facts. My team are testing it out right now.' She pointed back down toward the heap of broken locust bodies.

All three looked to where a pair of scientists were picking their way through the mess seeking out suitable specimens.

'What are they doing now?' said Delacroix.

'Humans developed weapons that can hurt humans, then they applied them wherever. We're presuming locusts did the same. That net with all the tendrils was fed with an electrical current to stun whatever was caught. We're thinking the locusts may also be susceptible to electricity – life generally is. What we don't know is to what extent their shell insulates them, and if there are any vulnerable points in the exoskeleton.'

'Electrocute them? Can we do that?'

'We'll know soon enough, sir.'

All across the bustling compound, groups of soldiers were linking up with scientists to learn how to manipulate the tendrils and fix grenades and counterweights to the ends. Others were busy harvesting more tendrils from the net.

'Why haven't they attacked before now?' said Delacroix. 'If they'd come in the night, we'd have had no defence ready, been overrun in short order. Do you think they can't see in the dark, professor?'

'First off, judging by what we have been able to observe of their vessels' flight patterns, they have been devoting time to rescuing all the locusts lost to the warbirds in space. Second, we think they can see okay in the dark. One or two of my team are speculating they may see across a wider spectrum than us.'

'So, if they have an advantage at night, why didn't they exploit it, attack before dawn?' said MacMillan.

Baillie pointed toward the sun that had now crept some degrees above the horizon; the atmosphere was bright but still bitterly cold. 'They are insects of some sort. That thick exoskeleton might provide good heat insulation, but who knows about the shell encasing their limbs? And their antennae? The nights here might be just too cold for them to function for any length of time. I expect, as the sun gets higher, they will become more active. Right now, they are safe in their ships, like warm nests.'

Almost on cue, away down on the plain, a hatch in the nearest locust vessel opened and two locusts hopped out.

'I need to get back to the control room,' said MacMillan. 'Well done on the grenades, professor, and keep me posted on the electricity. If that works, we need a delivery method.'

'On it already,' said Baillie. She turned her attention to information reaching her sleeve.

Chapter 33

Opsythia System – P-1

Captain Grainger stared into P-1's broad bridge screen. Opsythia e. was still distant, but distinct now. Its appearance had shifted from point of light to a distinct disc, still small but unmistakably a disc. She glanced round, sensing the arrival of someone new on the bridge.

Captain Ash stepped toward her, quickly followed by Fritz.

'You asked for me, ma'am,' said Ash.

'I did. How are your preparations going, captain?'

'We're as ready as we'll ever be. I'm assuming we have no element of surprise?'

'None. Secundo's emergency broadcasts to us would have been picked up by the locusts, as would our responses. They know we're coming.'

Fritz took a half-step forward. 'We'll be there mid-afternoon Secundo time. They'll know roughly our direction of travel from the earlier signal exchanges we had with Secundo and will see us long before we arrive. No secrets at all I'm afraid.'

Ash grimaced slightly. 'We've assumed that. All the same, some element of surprise would have been nice. We're pulling together a plan, just need to reconfirm your order is to go for the cone, not to relieve Secundo?'

'Colonel MacMillan was clear. We go for the cone. Leave Secundo to fend for itself, no matter what.'

'Okay. How do you want to play it, ma'am?'

'Tell me your thoughts, captain.'

'Ma'am, it strikes me we just go in hell for leather. Having seen how the cone deploys its attack vessels, I'm thinking once those beasts work out your plan, whatever it might be, they'll respond by launching their own attack to counteract and intercept. That's when the warbirds launch and screen you as best we can, while you press home.'

'Captain, the Leviathan can't press home an attack. We have no weapons,' said Fritz.

'All right, Fritz. Let's hear the plan out,' said Grainger.

'Thank you, ma'am. I think we take a leaf out of the locusts' playbook. I've been through the data; they were more than happy to sacrifice some of their own vessels to take out the warbirds. We'll be watching for that this time around – knowing the tactic, we should be able to respond appropriately. Simultaneously, we should adopt their tactics and do the same back at them.'

'Explain,' said Grainger.

'We have an observer in the hangar. Once P-1 gets in close to the cone, very close, launch it directly out of the hangar and have it ram the cone while their vessels are concentrating on my three warbirds and you in the Leviathan. It might give us an edge, launch the observer at the last moment, use it as a projectile.'

Grainger raised a hand to silence Fritz. 'That's a brave plan, Ash. It might work, and it does conjure up an element of surprise from nothing. But what about the pilot? It's a suicide mission. Even if they could get into an escape pod at the last moment, it would be engulfed in the explosion.'

'Hold on, captain, there might be a way,' said Fritz. 'Let me see if I can cut into the observer's autopilot system and rig a remote piloting control. Maybe we could launch and fly it from right here on the bridge.'

Chapter 34

Opsythia e.: Base Secundo

The sun was passed its zenith. What little warmth it offered had peaked. Its weak rays played across Sarsen's face as he stood behind the perimeter parapet, watching the movement on the plain below.

'There's more of them down there now, sir,' said the sergeant.

Sarsen nodded. 'Hard to count, the way they keep bobbing about. How many do you reckon? Two hundred?'

'Maybe more, sir.'

Sarsen turned his attention to an approaching sound on the steps below. Professor Baillie was climbing to join them.

'Ma'am,' said the sergeant, taking a step back to allow Baillie space beside Sarsen. He received a grim smile in return.

'Well, we're as set as we can be,' she said, pointing down into the enclosure where several of her scientists clustered together with a squad of Sarsen's soldiers. A briefing was in progress.

'Will it work?' said Sarsen.

'You know we've tested the carapaces, and they scarcely conduct electricity at all, but the limb casings on the extremities are lighter and thinner – any contact with them should give a good jolt. Shake them up for sure. And see, we've spread their net out directly in front of the main doors. If you have to fall back, do so in good time. Once we have a current flowing through that net, it will affect your men just as we hope it will the locusts.'

'You're sure you can do it?' said Sarsen.

'Oh yes, we've got a cable running back through the building, linking into the base power supply. It's been tested, works perfectly.'

'Pity you can't just put a really high charge through, fry them dead,' said the sergeant.

Sarsen looked expectantly at Baillie.

'That's a good idea in theory, sergeant. But we don't know how much power will be needed to do that. We'll have to play around with it, in live conditions.'

'Right, ma'am. What I don't understand – why did the locusts only use their net to stun our crew yesterday? Why not kill outright? It would be easier.'

Baillie looked across the wall to where the distant locusts had formed into three motionless ranks.

Sarsen did a quick recalculation now the locusts were still. 'Over three hundred.'

'Reckon so, sir,' said the sergeant. Then he returned his attention to Baillie. 'So, ma'am, why didn't they kill our people?'

Baillie took a deep breath and looked from the sergeant to Sarsen. 'Major, please be certain to get your men back into the base before we put power through the net.

'Last night, I thought about those first translations Steph's linguists got out of the Goliath back at Primo. The meanings make more sense now. Our locust visitors are predators. More than that, they are swarm predators. We've surmised they arrive at a habitat and pick it clean before moving on. Whether it takes years or hundreds of years, eventually everything is consumed.'

'You mean everything?' said Sarsen.

'Everything. I think they were gathering our crew, like a harvest. They first approached Secundo and tested our defences, which were zero at that point. Assuming their technological advantage, they closed in and began their harvest, as they've probably done on scores of other planets.'

'And then we put a few rockets up them,' said the sergeant.

'Exactly. Yesterday, they were gathering in a food crop; today, they know they have a fight on their hands.'

'People as a food crop – that's sick, disgusting!' said Sarsen.

'Very. You know, I think that empty hold we saw in the vessel yesterday is just like a fishing trawler's catch deck. Living prey caught in the net, stunned and hauled into captivity. They catch what they need and come back for more as and when.'

'They're treating us like animals,' said the sergeant, his voice breaking into a growl.

'If only that were all. Looking at their anatomy – limb-size and position – the pair of mini arms high on the thorax are perfect for holding something steady beside the mouth parts. And the mouth parts... The team and I have concluded that these locusts eat live prey. They didn't kill the crew because that was an unattractive feeding option.'

'Christ! That is just...' The sergeant's voice trailed off as movement on the plain below caught his attention. 'Sir, they're on the move. Coming our way and fast. Reckon it's warm enough for them now.'

'I don't understand, prof. – they're clever, surely, they should have worked out a way to avoid waiting most of the day for the sun to warm them up?' said Sarsen, his eyes fixed on the first rank of locusts, which was making good progress up the slope.

'You'd think so, but maybe they don't normally choose such cold planets. Maybe they depend on food energy to sustain periods of high-impact activity. In that case, if they haven't eaten since leaving Pardamax in the Perseus Arm, they probably need the sun as a substitute for food to reach peak performance. They need to eat us.' Baillie gripped Sarsen's arm. 'Remember, if you must fall back do so in good time. Once that net's energised, anyone left outside is... outside. Good luck both of you.' She turned and hurried down the steps.

Sarsen stroked his sleeve and issued instructions to the defending soldiers as the sergeant hefted one of the tendril grenades and moved along the parapet, offering gruff spoken words of encouragement to his soldiers. All the while, they watched the first line of advancing locusts closing the gap on their position.

***

Ensconced in Secundo's control room, MacMillan crossed to the LPA that was displaying information on movements in the sky above Secundo. When the last of his warbirds had been downed, he had lost his only reliable source for relaying information from near space down to him. Since then, he'd been having to rely on detecting limited signals, hampered by the planet's atmosphere.

Now however, Secundo was picking up a constant signal stream beamed from P-1, albeit still so distant that messages were time-delayed. They weren't so blind now, but that didn't make the viewing any easier. He saw the light arc representing a section of the planet's surface. Secundo's position was marked by a brighter light spot. High above it, the cone was displayed, from which half a dozen smaller red lights had detached, moving some distance further off, forming a screen between the cone and the far more distant signal that was the fast-approaching P-1.

MacMillan could do nothing but wait and watch… and pray. It was in Grainger's hands now; he trusted her. He peered yet more intently into the LPA.

'The cone is moving toward P-1, sir,' said the technician who was monitoring the LPA. 'Not fast but definite movement.'

Okay, keep me posted. What's P-1's ETA now?'

'It'll be in local space late afternoon, sir. A little before sunset.'

MacMillan turned his attention back to the screens as an update came in from Sarsen. The locusts would be on them imminently. 'Have everyone on alert – this is it.' MacMillan noted the look of fear on the face of the young technician who had taken Barrington's place handling communications. Barrington had been transferred, detailed to provide tech support to Delacroix on the rooftop. Crossing the room, MacMillan rested a hand on her shoulder. 'Don't worry. We saw this lot off first time around; we're better prepared today. It'll be fine.'

'Yes, sir. Just, it's still hellish scary.'

'I know. But we'll get through. What's your name?'

'Smith, sir. Jillie Smith.'

'Well, Jillie Smith, you stay focused on your job. Any signals come in from P-1, you just shout out and patch them through to my collar-phone. Leave the rest to us; it'll work out. Got it, Jillie?'

'Thank you, sir, yes.'

MacMillan turned again to the screens as he stroked his sleeve to open a comms channel. 'How are things up on the roof, Delacroix?'

'We're as ready as we can be, sir. My teams are all set. We'll hold this entrance, come what may. I've got a good vantage point here, and I can see the first rank of locusts are about four hundred paces off the perimeter wall. They'll be on Sarsen's men in no time.'

'What about their vessels? Any air support?'

'No, sir, they all seem to be sitting tight on the plain. It's as we thought – now they know we can hurt their vessels, they're keeping them well away.'

***

Sarsen looked along the parapet. He had under a hundred men facing the oncoming line of locusts. He gave a little internal shiver; the men close by saw nothing. He spoke quietly into his collar-phone. 'Steady, men. Remember, hold fast until you can launch the grenades, on my order.

'Marksmen, headshots only. See if you can do some damage there. Fire as your targets present.' Half a dozen crack-shots hoisted weapons and peered across their weapons' sights, singling out individual targets.

Twenty paces along the parapet, he saw the sergeant still stepping among the men, offering encouragement and support as he went. Sarsen turned his attention back to the first line of nearing locusts. *A hundred*, he estimated. Near even numbers. If this were man-on-man, he'd be pretty confident, but he'd seen these monsters in action. Hand-to-hand, it needed two soldiers to have any chance against one attacker.

A shot rang out, then another and another. His marksmen were engaging. He lifted his binoculars to better see the impact – none. The line of locusts continued unabated.

'Hell,' he said, tweaking at the focus, then touched his sleeve. 'Listen up! The locusts have got their helmets on – they seem to be resistant to bullets too. That's going to be a problem for hand-to-hand. We can't get at their antennae. Those of you with RPGs aim and fire now. Get off as many as you can. The rest stand by with your grenades, wait for my order.

'We can't win hand-to-hand if their vulnerabilities are protected. If we can't keep them back from the wall, we'll need to retreat, fast.'

Suddenly the sergeant's voice shifted, the quiet encouragement gone as he boomed out a general command, no need for collar-phones here. 'You heard the officer, stand by for action!'

'Ready grenades!' Sarsen's voice sounded in collar-phones all along the parapet. Every few yards along its length, pairs of soldiers were poised, waiting for the word. One soldier, arm arched back ready to throw, gripped the weighted end of an extended tendril. The other soldier knelt close behind, supporting the grenade at the other end, its safety pin positioned ready for instant removal.

The lead rank of locusts was very near now and steadily closing. As they came forward, they passed a marker the sergeant had placed immediately beyond the throwing range of a man. The locusts were within striking distance and still coming.

'Sergeant, detonate the first line,' said Sarsen, quietly into his collar-phone.

'Very good, sir!' The sergeant's instant reply coincided with a deft stroke on his sleeve, and the big man unleashed hell on the locusts.

Exactly where the monsters were passing, a line of buried mines detonated. The explosive percussions merged into a single roar as light flashed and earth flew. Scanning the line, Sarsen guessed they'd scored at least a dozen dead or broken locusts. The locust line wavered and some stepped back.

'Detonate the second line,' ordered Sarsen, and the sergeant triggered a second strike. In line with the sergeant's range marker, a further series of mines exploded, echoing the first blasts, catching those locusts that had stepped back.

More dead, but not enough. The main group of locusts continued their advance. 'Throw the grenades,' said Sarsen. All along the parapet, soldiers withdrew detonator pins and shouted countdowns to their partners. 'Seven, six, five…' then tapped their partner's shoulder and stepped aside as the throwers swung their arms up and over, hurling the grenades toward the approaching locusts.

Some grenades missed completely, detonating behind the locusts' line, causing no more than a disturbance. Others bounced off helmets to explode at a short distance, peppering the hard carapaces with shrapnel but doing no damage.

Then Sarsen saw one land against a locust's knee. The tendril responded exactly as planned, instantly wrapping round the limb, fixing the grenade hard against the exoskeleton. The locust tilted its dome-enclosed head down to consider the hinderance, the grenade exploded. The monster fell, its short upper arms reaching out toward the stump that had once been a leg.

Up and down the line, other grenades met their marks. Arms and legs were blown off, some bodies ripped open. One grenade managed to ensnare around a locust's domed helmet, and with that blast, a decapitated locust's body stood for a moment, aimless, before teetering over.

'Choose your targets. Launch grenades at will.' With Sarsen's order, his men hurled grenades like madmen. The explosions were now closing tight beneath the wall. His men were taking down the enemy but not enough. He reckoned there were still about fifty locusts coming on. The parapet was more than twice the height of a man, but suddenly it seemed no barrier at all. The locust closest to the wall leapt up and landed on the parapet.

'Sergeant, detonate line three!' Sarsen's voice, an unintended shout.

Immediately below the parapet, another line of explosions sounded. The parapet itself rocked as a shockwave rippled through the earth, and Sarsen's biggest mines did their damage. Vivid flashes, billows of smoke, and a mix of earth, locust body parts and an unfortunate yellowy ooze flew up before raining down on the defenders.

The locust on top of the parapet rocked against the shockwave. While fighting for balance, it glanced back and down toward a blanket of smoke and dust, and beneath that, the carnage that had been the locusts' leading line. Motionless for a moment, the locust tried to comprehend what had just happened. Then it sprung to action, triggered by a tightening around its ankle where a tendril was wrapping in an unbreakable grip.

The soldiers close by dropped flat onto the walkway. Above them, on the parapet itself, the locust jumped away as the grenade exploded. It landed footless among the broken bodies of its comrades.

The roar of explosions rolled away, and the ringing in Sarsen's ears subsided just a little. He scanned through the smoke to where the second line of locusts continued its advance unabated.

As the ragged cheers of his men sounded along the perimeter wall, he knew they had to fall back. The advantage of surprise was lost. The locusts now knew for certain that humans were not a passive food source to be taken at will. And most importantly, the three lines of mines had all been detonated. Up here on the parapet, it would be hand-to-hand, and with the great domed helmets protecting the locusts' antennae, it was a fight his men couldn't win.

'Listen up, men. Well done. That went better than we might ever have hoped. A total wipe out… Now, you know the plan, you each know your tasks. Everyone fall back to the base main entrance. Let's move while we can.'

The sergeant looked along the line of fighters. 'You heard the major; get moving now! Lead on from the steps, at the double.' The troops began to file down the steps and hurried across the enclosure toward the main base.

The sergeant stamped his foot on the parapet as the last of the soldiers funnelled down. 'Pity we have to leave this, sir. It served us well.'

'Agreed, sergeant. Under other circumstances I'd want to hold this position all day. But there's another rank of locusts coming up fast, and we have nothing left to touch them with.'

'Nothing here, sir.'

'Nothing here, for sure. Come on, sergeant, we'd best go while we still can.'

After a final glance across the parapet, Sarsen followed his sergeant down into the compound. Halfway across the pad, they paused to speak with four soldiers who had halted their retreat to muster behind the shelter of a short and flimsy barricade. Behind it was a small pile of grenades attached to their all-important tendrils. The sergeant nodded with approval and joined them.

'Right, sergeant, you and the squad know what's going to be coming over that wall any moment. You know your job. Do it, then get the hell back to the base doors. Don't linger for anything.'

Spread out some paces behind the barricade was the locusts' net. It reached right back to the base main doors, to where the rest of his men had already retreated. There, Professor Baillie had shooed most of them inside the building, allowing only a handful to remain at the entrance armed with RPGs. She and her team needed to maintain a clear line of sight across the enclosure.

Sarsen left the barricade and hurried back to the base entrance where he took command of the RPG squad.

For a moment nothing moved within the compound, everything was quiet. Then from beyond the main wall came a strange sound, growing in intensity with every passing moment. A mix of rustling legs and thudding feet signalled the second line of hopping locusts advancing as one, closing on the wall. Then the noise stopped; they were at the wall. Sarsen guessed they would be checking what had happened to the first wave and conferring, learning lessons.

Crossing to stand beside Baillie, he peered inside the doorway to where others of her team were anxiously waiting beside a console. 'All set?' he said.

'As best we can be,' she said. 'I just hope your people get back across the net before I have to make it go live.'

'They know what to do. Don't worry, the sergeant will get them back in time.'

Baillie pursed her lips. 'Let's hope so.'

Sudden movement caught Sarsen's attention. A single locust appeared atop the perimeter wall and stood surveying the compound

It had begun.

'Take that locust down,' said Sarsen to his RPG squad. One man immediately fired. A vapour trail reached across the compound, tracing the course of the rocket until it punched into the locust which disappeared in a blast.

'Good man,' said Sarsen. Almost before he had spoken, all along the length of the compound, locusts appeared on the parapet and quickly dropped into the compound. He scanned the horde – another hundred, he estimated. The second wave had come as one. 'Hold fire,' said Sarsen to his RPG squad. Then stroked his sleeve. 'Sergeant, draw them in.'

'Yes, sir,' came back the reply, and Sarsen watched as the sergeant hurled a grenade toward the line of locusts. It fell a dozen paces short and exploded. Some locusts were hit by shrapnel but showed no injuries. The explosion attracted the whole locust line's attention toward the blast and then quickly to the little group of soldiers assembled behind the makeshift barricade.

The locust line advanced, many converging on the barricade. The sergeant and his squad hurled their grenades toward the locusts. For a moment, the compound was filled with the sound of explosions, accompanied by billowing smoke.

A booming voice reached across the compound to Sarsen where he stood at the main doors. 'Run. Run!' The sergeant's voice was accompanied by the sound of boots as the squad of grenade-throwers, chosen for their speed of foot rather than their throwing accuracy, ran back toward the main doors.

Sarsen saw a man stumble, going over on his ankle. Even as the sergeant stooped to help him up most of the soldiers had already reached the netting and were running hard for home. The sergeant glanced back, the plan was working, the locusts were giving chase, converging on the netting.

'We won't make it, sir,' said the sergeant into his collar-phone.

'The hell you won't,' said Sarsen, running into the doorway and clambering up onto the shoulder of a hopper. 'Get out there now, fast!' he said to the driver, pointing in the sergeant's direction. Immediately, the hopper started moving, and Sarsen swung through the hopper's entrance hatch and into the shotgun seat.

He touched his sleeve. 'RPG squad, fire everything you've got, take out any locusts approaching the sergeant. Sergeant, hit the deck; I don't want any friendly fire casualties, and throw your smoke grenades – that might put the monsters off for a few moments. We're on our way.'

The driver had his hopper going flat out, and Sarsen knew it would cover the distance in moments. It was more than equal to a locust, but no match for the RPGs that whizzed past them. Two struck targets, blowing away the locusts and making those approaching the downed men pause for just a moment.

The hopper passed the retreating soldiers and stepped off the netting to stop directly beside the two men.

More RPGs flew past: some hit targets, others vanished over the perimeter wall. Most of the locusts were chasing across the netting toward the retreating soldiers and the main base doors, but several remained around the billowing smoke, interested in the downed men and the hopper.

Sarsen threw open his hatch and shouted down to the men below. 'Stand up so we can see you both. Show yourselves quick. It's now or never!'

The sergeant stood, pulling the soldier with the injured leg to his feet. As they rose, the locusts had a target and eagerly closed in just as the hopper's sturdy lifting arms swung into action, grabbing the two men and hoisting them up and away from the attackers. The hopper driver used the mechanical legs to fend off the locusts while Sarsen gripped the sergeant's arm and swung him into the cab. Then he leaned out further still to bring in the injured soldier before slamming the cab shut.

He looked down where the smoke had cleared and saw dead locusts crushed beneath the hopper's feet. 'Good work, soldier.'

'Yes, sir,' said the driver, as he used the hopper's arms to swat away the locusts that were beginning to swarm over the cab. 'But what now?'

'Major Sarsen, I have to put the charge through the net now. We can't wait for you. I'm sorry,' said Baillie in his collar-phone.

Sarsen glanced toward the base doors. His runners were clear of the net and funnelling into the base, but the swarming locusts were closing behind them. 'Do it right now, professor. Hit it!'

Even before he'd finished speaking, the net began to shimmer as power flowed through. The chasing locusts broke their stride for a moment then resumed the chase. A momentary worry that the plan had failed passed when the shimmering increased, Baillie ramping up the power. The locusts slowed, stopped; many jumped to avoid the growing charge, but as they landed again, it got them.

Spread across the net were dozens of twitching, jerking locusts. Held tight to the net by grasping tendrils, they could not escape while Baillie steadily ramped up the power, electrocuting them all.

It seemed to Sarsen that those locusts that had not been on the net were confused by what they were seeing. Likely, they had never faced such concerted resistance. For a few moments, they didn't know what to do.

'Professor Baillie, can you hear me?'

'Yes, major. What should I do?'

'How long can you keep that net live?'

'Not long, two or three minutes, I guess. The power cabling back here is beginning to heat up; it will burn out like a massive fuse at any moment. How can we get you back in?'

'You can't. Don't worry about us, I've got a plan. You execute yours. Understood?'

'Very well, but—'

'No buts, professor. Get on it now. The base is depending on you. Over and out.' Sarsen closed the channel and leaned over to his driver, everyone struggling in the tight space. Four well-built soldiers in a two-seater cabin was impossibly uncomfortable – but they were alive.

'Fast as you like, driver. Get us round to the other side of the building. I know you can outrun those beasts.'

'Yes, sir.' The hopper took off at speed, the handful of locusts in its path suffering violent crushing as it stamped past. For now, none gave chase.

Sarsen glanced toward the entranceway. Behind the protection of the net, Baillie had brought forward a construction machine. As the last of the RPG squad hurried inside, it had already begun sealing the doorway with the construction mix. In moments, the doorway would be gone forever, swiftly hardening into just another stretch of wall. Sealed – a redoubt or a tomb? The hopper turned the corner and left the scene behind.

'Sarsen, MacMillan here. Great work. We're monitoring you on the perimeter cameras. You're on your own for now. None of the locusts followed you. The survivors of Professor Baillie's fry-up seem pretty stunned.'

'Message received, sir. Where is the third wave?'

'They've held off a bit beyond the perimeter wall for now. I'm thinking this has been a bit of a culture shock for them. Probably never had to face any organised resistance like you and your team put up.'

'That's great, sir. Has Baillie got the main doors sealed off?'

'Yes. She's on her way to join me here in the control room. What's your plan?'

'Nothing clever, sir. We'll use the hopper as a climbing aid to come up onto the roof at the rear. Best make sure none of Delacroix's people up there get trigger-happy and shoot us up as we come over the top.'

Chapter 35

Primo Main Base

Dower wrapped Lily in his arms when she ran out through the berthing access door to greet him. She was crying and smiling simultaneously. 'You did it, Lily, you did it,' he said.

'I know we did. It's amazing – the column, all one above the other – and it works perfectly. You'll have to visit it.'

'I will, that's for sure. What matters most right now, though, is that the counter-virus delivery has been achieved.'

'It has. Very late, but otherwise delivered as per Weeman's plan,' said Steph, following Lily through the berthing access door.

The general broke away from his daughter and hugged Steph; she reciprocated. 'Steph, you've done a great job, all of you. Outstanding, quite stunning. If I had medals here, you'd all get one.'

'Big ones,' said Gail Dower, hurrying to join them and exchange more hugs.

General Dower's elder daughter Fay arrived with Captains Kingston and Besinski, all eager to join the welcoming committee. Steph slid from the general's arms and moved to greet his wife, while he in turn greeted Celine as she too disembarked.

'What now?' said Gail.

'What now? We're going to my office this instant to break open a bottle of something special I had shipped up before everything went pear-shaped. All of you, come on.' Dower pointed across the gathering toward

Borland who was still resolutely shadowing Steph. 'You too, soldier – we're all in this. Come on.'

Along the way they were joined by Brigadier Smith-Brown. Dower waved everyone into seats, lined up glasses on his desk and grazed the bottle along the line, giving each glass a generous measure. He raised his.

'We've had a hellish time. Everything's gone wrong. Everyone here has suffered. Suffered losses of family and friends on Earth, too many losses. So much disaster. Humanity almost gone…' His gaze ranged about the company, connecting with each in turn, then he smiled. 'Today we… *you* have taken the first step back for humanity. If we are to recover, and we will, we must rescue Earth. What you have achieved is wonderful, a corridor back to the surface. It's a first step. *The* first step. The first of many. Thank you, thank you all. Here's to you, to us, to humanity!'

He raised his glass higher and gulped down the spirit to a chorus of, '*To you, to us, to humanity. Humanity!*'

The hubbub persisted for a minute before the general brought them all back to the day. 'All right everyone, listen up, let's have a little order, please.' In the ensuing silence he looked to Steph. 'Well, Steph, what's the prognosis?' He reached out an open arm as he spoke, offering her the floor.

'You all know the plan has been executed to perfection. In theory, the second virus will quickly spread along its distribution pattern and begin to interact with the first. Sadly, too late for the vast majority of people, but there's nothing we can do about that. Let's find the positives. That viral interaction will very quickly weaken the threat, rendering it mostly harmless. For those on Earth who have survived the virus, respite is coming.

'We've also sent in three other automated craft to monitor the atmosphere for changes in the virus. As soon as it's safe, we can progress plans. But I'm afraid not before that. There's no point in sending in rescue teams just to have them die of the virus.'

'How long?' said Dower.

'I don't know how long it will take now,' she said. 'The original distributions were meant to be about two days apart, timed to ensure the first virus encountered the second at its most vulnerable point and before the virus could form into its killing mode or have any impacts on life. That timing is clearly broken now. The first virus will have spread widely, so the neutralisation process is bound to take correspondingly longer. I'm thinking weeks, three, maybe two if we're lucky, maybe more. Let's see what the tests show. Celine will be overseeing the rescue. Celine, where are we on that?'

'Thank you, Steph. We have teams standing by on O-2 ready to go down the tube as soon as it's safe. But right now, there's another problem. Once we send in teams, how do they get out? The gravlift stack is all focusing down. In theory we can just reverse the direction to start exiting ships and people. But we've yet to trial that. Some numbers still to process. I'll know better in the next day or two. The theory for reversing direction is clear; putting it into practice will be the problem. I'll return to Earth orbit shortly, to join O-2 and oversee that. Meanwhile, there's an exciting possibility, two actually, that Lily and I have been considering. She's going to stay here and start that work.'

'Tell us more,' said Dower.

'I think I'll let Lily talk about that,' said Celine.

Lily stood. She glanced at her father who nodded encouragement. She felt her mother take her hand and squeeze. Lily didn't enjoy the limelight. Her gaze linked across the room with her sister; she could feel her family's encouragement willing her on.

'Lily?' said Steph. 'What have you got for us?'

'Celine and I were charged with getting the second virus craft into Earth's atmosphere to neutralise the first virus. We've done that... we hope. We were also to come up with ideas to get the atmosphere opened for regular traffic. Maybe we've done that too, on a small scale, if Celine's gravlift reversal works on the column...'

'Why wouldn't it?' said Dower.

'Each gravlift in the stack is projecting its energy down. At the very limit of each gravlift's reach is the next sample craft. It's positioned exactly at the end of the protective gravlift forcefield projecting down from the craft above. That means, right now, each craft in the column is simultaneously not being subjected to any significant downward force that might move it and break the whole tube, yet it's still just within the protective shielding projecting down from above, keeping it safe from debris. Celine needs to work on the timing of reversing the gravlifts' direction of force from downward to up. Getting the timing wrong could leave craft unprotected and vulnerable to debris strikes during the reversal process – it's got to be perfect.'

'Okay, got it, thanks. Please continue. Your two big ideas?' said Dower.

'Yes. We have two theories, linked but not interdependent. If only one works, brilliant, but if they both stand up, we could quickly be on the way to a permanent solution.' Lily paused for a moment as a ripple of excitement ran around the group.

'So, all the debris we have to contend with is racing round Earth on entirely random, unpredictable orbits, making every bit of the atmosphere potentially dangerous. A descending craft might miss a particular piece of debris. But another craft coming later along the exact same track might be unlucky and collide with it. We can't predict at all. Each part of space is either safe at a given moment or it isn't, and we can never know which it will be with any degree of certainty.

'So, perhaps, if our current tube is in place long enough, it will block every piece of debris that would otherwise cross through its path. Leaving that narrow channel of space cleared and navigable, without the need to maintain the gravlift column.'

'What about debris collisions elsewhere that might redirect the orbits of other material across our cleared tube?' said the brigadier.

Lily shrugged. 'It's just a theory at this stage. The second plan might offer better prospects, but it would mean breaking the existing tube.'

'Go on,' said Dower.

'Many planets' atmospheres are thought to have been swept clear of natural debris over time by the gravitational forces of things like moons deflecting matter away or down. That's really what the gravlifts in our column are doing now, but in just a narrow tube. So, could we pull all the sample craft up from the tube, refocus their gravlifts again, and set them in a broad line abreast, orbiting Earth. Over a period of time, they could go round and round, gradually getting lower, sweeping the debris from the sky as they go.

'Given enough time, it's an approach that might completely clear the atmosphere of debris.'

The general stood. 'Lily, Celine, those ideas sound great. I want you to press on now. Meantime, Steph, you need to get back onto the weapons problem.'

Chapter 36

Opsythia System: P-1

Captain Grainger glanced from the screen to acknowledge her chief scientist's arrival on the bridge. 'Well, Fritz?'

'My team's still working on it, ma'am. We're not there yet, but I'm certain we can deliver you a remote-control flight system for the observer.' He looked up at the screen. Ahead was the cone, now appearing much larger than when he'd last been on the bridge. A formation of combat vessels flying ahead of the cone was quite distinct. 'Though it'll be tight in the time available.'

'We have contact in fifteen minutes. That's all the time you've got. What's the problem?'

'No problem with the technology. We've been moving the observer around the hangar remotely. I'm happy it'll do exactly the job you want.'

'What's the difficulty then?'

'We're trying to build in a firewall, just in case the cone tries to snatch control from us once it's launched.'

'Can they do that?' Grainger looked sharply at Fritz.

'I think they would try. Certainly, I'd try in their place.'

'Do your best. What are the chances of them overriding our control?'

'In the time available to them once they realise we've launched a remotely controlled craft? Slim, very slim. But I have to cover every eventuality.'

'Okay, keep your team on it. When the time comes, I'll have to launch with or without your firewall. We'll only get one chance.'

Fritz left the bridge, passed through the navigation room, and headed for the exit stairwell, all the while speaking to team members via collar-phone. As he crossed the navigation room, he suddenly changed direction and disappeared into the comms control room.

Grainger had followed him off the bridge to where her second officer was tracking events in the navigation-room LPA. She stood in silence for a moment considering the array of light signals. 'What are we looking at?'

'Ma'am, what Fritz suggested earlier… it's certain now – we've misjudged the number of vessels that are attached to the cone,' said the second officer.

'Explain.'

'We had previously reckoned around one hundred and twenty vessels. That was informed by our first encounter readings at Pardamax. Recently, Fritz had speculated it might be more. But now I can see the cone's carrying capacity is nearer twice what we'd estimated, ma'am.'

'What? Hell's teeth, how have we got that so wrong? Show me.'

The second officer waved into the LPA. 'I've just reset our scale to take a better look at the cone now we're closing. That's only the cone showing in the LPA. You see, ma'am, I think when we flew past the cone at Pardamax, it was berthing its vessels, and it looked pretty well full at one-twenty.' He passed his hand into the LPA and almost touched the array of lights that picked out the individual vessels attached to the cone. 'Based on the number of vessels that have left the cone already, there are far too many still attached. The only answer is we misjudged the numbers before.'

'Interesting,' said Fritz, who had emerged from comms control. 'Let me see.'

The second officer withdrew his hand and stepped back, allowing Fritz to look closely.

'I think you're right. There are far too many craft still on the cone,' said Fritz.

'Surely, that can't be? It's not possible to have launched vessels and those vessels still to be there,' said Grainger. 'Especially as we know so many were destroyed, and others are on the ground at Secundo.'

Fritz frowned. 'Well… including the vessels currently providing the cone's screen escort, they have launched around eighty craft in total, give or take. The cone should have less than half its remaining vessels attached, say forty to sixty vessels. Yet, it seems to be at least two thirds full still.'

'How so?' said Grainger.

Fritz straightened up. 'There is only one possible answer. What we thought was a fully laden cone ready to travel was only half-laden. They must double-up their vessels, piggyback. One attaches to the cone, a second attaches directly over it, creating a second layer of vessels on the cone.'

'That means there could be another hundred and fifty vessels still on the cone, maybe more!'

Fritz nodded. 'That fits. Perhaps one-eighty'

Grainger tapped her sleeve. 'Captain Ash, you need to be aware the locusts have more vessels still attached to the cone than we thought.'

'Ma'am?' Breeze Ash's voice sounded in Grainger's collar-phone.

'Turns out they double layer their vessels on the cone. There are way more remaining than we thought.'

'We'll cope, ma'am. From down here, it seems they still only have six deployed in their defensive shield. We can deal with that easily enough. Let's get out and clear your path while we can. The warbirds are ready to launch on your word.'

'Thank you, Ash. Stand by.' Grainger glanced toward the second officer. 'ETA?'

'Five minutes. And, ma'am, there's more movement at the rear of the cone. I see more vessels detaching.'

'Numbers?'

'I'm counting twenty. They're moving to join the existing screen.'

'Ash, did you hear that?'

'Yes, ma'am. We're seeing them here too.'

Grainger headed back onto the bridge where the cone was looming large. Ahead of it, a phalanx of locust attack vessels.

'Number One, this is going to be difficult. I want you to handle manoeuvring the Leviathan while I maintain oversight. You're happy with the plan?'

'I am, ma'am. It's high risk. Especially now we know how outnumbered we are.'

'It is, but Colonel MacMillan's orders are explicit: if humanly possible, we must stop the cone folding away, at any cost. The one thing we've got to our advantage is speed. Let's use it. Now stand everyone to. It's time.'

Moments later, the third officer hurried onto the bridge, closely followed by Fritz.

'Launch warbirds,' said Grainger. She stared steadfastly into the great screen. Directly ahead and closing very fast was a mass of locust attack vessels, behind it the cone. Far beyond that, the disc of Opsythia e.

'This is P-1:C1, warbirds moving to station now.' Ash's voice sounded in Grainger's collar-phone.

'Thank you C1. I see you,' said Grainger as C1 moved ahead of the Leviathan mother ship. C2 and C3 appeared to her port and starboard bows.

'Attention, warbirds, maintain your positions on me; we are executing a course change in three, two, one, now,' said Grainger. On *now*, she saw the chief officer mouth an order into his collar-phone.

Immediately, the Leviathan altered course. It was only a five-degree shift, just enough to ensure there was no unintended head-on collision with the onrushing cone – that would be the very last resort. She hoped it was not enough change to signal any weakness to the enemy. Her screen quickly steadied as the Leviathan settled on its new heading. The three warbirds had maintained station. C1 directly ahead, C2 and C3 to either hand. Now the cone showed just offset to port on the screen.

It was quickly clear that the cone was not shifting course, perhaps content in having sensed weakness in its enemy. However, a shout from the second officer beside the LPA signed more trouble. 'It's shedding more combat vessels; I count twenty more signals.'

On the bridge, Fritz jabbed out a pointing hand. 'There, see how they're shedding. Where will they form up, though?'

Grainger nodded. 'Captain Ash, do you see that? There's a second wave, twenty more vessels; we're monitoring them. Looks as though they're trying to flank us, so they'll be coming in on our port side.'

'I see them, ma'am. C2, they're for you. Proceed to intercept now,' said Ash.

'Preparing to engage to port,' said the pilot of C2, peeling away to face the newly launched wave.

'Holding position to starboard,' said the pilot of C3.

'Locust missiles launched directly ahead, salvo incoming, counting fifteen… twenty. Twenty incoming,' said the second officer, reporting across an open channel.

'C1 that's for you. C3, support C1,' said Grainger.

'Wilco,' said C3's pilot.

***

Ash turned to her co-pilot. 'I'll take the laser on manual, shout if I'm missing anything.'

She nudged her warbird further ahead of the Leviathan and registered the arrival of C3 to her starboard side. The two warbirds were directly between P-1 and the fast-closing missiles. Beyond the missiles, a whole raft of combat vessels and, finally, the cone. With every moment the gap was closing.

Using line-of-sight guidance Ash focused on the nearest missile, and with the slightest touch of her finger, the laser beamed out from the nose of her warbird – just a passing touch of its energy sliced the missile in two. Shifting her gaze, she beamed again, destroying a second. The pilot of C3 was doing exactly the same.

The single-shot method worked effectively, but almost at once, Ash calculated they could not take out all the missiles in time. She changed tactic, keeping the beam active while allowing her sighting gaze to roam across the onrushing missiles. The kill rate was faster; she called an order for C3 to copy her tactic. Between the two warbirds, the last of the missile salvo was downed just as it came abreast.

'Second salvo launched, a double salvo, I count forty,' said the Leviathan's second officer.

Ash braced for the next engagement. Ahead, the cone was now huge, and she could make out individual combat vessels attached to its frame. The cone would pass imminently. Meanwhile, the onrushing missiles and the combat vessels directly behind them were all on a collision course. Crunch time.

Ash chanced a brief glance toward her co-pilot. 'Jess, I'll try to take out these incoming missiles with the laser. You commence firing our own missiles, hit back. Take out some of their vessels. Let's try to stop any more enemy missile launches. C3, you do the same.'

Jess acknowledged and began arming the warbird's missiles.

Again, Ash used her laser, sweeping her sighting gaze from missile to missile. The constant beam trailed her gaze; the kills were easy but there were so many to hit. In a slightly detached way, she registered outbound missiles streaking away, as her co-pilot began engaging with the closing squadrons of combat vessels.

Like swatted flies, the locusts' missiles were going down, but there were too many. Several missiles got past Ash, en route for the Leviathan.

'Hell, C3 stay engaged with the combat vessels, just try to hold them back,' said Ash as she forced the warbird into a one-eighty turn. As her warbird turned to port, she kept the laser live, taking out two of the missiles as they passed. Then she began the short and desperate chase toward P-1, killing missiles with every glance.

The distance was too short, she couldn't get them all. In despair, Ash watched the two leading missiles detonate. The first was deflected by the Leviathan's bow shield; the second struck home, penetrating forward compartments. A blast flashed out to leave a hole gaping into space. As Ash turned the warbird to again face the oncoming combat vessels, she registered bodies being sucked out of the ruptured compartments, lost to space.

Immediate responses to the missile strike had momentarily impeded P-1's surprise strike plan and the cone was slipping by.

'Launch the observer,' said Captain Grainger.

Ash heard but didn't look. In the arc of her warbird's turn, she saw the cone was nearly abeam of the Leviathan. She gritted her teeth, needing to get back to support C3 against the host of locust attack vessels.

The warbird missiles had certainly thinned out the oncoming locusts. Clearly, C3 was doing a great job against the slower and less agile attacking vessels. Given time and space, Ash half thought C3 could manage the whole business with its laser beam at close quarters, slicing into hulls, carving them up like Sunday joints. But there was neither time nor space.

As she hurried C1 forward in support, she admired her colleague's skills. C3 had slipped amidst the onrushing pack of combat vessels, the warbird so close in that the locusts were unable to bring their missiles to bear. C3 began a lethal display, executing a pirouette with its nose laser running hot and live throughout.

One after another, locust vessels were taken out, victims of the deadly dance. Some lost wings or tail fins, others suffered hull gashes, still more exploded where fuel or oxygen tanks were ignited. But at such close quarters, nothing was certain.

Ash suddenly felt sick to her stomach, registering what was about to happen and unable to do anything about it. While C3 continued its killing spin, one locust vessel altered course to deliberately ram it. As the warbird's rotation brought it nose-to-nose with the incoming vessel, its laser dissolved the locust cockpit but could do nothing to stop the collision, and C3 vanished in an explosion of light and dust.

Only six of the original attack vessels remained, and then C1 was among them. Ash determinedly sliced with her laser, every kill reducing the threat to the Leviathan. What had seemed to her an almost unending flow of energy and concentration had, in reality, lasted only seconds. One of the attacking vessels broke off, the remaining five left as ruined hulks.

'What's happening, Jess? Where next?' said Ash to her co-pilot as she looked around the space panorama.

'We've lost C2 as well,' said Jess, pointing to the active flight lights in the low-slung console before them. Only their own blue light glowed. C2 and C3 were extinguished. 'It must have gone down to the second flight of locust vessels.'

'Hell, come on, we'll need to intercept them before they get to the Leviathan.' Ash turned the warbird's head to close on P-1. She forced the warbird forward at maximum speed, while scanning across the wider battlefield.

Eight or nine attacking vessels had survived their encounter with C2 and were making a beeline for P-1, now left defenceless save for its speed. But P-1 couldn't flee – it still needed to direct the remote-control observer to its target. Ash was still too distant to intervene as the furthest forward attack vessel fired two missiles.

For the second time, Ash felt sick. Ahead of her, the missiles raced on to strike direct hits. One plunged through the open portside hangar doorway from which the observer had been launched. Simultaneously, the other punched through the hull someway below the bridge. Flashes and debris plumes billowed out.

Then nothing. No more missiles. The attacking vessels were turning away, ignoring the defenceless Leviathan, and heading back to the cone, which had suddenly altered course to pass out beyond Opsythia e.

Ash tried to assess what was happening as she altered course to engage the enemy. 'Can you make anything out?' she asked her co-pilot.

'The cone's running from the observer,' Jess replied, having spun his bucket seat about to consult the LPA behind them. 'Captain Grainger's guiding it directly into the rear of the cone.

'I can see it now,' said Ash. The co-pilot looked too. 'Everything on the cone is forward facing, the cone's got no weapons that can touch our craft. It's going to make it.'

Ash leaned forward anxiously. She knew that deep within the cone's framework was embedded one of their sample craft that the locusts had captured and somehow commandeered as the root source of their own folddrive. The observer had to hit home, had to take out the sampler to ensure the locusts could not use folded space to reach Base Primo and Earth. They were winning the race; the plan was working. Using the observer craft as a weapon to ram its target would maroon the remaining locusts in this system.

'The retreating locust vessels are trying to intercept our observer!' said Ash. 'Come on, after them, let's block their run-in.' Ash focused on the line of withdrawing locusts. 'Too far off for my laser. Can you get any of them with a missile?'

'I can try, but if they dodge it, there's a risk of hitting our own observer,' said Jess.

'We'll have to risk it, pick your targets and fire.'

'Hello, Ash, Grainger here. Are you receiving? Report, over.'

'Yes, ma'am. We're closing on the cone now, trying to give the observer some cover.'

'Okay, please report the craft's progress to target. We believe Fritz's instruments have full control of the craft, but several data channels have been taken out completely by the missile strikes. We can't receive any responses from the observer. We're driving it half-blind here.'

'You're bang on now. Just keep it steady as she goes. Contact coming up fast, maybe less than thirty seconds, and you'll ram right into the cone. I'm thinking the enemy have left it too late; their attack vessels don't have the speed to catch up with our observer.'

'Great, just talk us in. Pray God we score a hit.'

'Yes, ma'am.'

Using gravdrive, flat out, the observer was simply outpacing the locust combat vessels. Still too distant to engage her own laser, Ash was content to watch as her co-pilot aimed and fired a succession of missiles, each of which hit home to take out one of the chasing locust combat vessels.

'Hello P-1, estimate twenty seconds to impact, you have a clear run, but the cone is changing course slightly, it's running for the Fold; you need to bring the observer's heading to starboard by ten degrees, now.'

'Roger that C1, changing heading ten degrees starboard now.'

'That's good ma'am. Steady now and contact in ten, nine… Oh hell!'

'What's happening, C1? Report.'

Ash watched in despair as the cone shed four vessels. All launched simultaneously, all with an inward trajectory that focused on the forward track of the fast-closing observer. Almost as one, the vessels crashed into the observer, stopping it, diverting it, destroying it.

'C1, report, now!'

'It's gone. The observer craft has been destroyed. A total kamikaze strike. They launched vessels off the cone directly into our craft's path. It didn't stand a chance. The cone has survived. I'm following in to attack now, over.'

Ash had the speed to catch the cone but first needed to divert around the spreading debris field.

'Hell, look! It's all over,' said Jess pointing toward the cone as the warbird skirted the debris and readied for an attack run.

Ash was suddenly deflated. Ahead of the cone, a milky disc was forming – it was moving into the Fold. 'Launch a missile now,' she said.

Jess fired and they both watched as the weapon streaked toward the cone. As the cone disappeared, slipping through the disc into the Fold, the missile made contact but only with the rearmost round of attached vessels. Damage was done, but Ash knew they had failed.

Her report was met with a terse response from Captain Grainger. Then, after a few moments, orders arrived. 'Hello, Ash. Our main LPAs have not reset yet, and engineering is reporting sufficient damage that we won't be able to fold until repairs are completed. The cone has evaded us for now. Return to us at once; we are a sitting duck if any enemy vessels have survived or if the vessels on the planet come up after us. You'll need to relay a report to Colonel MacMillan for me. We only have local comms; our longer-range channels are still out.'

'Yes, ma'am, on our way back to you now.' Ash immediately set the warbird's course. They may have missed the cone, but there could yet be fighting to do. She took a moment to compose her thoughts then opened a channel to Secundo.

Chapter 37

Opsythia e.: Base Secundo

MacMillan banged a fist into the palm of his hand. 'Damn! Damn these locusts all to hell.'

'I'm thinking that's where they came from,' said Delacroix.

'You're not wrong. And we know for sure we're on our own down here. There's one warbird left, and it must stay with the Leviathan. Short term positives: at least we know the locusts here are not going to be reinforced, and the main entrance is sealed. Negatives: they can still come in through the roof deck, and we have little left to hit them with.'

'My people can put up some resistance, but not for long,' said Delacroix.

'We need something that will give us an advantage, some edge over these monsters.'

Both men looked toward Professor Baillie.

Grim-faced, she waved toward the control-room screens. 'The science team has been working flat out, trying to come up with a clear kill option for you. It's just not easy – they are naturally armoured, physically strong, and very fast-moving. We've got explosives, but we can't mine the roof when we're underneath – it'll take us out too. They'll be alert to that now anyway. Similarly, they know we've turned their stun net on them, so there's no surprise there anymore.'

'Now give us the good news, professor,' said MacMillan.

Delacroix threw up his arms in exasperation. 'It's all about their vulnerability. We know that's their antennae, but now the locusts are wearing helmets we can't get at them, even at close quarters. Don't you have a ray or something we could use to get through the helmet?'

'It doesn't work like that, I'm afraid,' said Baillie. 'The obvious solution would be to withdraw everyone down into the building and employ a construction machine to seal the roof entrance, leaving the locusts outside.'

MacMillan scowled. 'And us inside, trapped. We'd simply be entombing ourselves. Sardines in a can, waiting to be eaten. That's no answer.'

Baillie nodded. 'Yes, sorry. We're struggling for any hi-tec solutions just now, but we're working on some conventional ideas too.'

'What have you got?'

'With respect, colonel, I need to get back to my team and see how things are progressing. I don't want to explain anything until it's more than just a thought.'

'Okay, get to it. I want to know as soon as you have something that might work. How long do you need?'

'Another hour, I guess.'

MacMillan glanced at the screens. In the distance he could see movements rippling through the third wave that still waited beyond the perimeter wall. On the plain beyond, what appeared to be a fourth wave of locusts was assembling. 'I think they'll be coming soon. Get to it, Baillie. I doubt you have even half an hour, now go!'

***

Delacroix leaned forward, his hips pressing against the parapet that skirted the roof edge. Dotted all along it were soldiers. Beside him stood Sarsen.

'Any moment now,' said Sarsen, peering across the enclosure to the outer-perimeter wall. The third wave had advanced up the slope and vanished into the shadow of the wall.

Delacroix touched his sleeve. 'Stand by everyone. When they come, they'll likely come fast. RPG squad, choose your targets and fire at will. Riflemen, aim for the domes: they're bullet-proof, but direct hits will slow them down – give the tendril grenadiers a target to aim at. Finally, when the order comes, fall back fast to the roof's central access door.'

'They're here!' A shouted voice further along the line signalled the beginning.

A single locust scout had jumped up from behind the perimeter wall to land on the parapet. It looked about cautiously. Detecting no humans at the wall, it turned, rose on its back legs and loudly rattled its carapace to call forward the swarm. All along the wall, locusts appeared, leaping up. As the locusts were landing on the parapet, a report sounded, and an RPG fizzed across the enclosure, hitting home to blast the scout off the wall and into a dozen pieces.

The locust advance party dropped into the enclosure and hurried across the compound while more locusts appeared behind, leaping over the parapet to reinforce the attack.

'Keep firing!' shouted Delacroix, as he turned and waved a signal to the observer that had remained grounded next to the rooftop entrance. 'Come on, pilot! Get up, engage!'

'Readying now, sir.'

All around was the report of gunfire, the whizz of launching RPGs and their more distant explosive detonations. Louder and louder grew the rustle and clicks of the oncoming hoard.

With long leaps, the leaders crossed the enclosure in seconds and immediately jumped for the building's roof, just high enough for them to reach the parapet and pull themselves up with their short upper arms. Some were blown back and down by the sheer force of point-blank rifle fire. Others were forced back from the roof with viciously delivered rifle-butt blows. Uninjured, they recovered and relaunched for the roof.

For every locust displaced, another established a footing on the parapet. One particularly big creature hopped down onto the flat roof, two soldiers felled by kicks from its heavy legs – one eviscerated, one simply winded. The hungry locust thrust its body forward toward a third man, bringing its head down to the soldier's face. Before he could back away, the locust's short arms grabbed his neck and face and tore hard into the man's flesh.

A piercing scream was drowned out by the triumphant clack and rustle of the locust as it straightened, swept off its helmet and fell upon the injured man, its mouth parts biting and snapping in a feeding frenzy. Above and behind him on the parapet, two more locusts appeared at the undefended gap. They too dropped onto the roof, expertly removing their helmets in the process, then stooping to savage the already downed soldiers.

'Come on,' said Delacroix to Sarsen. We need to fill that gap. The two men hurried over. Pulling their knives, each leapt onto the back of a feasting locust, catching them off-guard. Before the monsters could react, the men sliced off their antennae. In angry distress, both locusts let out pained squeals and rattled their carapaces in alarm. They abandoned their feasting to lurch and waddle aimlessly across the roof. Alerted, the big locust looked up from its feeding and rose to confront the two officers.

Fully eight feet tall, the locust stepped away from its still twitching meal and, with a threatening rattle of its carapace, advanced apace. Its bloodied mouth parts cracked together emitting an angry message.

Sarsen raised his pistol and supported his gun hand with his left, locking it tight across his wrist. Steadying, he aimed at the locust's head and fired off a desperate series of rounds as the insect closed the gap. The locust's great kicking legs twitched ready to strike out even as its horny-headed shell stopped two rounds that embedded ineffectively in its thick natural armour. There was nowhere and no time to run. All they could do was watch as the locust's antennae twitched an urgent angry dance. Instead of kicking out, it tried to jump, launching itself up and toward Sarsen.

'Sirs! Drop, drop! Hit the ground!' The observer pilot's voice sounded in Sarsen and Delacroix's collar-phones. Conditioned to following orders, they responded at once, dropping flat beneath the parapet.

As they hit the deck, a shadow passed low overhead, and a thumping sound signalled the end of the huge locust. The officers raised their heads, and it was immediately clear the area was locust-free. Like a great snow plough, the observer's bow had swept away the big attacker, splintering its shell in a dozen places. The craft ran along the line of the parapet cracking and crushing locusts. Then it dropped down into the enclosure crushing attackers before skimming about at ground level to bump and crush yet more.

A faint cheer rose from the roof as it became clear the locust attack was wavering, the monsters falling back across the enclosure. The cheer was cut short by an explosion, then another and a third. The observer was downed, damaged by impacts from the locusts' own version of RPGs.

Immediately, the enemy regrouped and began to close again on the building.

'Fall back,' ordered Delacroix. 'Back to the doorway!' He turned and paced steadily away to the rooftop entrance.

Sarsen looked along the line, waving his men back. They all retreated briskly to join Delacroix who was directing men at the entranceway. The uninjured were being mustered behind a barricade, a final flimsy line of defence formed from a variety of movables. Other soldiers were carrying the wounded down into the base. Some of the injured had broken limbs or torn bodies where locust kicks had felled them. Yet more were unconscious, rigid in the arms of their rescuers.

'What's happening with them?' asked Delacroix.

'Don't know, sir. One moment he was standing by me at the parapet, next he's flat out, stiff as a board.'

Delacroix looked toward the doorway where the sounds of a commotion had been building. Professor Baillie pushed her way through the throng of retreating wounded. She emerged on the roof as Sarsen and the last of the troops arrived from the parapet.

At the doorway, she stopped the soldiers carrying a rigid body and ran her hands over the soldier's quivering form. Her hands paused, felt again then scrabbled to grip something. After a moment she extracted a slender dart that had passed through the soldier's suit to embed in his body. As it came away, the tension in the man's body faded, and he slumped.

She thrust out a hand toward Delacroix, displaying a dart with a double needle point. An electrical arc sparked between the two needles.

'They're using stun projectiles, so make sure your men keep low behind the barricade.' She waved the dart and the white flashing arc sizzled. 'Enough power to put you down in a moment. Not enough to kill.' She grimaced. 'We know why.'

She traced Delacroix's gaze across the roof to where locusts were again appearing at the rooftop parapet. 'I've got something for you,' she said, looking back to the doorway where the last of the wounded had been carried down. Now emerging was her team carrying a jumble of paraphernalia. They were followed by two bots, each transporting a forty-gallon drum.

'This is all we've come up with. I hope it works,' she said, waving her assistants into action. They rigged the hoses they had carried with them, linking them up to a pressure pump and in turn to the drums.

'Here they come,' shouted Sarsen. 'Stand by with the grenades, throw on my order. And keep your heads down. They have stun darts. Steady. Wait for it, wait…'

Baillie waved her assistants back through the doorway and thrust the first of the hoses toward Delacroix. 'This might help.'

'What is it?' Delacroix took the hose as the scaly rustling and thudding sound of advancing locusts reached them from across the roof. They were coming, fast.

'It's not much but it's all we've got.' She kicked a drum. 'This is a highly viscous bonding agent, under pressure.' She pointed to the pump. 'Spray the locusts with it. It will cover their helmets, block their sight. Force them to take their helmets off. At least you'll have a fighting chance then. You'll be able to get at their antennae. Sorry it's not more.'

'It's more than we had a minute ago,' said Delacroix, beckoning over the nearest two soldiers who had been listening intently.' He waved them up to the barricade with orders to spray locusts. 'Well done, Baillie. You'd better go now.'

Crouching down beside Sarsen, Delacroix shared the news of the spraying device. Both men instinctively felt for the sharp combat knives attached to their belts.

'What do you think?' said Sarsen.

'I think it's a last chance, and right now we're in the last chance saloon. Anything's better than nothing.'

Delacroix gestured to the two soldiers detailed to operate the spray. They hoisted their nozzles and fired the viscous material directly at the first rank of attackers. The locusts kept coming. The thud of landing feet and rattling of carapaces grew to be the only sound anyone could hear. The spray detail kept spraying, then one soldier dropped, twitching.

'They're using the darts again! We have to neutralise that. Lieutenant! Smoke cannisters, as many as you like, over there – get us some cover. Now!' Sarsen pointed across the barricade.

Smoke canisters were hurled. Sarsen nudged the soldier beside him, pointed at the abandoned spray wand then shoved the next man toward the downed soldier. 'Get the dart out and move him into the stairway.'

Sarsen turned back to the barricade, ready to repel the first of the locusts, but they had not arrived. He carefully raised his head above the barricade and gave a wry laugh to himself. Delacroix joined him.

'Keep spraying,' said Sarsen. Directly in front of the barricade, the first line of locusts had stopped, their helmets covered in a black film that completely obscured their vision. Blinded, confused, they had stopped to pull their helmets off. Beyond them the second wave was emerging from the smoke, short-armed hands wiping at their helmets in a futile attempt to remove the coating – they too paused to strip them off.

'More smoke canisters! More spray! Knives ready, men; it's hand-to-hand now!' Sarsen looked at Delacroix. 'This is it, sir.'

'It is.' Delacroix flexed his knife hand as the first wave advanced again, their heads now bare, antennae vulnerable.

Locusts jumped over the barricade, landing behind the soldiers and turning immediately to attack those soldiers who had turned to face them.

The nearest soldiers got in close fast, ensuring the locusts could not aim and land any eviscerating kicks. Sarsen and a corporal found themselves teamed up in a life-and-death grapple with one locust. The corporal had pressed in, wrapping his legs tight around the beast's thorax while squirming round to the back. His hands reached forward to grip the locust's small arms and constrain their movement while Sarsen faced-up. Enraged, the clicking locust jutted its head forward, mouth parts snapping at Sarsen's face. Sarsen fell backward, sprawled on the roof. With a stream of angry clicks, the locust stepped forward to stamp Sarsen with its heavy legs.

Life and death suddenly crossed paths, and in the instant's reprieve, Sarsen reacted. Rolling to one side, he sprung up and slashed out at the locust's waving antennae, while it looked down in puzzlement at its suddenly under-performing legs. The bonding agent was working far beyond Baillie's conception by setting hard in the locust's exoskeleton joints, rapidly diminishing its mobility.

Hissing in anger and struggling against the bonding agent, the locust stretched up, trying to straighten its torso, calling out in distress. Its arms were completely locked now, allowing the corporal to redeploy his own hands, freed to reach for his knife. With a violent slash, he severed the antennae. The locust squealed, twirled about, and dropped on its front. Its mouth, untouched by the bonding agent, continued to click and snap, biting at nothing.

Sarsen glanced along the line; a similar story was playing out everywhere. He saw three men down, he feared dead. Other men were going through a strange procedure that involved wriggling and stripping out of their uniforms that had bonded to the locust exoskeletons. He waved them into the doorway as they broke free.

'More smoke! Keep spraying.' Delacroix's collar-phone order pulled Sarsen back to the action, and he looked over the barricade. Immediately beyond their defensive position, a little over a score of locusts were gathered. All had discarded their helmets. Some hobbled about, still fighting against the bonding agent's locking effect on their joints. Most were down, joints seized, frozen. Unsprayed heads and antennae continued to move and snap to a tune of angry hisses and clicks.

Beyond them, seen through the wafts of clearing smoke were massed many more helmeted locusts, waiting for some insight, some order to help them overcome this latest challenge, waiting for clear targets at which to aim their stun darts. Then a fresh round of smoke canisters deployed, and they vanished from view.

'Sarsen, take a squad over the barrier as quick as you like. Let's take some of these monsters out while we can.'

'Yes, sir! Every second soldier in the line, on me. Let's move!'

Sarsen stood and vaulted the barricade with his men. He landed directly in front of a downed locust. Leaning forward he gripped the waving antennae and sliced them both off. Its hiss raised almost to a screech as Sarsen moved on to the next. To either side, soldiers were executing the same manoeuvre.

'Fall back,' said Sarsen as the smokescreen began to thin and the last of the downed locusts had been cut.

He returned behind the barricade to find Delacroix inspecting the bonding agent storage tanks.

'Empty,' said Delacroix.

'What now, sir?' said Sarsen.

'I think we're done here. Have the men fall back through the doorway. We'll have to fight them in the passageways now.' He turned away, stroking his sleeve to open a channel to report to MacMillan.'

By the time he'd finished, the last of the soldiers was inside. He stood beside Sarsen at the open door and looked out. The blanket of smoke they'd laid down had almost cleared. The rooftop around the entranceway was scattered with dead and dying locusts. Further off, the massed ranks of helmeted locusts had registered his men were pulling back and the advance resumed.

Delacroix pulled the hatch shut just as it drummed to the sound of half a dozen stun darts. He looked at Sarsen, and together they turned the heavy, locking seal.

'That should hold them for a while,' said Delacroix.

'I hope so.'

At the top of the stairway stood a lieutenant. Delacroix called him forward. 'Keep watch here. Major Sarsen and I are heading to the control room to work out our next move.'

'Very good, sir.' The lieutenant and his squad edged up to the door, clutching rifles that they knew would have little effect should the locusts get in.

Chapter 38

Opsythia e.: Base Secundo

Professor Baillie waved away the praise Sarsen and Delacroix tried to give her for the bonding agent plan. She and her team really had nothing left now – the cupboard was bare. If the locusts got through the door, it was game over.

MacMillan clapped her on the shoulder. 'Baillie, your idea saved soldiers' lives. No matter what happens next, you delivered. Keep your team on it; I'm sure you'll come up with something else.'

'Surely we can use more of the bonding agent if they get in. You do have more in the stores?' said Delacroix.

'We've got plenty of it, but in a confined space we can't restrict its distribution to just the locusts. You saw how soldiers who came into contact with the stuff were quickly gummed up, just like the locusts.'

'Except our people were able to wriggle out of their uniforms,' said Sarsen.

Baillie shook her head. 'Then what? Have them fight naked? Anyway, the stuff's toxic. Spray it inside, and the soldiers would need to keep their helmets up. As soon as we started spraying, their visors would be as obscured as any locust's, and helmets down means poisoned soldiers. We can't use it inside.' Baillie's pragmatic statement masked her growing concern. She had quickly come to grasp the theory and demands of conflict, but her instincts were all for peace, and most of all, she was not a physically courageous person. Having the locusts so close was frightening – she was really scared.

MacMillan rested a hand on her forearm. 'Professor Baillie, get back to your team, have them go back to basics – look at what kills these monsters and how we can apply it? Sarsen and Delacroix will keep them out for now. We know what we can't do. You just focus on what we can, okay?'

Baillie left the control room, and MacMillan turned his attention to Sarsen and Delacroix. 'Thoughts, gentlemen?'

Sarsen waved up toward the rooftop display screen. 'What are they up to?'

The screen showed the locusts busy on the roof. Most were marshalled a little way from the access doorway, others were dragging the dead and disabled locust bodies off to one side. Several were gathered around the sealed door. One kicked it in frustration.

'Movement down on the plain, sir,' said Barrington.

As one, the three men switched their gaze to the screen displaying the scene beyond the main gates. With Secundo's recently installed air-defence batteries overrun, it was clear the locusts were now confident they were in control of the air space. A combat vessel had taken off from the plain below and was flying directly to the base. It hovered over the roof, lining up on the locked doorway. The locusts were all hurrying away.

'Oh hell,' said Sarsen. Touching his sleeve, he issued orders. 'Lieutenant, fall back. Move your men away from the door and down the steps immediately. Get away from there, now!'

'Falling back now, sir,' came the reply, while the three leaders continued to watch the screen. Impotent, they could do nothing when the inevitable happened. A bright light flared beneath the combat vessel's wing, and a missile launched. They scarcely had time to register the event before the camera feeds shook and dropped out. They were blind. All three feared what it meant.

Coughing sounded in their collar-phones, followed by an anxious report. 'Sir, sir, there's been an explosion; everything is smoke and dust.'

'Are we breached, lieutenant? Are they in?' said Sarsen.

'I'm not sure, sir. We're on the floor below. In the stairwell. I'll go up and see.'

'Be careful,' said Sarsen.

MacMillan turned and pointed a hand toward Jillie Smith who was running the comms. 'Jillie, access the lieutenant's body cam and feed it up onto the screens, please. We need to see what's happening.'

One section of screen flickered and displayed the lieutenant's camera feed. The image bobbed up and down as the lieutenant climbed the stairs. It showed dust swirling up, carried by the warm air toward a cold, hazy light above.

'Do you want the audio too, sir?' said Jillie Smith.

MacMillan raised his hand, thumb up, all the while keeping his eyes on the screen. For a moment, audio fuzz filled the control-room speakers, then came the sound of shallow breaths and cautious footsteps climbing the stairs. The noise of the blast had faded. In its place a distant thrumming filled the background.

'Can you hear that noise, sir? I'm not sure what it is, but it's up ahead. I can't make anything out. There's just a hazy light above,' said the lieutenant.

Sarsen turned to MacMillan. 'Sir, there's no lighting in the stairwell that matches that quality of light. It can mean only one thing—'

'Yes, the entrance way was destroyed in the blast. It's open to the daylight!' said MacMillan, touching his sleeve. 'Lieutenant, stop. Do not proceed further. We believe the doorway is open to the elements.'

'I'm only a couple of steps from the final turn in the stairwell, sir. I can give you a definitive report from there. Permission to proceed?'

MacMillan looked toward Sarsen and Delacroix, then shook his head. 'Negative, lieutenant. Withdraw, rejoin your men on the level below and await orders.'

They watched as the camera stilled, then it bobbed again as the lieutenant took a step backward, beginning his retreat from the dust-hazed daylight above.

MacMillan took an involuntary half-step back as the body-cam feed suddenly became animated. Just feet ahead of the lieutenant, a dark silhouette appeared through the haze. Its heavy foot swept out and struck the lieutenant. His sharp gasp and despairing groan echoed round the control room to complement the camera image, which suddenly showed the steps and his boots as he doubled over in agony.

Clicking and clacking poured from the speakers to fill the control room while everyone watched horrified as the lieutenant met his end. Horny little claws gripped his upper arms and lifted him up, pressing him against the wall. The locust's head was perfectly framed in the body cam, the shadowy shapes of more locusts passing behind it, on their descent into the base.

The locust's mouth parts opened wide, then chattered together in a gleeful prelude to the kill.

'Stop that audio, now!' Everyone welcomed the sudden end to the sound. But the picture stream continued. It framed the hard casing of the locust's head, antennae twitching and sweeping from side to side. Then with a vicious strike, the head moved forward, passing beyond the camera's angle to press, unseen, against the lieutenant's throat.

'Cut the picture,' said MacMillan. He touched his sleeve. 'Sergeant, the lieutenant's down. They're coming for you. Retreat to the passageway immediately. Close the stairwell access doors and lock them. Brace the doors with anything you can find and wait there for my orders.'

MacMillan looked at the two officers. 'Can we get a print constructor to the stairwell door, seal it?'

'No, access to the machine room is from the stairwell, we're cut off from all the construction kit,' said Delacroix.

'So, they're in. I don't know how it's going to end, but we must make it as hard as possible for them. Make them pay at every turn. If nothing else, from this, they must learn humans are not cattle to be herded to the slaughter at their whim. Major Sarsen, please get to the inner doors, see what you can do. Delacroix, get all the civilians in here and check on Baillie and her team. There's no time left for experiments now, just get them out of the lab and back here with everyone else. This is as good a place as any for a last stand.'

For the first time since the day the Perseus Squadron had originally mustered, the three men saluted one another. Then they shook hands, and without further words, Sarsen and Delacroix left the control room.

A technician called MacMillan's collar-phone and asked for his presence. The colonel joined him immediately. No words were exchanged. A pointed finger into the LPA was enough. Red lights were rising – the grounded locust vessels were on the move.

'They're coming, sir. All of them,' said the technician.

MacMillan nodded. He looked up at the screens where the vessels could be seen moving up the slope toward the base compound. 'They are.' He looked back toward the technician. 'All the more for us to deal with, eh?'

The technician tried to keep his cool. 'Yes, sir. But...' He stroked his sleeve, changing the LPA's display scale to reveal the signal light of the distant P-1, and beside it the smaller signal of P-1:C1. 'Can't we ask the warbird to help? It could sort out that lot.' He waved toward the screen and the closing vessels.

'It's a nice thought. But I tell you, son, it must stay with the Leviathan, protect it from that lot outside and from any other rogue survivors. P-1 is a sitting duck; it must survive to get a warning back to Primo. It's humanity's only chance right now. I'm sorry, but if it comes to it, down here – you, me – we're all expendable.'

He reached out his hands and gripped the man by the shoulders, squeezed them gently and locked eyes. 'But believe me, mister, this ain't over yet. They've paid a heavy price to push us back this far, and it's going to cost them a lot more to come any further. A hell of a lot more. We'll make them pay for every inch.'

***

Delacroix stood in the passageway, waving civilian team members past him and on toward the control room. 'Move it now. Keep moving everyone.' He looked further along and spotted a small group of soldiers hovering, unsure of what to do. 'Sergeant! Spread your squad along this corridor, check the side rooms. Make sure you get all the civilians back to the control room; I don't want anyone left behind.' He heard the sergeant's shouted acknowledgement, saw the soldiers spring to, relieved to be doing something.

With a deep breath, he pushed open a lab door, entered, then paused, puzzled at the calm scene. At the far end, Baillie and her science team were gathered around an LPA. They were chattering as though it were a routine day.

'Professor, we need to move along now. The locusts are in the building. Everyone's falling back to the control room.'

Baillie looked round and greeted him with a determined smile. 'We might have something. Come and see.'

Delacroix peered, intent but unknowing, at the sequences of white lights. Some formed solid chains, others pecked lines that seemed to move. 'What am I looking at?' he said.

'This is the water piping plan for the base. The plumbing. The solid lines mark the drains, the moving pecked lines are the freshwater supply pipes.'

'And?'

Baillie tapped her sleeve, and a sequence of blue lines superimposed over the white plumbing lights. 'The blue marks the base's room layout. That's us here,' she said, thrusting her hand into the display. 'And that's the corridor outside. 'The pipes are all sub-floor, quite inaccessible, but see in this room, they surface at terminal points, the sinks. The same further along, at the toilets and elsewhere.' Her hand traced across the LPA to highlight the rest rooms.

'I'm not with you, professor – spell it out.'

'We know they don't like electricity. Here in the base, our floors, handrails, stairs… everything is made of non-conducting material, so we can't get them with electricity inside the building. There's no way we can catch them out again with a net like we did in the enclosure, even if we had another one. But water on the floor…' She looked at Delacroix.

'By God, with water we can fry them in their shells!'

'Well, it's not that simple. We need to get the water spread across the passageways without triggering caution in the locusts, and then we need to charge it with a sudden burst of huge electrical power at just the right moment.'

'But you can do it, right?'

'It's not going to be easy. We'll need to put explosive charges on the pipes where they come through the floors, rig them to be remotely detonated so we can flood the corridors once the locusts are in.'

'I'm on it,' said Delacroix, stroking his sleeve and summoning his explosives expert. 'Captain Barton and his team will blast whatever you want. Just tell him.'

'That's only half the battle. There's the source of the charge to consider. We'll need some heavy-duty cabling and access to the power conduit.'

'The what?'

'There's a tunnel, a conduit, which runs beneath the ground from the power station directly into the base. We tapped into it before to electrify the net. There's a junction beneath the control room where most power is used.' She touched her sleeve, and the LPA display changed to show a wider plan of the base buildings, including a tunnel linking the power plant with the main base.

'What else do you need, professor?'

'Some men to help my people move a power cable to the control room… and time.' She eyed Delacroix.

'Plenty of men, but sorry, professor, we're out of time. Let's move while we still can.' Delacroix broke off to summon more help for the professor as the lab door opened and Captain Barton and his squad entered. They were accompanied by the sound of distant but violent banging.

'Sir,' said Barton. 'I think they'll be through that door soon.'

Grim-faced, Delacroix nodded. He briefed Barton. Then, as more men arrived, he detailed them to help with the power cable. 'Let's move, no time to lose!' He headed back to the control room to update MacMillan.

Chapter 39

Opsythia e.: Base Secundo

From his position behind the locked stairwell door, Sarsen could see down all three corridors at once. This door was set at their junction, like the nexus of a capital T. He knew the washrooms in the stores corridor were already mined, as were the water points in the living quarters. A little way down the stem corridor, Captain Barton emerged from the washrooms, gave him a thumbs up, and disappeared into the labs.

The door was shaking under the unremitting heavy blows; the corridors echoed with the sound. He'd had the soldiers wedge the door and brace it with poles, but it was just about ready to give. A particularly vigorous blow shifted his men back an inch, and they redoubled their efforts, pressing back.

'Sir!' said a corporal. 'We can't hold it any longer.'

'You must. Every man, brace! Brace like the very devil!'

Barton emerged from the lab and beamed Sarsen a near maniacal grin. 'Ready when you are!' he shouted.

'Steady. Steady. Hold for the next blow, then we run!' ordered Sarsen. His men braced. The blow came, and the door quivered violently but held again. 'Fall back. Everyone to the control room at the double. Double away!'

Sarsen frantically waved his soldiers along the corridor toward the control room, and as the last passed him, a further round of blows landed on the door. Without the men bracing it, he knew it wouldn't hold. He sprinted after his troops, gripping Barton's arm as he passed to drag the slightly detached explosives expert with him. The stairwell door split and burst open as Sarsen pushed the soldiers through the control-room door. He relieved Barton of the control-box and then propelled him through the door too.

Just outside the control room, Delacroix and two volunteers crouched behind a makeshift barricade. Sarsen knelt beside them. Safe from any flying stun darts, they delivered a fusillade of fire, attracting the locusts toward the control room. The locusts advanced steadily, untroubled by the bullets.

'I'm not sure about the timing here,' said Delacroix.

'Me neither. They're coming the way we want. I guess this is as good a time as any,' said Sarsen.

The locusts passed the laboratory doors and moved inexorably closer. The group abandoned their barricade and slipped through the control-room door. Banging it shut, they used makeshift props to secure it as best they could.

Delacroix called more men across to bolster the door's support while Sarsen knelt to inspect the power cable's end that an engineer had placed immediately behind the door, its exposed tips waiting to deliver the charge. The cable snaked away to where the far end had been connected into a power console.

A thud against the door announced the arrival of the locusts. Another, then another. The muffled sound of clicks and rustles, and frequently rattling carapaces, told Sarsen a crowd was building in the corridor. He glanced across the control room to where MacMillan was dividing his attention between a corridor camera feed that displayed the massing locusts on the screen, and the line of people funnelling down into the power-cable conduit. All the wounded were already gone; he was now directing the last civilians and soldiers down.

'Colonel MacMillan, sir. We're set,' said Sarsen, then he flinched involuntarily as a much louder crash shook the door beside him. The screen showed two locusts had wedged themselves against the far side of the passageway and were now delivering full-strength kicks to the door with their powerful legs.

With a crack, the locks gave way, and claw-like fingers appeared around the frame. 'Hold it! Hold the door!' Delacroix's voice emerged from the scrum of men behind the door. Redoubling their efforts, the men pressed back, trapping the locust digits tight. Delacroix's arm reached from among the soldiers to chop at the digits with his knife.

'Sir?' said Sarsen.

'Okay. Take it away, Sarsen,' shouted MacMillan. The locusts' calls were sounding ever louder through the door crack.

Sarsen didn't wait. Using the control-box he'd taken from Barton, he triggered the trap. Immediately, reports sounded from assorted washrooms, laboratories and accommodations. The locusts' chatter was momentarily drowned out in the percussive roar. As the sounds of explosions subsided, the insect calls redoubled.

Watching the screen, MacMillan saw many locusts divert into side rooms to investigate the blasts. The main group returned their attention to the door, and the kicking resumed.

Baillie joined Sarsen; she looked worried. 'I think we've got a problem,' she said.

'You don't say?' said Sarsen as the men struggled to hold the door against the kicking locusts.

'Not the locusts,' said Baillie.

'What then?'

She pointed at the floor behind the door where Delacroix and his men stood, some with shoulders to the door, others applying their bodyweight to brace poles against it. Water was seeping beneath the door and flowing about their feet. It showed their plan was working – the corridors and rooms beyond would be awash now, perhaps half an inch deep, and deepening.

'That's good, isn't it?' said Sarsen as the door reverberated again.

'No, if I power up the cable now, it'll fry Delacroix and your men. I can't use our weapon against the locusts.'

'Rubbish!' said MacMillan who had crossed the control room to find out what the problem was. 'First, Baillie, you show Sarsen how to trigger the power cable. Then you get yourself down into the cable tunnel.'

'But—'

'No buts, professor, do it now.'

'It's a death-trap down there!'

'And up here isn't? I want you down there. I've men briefed to seal the access panel once you're inside. Even buying a couple of hours more might allow time for P-1 to complete repairs and get here. Then its warbird will play havoc with these monsters.'

'*Might allow*! That's your best shot?'

'Baillie, get down there now – that's an order.' MacMillan looked around the room, then shouted across the floor. 'Jillie Smith! Why aren't you already down in the tunnel? Leave your post and get into that tunnel now! You too, Barrington.' He watched the two hurry away, fear writ large across their faces.

'It's going to give!' shouted Delacroix from amidst the huddle behind the door.

'One minute more!' came back MacMillan's response. He rested his hands on Baillie's shoulders. 'Go now, professor, you've done well, thank you. This last task is for the soldiers.'

She frowned, pursed her lips, looked into MacMillan's eyes for just half a moment, then leaned forward and kissed him. 'Good luck, colonel.' Then she broke away and signalled Sarsen to follow her as she moved to the power-control console. There, she showed him how to energise the power cable before retiring toward the tunnel mouth. As she disappeared into the tunnel, the panel swung over and sealed.

'Delacroix, men, listen up. On my word, I want you to fall back instantly. Get yourselves away from the door fast. Get up off the ground on to LPA tops, consoles, anywhere – just feet off the ground and clear of the water,' shouted MacMillan while stepping smartly into the middle of the control room where the floor was still dry. To be sure, he jumped up onto Barrington's console.

'Are you set, Sarsen?'

'All set, sir.'

'Stand by at the door. On my count, retire. Three, two, one. Run!'

The men abandoned the door and rushed for dry height, scrambling up wherever they could.

Behind them the door flew open under the next blow. For a moment, there was stillness, the locusts taken unawares. Then the attackers rushed in, slowed momentarily by the press of their own bodies jamming in the entrance.

As the first locusts cleared the doorframe, the last of the men got off the ground and Sarsen threw the switch. Nothing happened; there was a terrifying pause that seemed to last for eternity. He feared the plan had failed. Then the electricity worked its magic. The two nearest locusts hissed, clacked and jumped. Landing back in the water, their carapaces opened, wings beginning to spread, then the twitching began. Immobilised, they dropped into the water and fried. Around the door, the press of locusts exhibited similar suffering.

Sarsen looked across to MacMillan and beamed an uncontrollable smile. The colonel reciprocated and pointed up to the screen which showed a whole swarm of locusts caught and dying in the corridors.

'We've done it, sir,' said Delacroix from his console perch. 'We've done it!'

'By God, look! They're all running; what's going on?' said Sarsen, pointing at the stairwell feed. The locusts beyond the water trap were hurrying away, up and out toward the roof.

MacMillan looked toward screens displaying the enclosure's landing pad and its rows of recently landed locust combat vessels. 'I think they're readying for take-off. Something's happening out there, and it can't be anything to do with us.' He pointed to where locusts were hopping down from the base's rooftop in a desperate rush for their vessels. 'What the hell? Sarsen! Cut that power feed – we need to get after them. Use any grenades you have left. Let's make hay. Delacroix, you get the soldiers up from below to reinforce Sarsen's detail. Move it, everyone.'

Sarsen cut the power, and as people began to climb up from the power conduit, he set off, leading a team into the corridors, dispatching any locusts who had not fully succumbed to the electric current as they hurried for the roof in hot pursuit of survivors.

The growing bustle in the control room suddenly stopped dead, everyone stunned by a whoop from the comms console – left on open channel by Jillie Smith before she retired to the conduit.

'Hello, Secundo. Secundo, this is P-2:C1. Coming in hot, keep your heads down.'

***

Sarsen reached the top of the stairwell as the last of the locusts jumped down from the roof. Leading his men forward, they ran as one for the edge, where they all stopped, shielding their eyes against a brilliant beam of light that slashed down from the sky.

'Helmets up!' ordered Sarsen. The visors toned down the brilliance to a manageable level and revealed exactly what the locusts were running from, or toward.

Perhaps two hundred feet above them a warbird was cruising slowly across the enclosure. Its laser, live and constant, was sweeping left to right, mirroring its pilot's gaze. With each sweep, the laser cut through enemy vessels. Some exploded when fuel tanks or missiles ignited, others crumpled, wings or tails severed. Occasionally, whole fuselages were sliced in two.

Everywhere, locusts rushed, escaping from burning vessels and hurrying toward those that remained intact. Some had the misfortune to be caught in the warbird's roving beam, instantly vanishing, incinerated to nothing.

Sarsen looked up to the warbird as it passed slowly overhead. He waved a hand, then looked down at the carnage in the enclosure. At the furthest end, vessels were beginning to lift off. He touched his sleeve.

'Hello, warbird. Look out at the end – they're getting airborne.'

'Got it, Secundo. Thank you.'

The laser beaming from the warbird's nose suddenly swept ahead toward the three locust vessels that had managed to get airborne. Before the first could orientate to fire a missile, it was sliced through, parts crashing onto the craft rising beneath it, taking that back down too. As the third vessel lined up to fire, it was downed by the raging blast of a warbird missile.

Then Sarsen had his men line the rooftop parapet and act as spotters while the warbird roamed back and forth with its laser, burning out every remaining locust wherever they tried to hide amidst the field of debris that had been their squadron. A few made it over the perimeter wall, but with the setting sun and nowhere beyond to shelter, he doubted many would survive the cold of the night. Hunting them could wait till morning.

***

Captain Grainger nodded toward Fritz then looked beyond him to where several of the scientists and crew were high-fiving. She mellowed for just a moment and met his raised palm even as she spoke into her collar-phone.

'Yes, sir, that's brilliant news. We've been worried sick about you all. We'll be on station above Secundo in approximately one hour. My science and engineering teams report the bots have been busy and progress on repairs is good. Though at this rate, they estimate it will still be some hours before the hull will be strong enough to take the stress of folding.'

'Keep on it, captain. We need to get back to Primo fast. If the cone has gone that way, which I believe it has, Primo's a sitting duck with only one warbird for defence.'

'We're on it, but Colonel MacMillan, Fritz has a suggestion. Do you have any bots you can spare from your own repairs? Any extra will help us in speeding up repairs to P-1.'

'Good idea. I'll see if Baillie can free some up and have them flown up to you in the warbird.'

Chapter 40

Primo Deep

Steph stared intently down into the whirling lights of the Deep Goliath. She had all the teams out searching every corner of the Deep. From the reports filtering back to her it was clear the Deep was the oldest part of Primo. These reports backed up information she was finding in this Goliath's archive. But there was still nothing that flagged weapons or warbirds.

The silence from the Perseus junction was worrying. The general had ordered that there should always be one Perseus Squadron Leviathan maintaining watch in the Fold. But it had been a while since a Leviathan position beacon had returned from the Perseus Squadron, meaning their Leviathans were not in the Fold. *Why?* That was a concern, but for now, they could only hope their absence was caused by technical matters. That hope didn't completely smooth away the pervasive worry, though.

Her current responsibility was to find weapons, and in desperation, she had devised a fresh search plan. The big question: would this Goliath deliver?

At the foot of it, Kingston hurried past Earl, Steph's duty guard, and ran up the steps to join her.

'Just in time,' she said, smiling a greeting.

'What are we looking at, ma'am?' said Kingston.

'Last time, Weeman showed me the warbirds in a secret section that was only accessible to suits of my grade. We have survey teams scouring the Deep for clues but nothing obvious presents yet. So, I'm using their survey reports to develop a new search approach.'

'What's the plan?' said Kingston.

'The problem we have is, if the chambers we really want to find are hidden, then we can only identify them when I or the general pass close enough for our suits to trigger the doorway display. That might take weeks, months even. So, I'm doing this.' She waved into the Goliath where the dizzying twirl of lights was beginning to slow.

The lights settled into a pattern that mapped the layout of the Deep's tunnels and chambers.

'This is important. I'm plotting all the data our survey teams have been sending back as they search. We're finding that the layout plans of the Deep appear consistent. But as with the similar style of plans for Primo Main Base, scale has given way to form and presentation.'

Kingston looked at her blankly.

'What I mean, captain, is that, to find any hidden warbird chamber, we need a map or plan reflecting the actual scale, directions and distances involved.'

'I don't understand. Isn't that what we've got?'

'Not quite. Our current display plans are more akin to a bus-service route map or maybe the plan of an underground railway system… a subway system. In other words, the display used is more like a schematic transport map. It distorts actual geographical positions and distances to provide an easy-to-read route map that shows sequential positions without regard for actual scale and position in the real world. Its priority is route planning and presentation. That same approach has been used in plans throughout Primo; everywhere – true locations and distances are discarded in the route-planner display to make it easier to read and use.'

Steph pointed to the lights beneath her feet. 'See, to this side I've displayed the plan available on your sleeve display.' Kingston recognised the plan with its uniformly spaced chambers, facilities, and mostly straight-line linking passageways, exactly as it displayed on his own sleeve.

Then she waved his attention to the right. 'See over here. It's the same information but presented using the actual survey results as the teams report them to true scale: real chamber sizes and their linking routes with all their twists and turns, actual directions and distances – a real-life representation of the layout but less user friendly on the move. This plan shows all those chambers we've surveyed using true location data, and if we add the Grand Canal to the scheme, you'll see it's a bit more complex to read.

'There's a lot more survey information to gather in yet, but...' She stroked her sleeve and the edge of the Grand Canal appeared in the imagery. 'We're looking for unusually large spaces between chambers and hangars – voids. If there is a secret chamber, it has to occupy real space and that can't be identified using the regular schematic plan. Unused space between chambers will quickly become apparent in a true plan; it will highlight any unused spaces where a secret hangar might be.'

'Like that?' said Kingston, pointing at the true-scale display where two series of chambers were linked by a long stretch of tunnel. The gap between the two developed areas was around eight hundred yards of nothing – solid rock.

'Exactly like that,' said Steph. Then she pointed back to the standard display. 'In reality, there's a big empty space between those chambers, but see on the schematic map – you wouldn't know there was any significant unused space there at all. Yet, the true space is big enough to hide a whole series of chambers. And see, it backs directly onto the Grand Canal. Any hidden hangar would need access to the Canal.'

Do you think that's it?'

'I think we need to go see.'

'Are there any other candidates to check out?' said Kingston, casting about the Goliath's display.

Steph swept an arm around the display, indicating other voids backing onto the Grand Canal, but none were quite so impressive. 'Let's go now – it's a fair distance.'

***

The travelator carried Kingston, Steph and Earl some way beyond the Deep's control room. After several switches and turns, the tunnel widened into a long, slim chamber, little more than twice the width of the unremarkable tunnels that had led them there.

They alighted and scanned the chamber walls carefully, searching for any sign of an accessway or a concealed entrance revealing itself in the proximity of Steph's enhanced suit. Nothing stood out from the normal. Then, just as spirits began to flag, at the furthest end of the chamber, the sides suddenly broadened out considerably to allow plenty of room for travellers to step off the travelator and muster. Thereafter, the chamber ahead gently narrowed away into the continuing tunnel. A natural anomaly? To some, perhaps; to Steph, it was a clear sign.

'Well, this is the right location,' she said, consulting her sleeve and the newly loaded true map display again. 'It looks perfect. Question is, can we find an entrance?' She stepped on alone, watching the walls carefully as she progressed. In passing, her hands touched and stroked the smooth sides of the chamber. Solid, impenetrable.

'It's not looking good,' said Kingston.

'We'll see,' she said, as she continued checking to the end of the space. There, her heart started racing. 'Got it – we're bang on!'

A sense of jubilation spread between them as the black-edged outline of a doorway formed in the otherwise seamless wall.

Steph activated her collar-phone. 'Hello, general? Good news, we've found a doorway. I'm going in now. We'll keep you posted... Yes, I'll be careful. Don't worry.'

Steph took a deep breath, reached out and stroked the door. It slid open to reveal darkness inside and the smell of ancient air rolling out to greet them.

Earl stepped in front of Steph just as she made to move ahead. He looked at her almost apologetically. 'Sorry, ma'am. You'll have to let me lead.'

'It's okay, Earl. I've done this before. I know what to expect.'

'Yes, ma'am. And I'll lead from here.' Earl turned back to the newly exposed passage as ceiling lights began to flicker on and illuminate the space. The lighting reached away just forty paces to highlight the point where their passage met a cross tunnel which was still in darkness, but there, too, lights were beginning to activate.

'Very well but expect bots to appear any moment now. They'll be friendly, just here to do the dusting and cleaning,' she said. On cue, the bots appeared, and as the lights came up to full intensity, Steph felt the gentle touch of air beginning to flow from some unseen place.

Earl moved forward, razor-fine attention tuned for the slightest danger, he led them on. There were no side chambers here, just a beeline to the cross tunnel. Earl paused at the T-junction and carefully edged himself round into the broad main tunnel. 'All clear, ma'am, come on round.'

The cross tunnel reached off in either direction. It was wide enough for a dozen people to walk comfortably side by side. A few paces along on the near-side wall was a shallow chamber housing a pair of regular but dimmed LPAs. Even though they must have lain dormant for a long time, the proximity of Steph's suit acted as a trigger of sorts, and one had already begun to run through its warm-up process.

'Hey, look at this,' said Kingston, hurrying along the tunnel and across to the far side. 'They're sealed viewing ports. He banged a fist against one in frustration. 'What's on the other side of this? What's it hiding?'

'Not just viewing ports,' said Steph, passing him. 'Look here, a small door. It won't open either. See, there are more, all along this side.'

Kingston caught up with her and tried to open the door. 'Yep, door won't open,' he said.

'Let me try again,' said Steph, reaching out and stroking the door – nothing happened. 'Hmm, that's not so good.' She tried again, still no movement.

'We could blow it open,' said Kingston.

'I don't think so,' said Steph. 'If that does feed into the Grand Canal, blowing it will leave this whole area subject to atmosphere loss.'

Kingston kicked the door in frustration. Kicked it again. 'Just open, why don't you?'

Steph rested a hand on his arm. 'Just a moment, let's see what else is up ahead.' She walked on, passing several more of the uniform-sized doors before reaching a larger one. 'I wonder… do you think this is a purpose-built hangar for warbirds? It's slightly different to the storage hangar we found up top. All these doors are like the ones the bots eventually cut to make you a proper base for berthing warbirds. The small doors here might actually be berthing access doors linked directly to a warbird's stern airlock on the other side. If the craft behind is dormant, its access door may be sealed inactive too.'

She reached out to stroke the larger door. After a long moment, reflecting the passing of so many years, it slid smoothly open. The blackness within was brightened by the shaft of light from the open doorway which illuminated a familiar profile.

With a whoop, Kingston pushed through the door. Arms outstretched he spun, calling out the longest *Yeeeeess* as he took in the enormity of the scene, which expanded more with every hangar roof-light that kicked in. They had their warbirds.

As Kingston celebrated, Steph counted. 'Thirty,' she said with satisfaction. 'Thirty!' She activated her collar-phone. 'General Dower…'

Chapter 41

Primo Main Base

General Dower had little time to process the implications of Steph's warbird discovery before confusion descended inside Primo's main control room. A pair of technicians shared anxious glances as General Dower hurried in to check their news.

'Give me details,' he said.

'Something's coming; it's not one of ours,' said one of the technicians.

'I said, details.'

She took a deep breath. 'It's coming directly for Primo. Could it be them, sir?'

'What signals have we got?'

'No communications with us. In fact, no comms anywhere. Just a traffic signal, a very big signal. And it's getting closer all the time.'

'I see. What's its ETA?'

'About two hours, sir.'

'What? How can that be? How can something so big get that close undetected?'

'I don't know. It wasn't there; then it just appeared. It must have come from the Fold.'

The general let it pass. 'Show me.'

He looked into the LPA and reviewed the light signal and its track – heading direct for Primo. It couldn't be an accident. Planet Nine was small, remote, and so far out of the plane of the solar system that to head for it was to know of its existence, and to intend to arrive. He tapped his sleeve. 'Steph, can you get here quick. I need to know how those warbirds are shaping up.'

'On my way, general. Kingston's with me now. We still can't get the hangar doors to open onto the Grand Canal. Something is keeping them sealed shut.'

'Okay, leave your teams there to work on it. Tell them maximum effort – this has become urgent as of now. Meantime, I want you and Kingston on me, ASAP. On your way, speak with the control-room technicians; they'll get you up to speed.' Dower's collar-phone reported the faint background sound of running feet as Steph led Kingston on a race for a distant travelator. He ended the call, looked about and pursed his lips. So few left here in the main control room. He had sanctioned moving as many as possible to search the Deep; this was down to him.

With only a skeleton staff left on-duty up here at Primo's main control room, it was inevitable some things would get missed. *But why did it have to be the big things?*

Dower turned to the technicians. 'Everyone's short-handed right now. The main thing is you spotted it, recognised the threat and contacted me immediately. That was good.' He reached out a hand and squeezed the young woman's shoulder as she blinked away tears. 'Point everything you've got at that signal. Whatever you pick up is going to be crucial intel now. Can you do that?'

'Yes, sir,' she said, finding some consolation in the firm touch of his hand. 'Yes, sir.'

'Good, Professor Simpson's on her way now. Contact her, and she'll keep the pair of you straight. Meantime, keep up the good work.' He nodded to them both and turned back to the LPA. After a long moment, he looked back to the technicians. 'We have Leviathans standing off Primo, O-1, O-3 and S-1. Set up a conference call to their captains now please. Celine's on O-1 – I want her on the call too. And Brigadier Smith-Brown, he's on S-1. Meanwhile, I'm going up there,' he said, waving to the top of the Goliath.

As the conference call opened, Dower cut short the formalities. He briefed his commanders of the threat and ordered them all to leave Primo. O-1 and O-3 were to make for the nearest safe point to enter the Fold – enter and hide. Celine was to transfer to S-1, which was to make for Earth –

its job to ensure that, if the locusts headed toward Earth, the column of sample craft was made inaccessible, closing the atmosphere again. On arrival at Earth, the duty Leviathan O-2 was to be immediately relieved and sent for the Fold, and once the column of craft was dealt with, S-1 was to follow, leaving Earth to its own devices.

'But we've got the warbird on board,' said Smith-Brown. 'Let's stand off Primo. When the cone arrives, we can at least have a go.'

'No. Your Leviathan would be too vulnerable. If it's the cone Colonel MacMillan saw at Pardamax, you'd have no chance. And if that's what's coming our way, it's likely they've already overcome the Perseus Squadron and all its warbirds.'

'But Steph's analysis shows our craft are way more advanced than theirs. We can buy you time to get these new warbirds launched.'

'Thank you, brigadier, but we will use the warbird here, not you. You must take S-1 to Earth – that's an order. Right now, most of our people are in the Deep. I have an observer here. I'm going to send it up to you with any people I can spare from Main Base. Get them away to safety too. Those that remain here will join the others in the Deep.'

'Yes, sir, understood,' said the brigadier.

'It's not completely bleak down here. We're getting the new warbirds set up as quick as possible. Problem is, they're mothballed and still locked in a hangar. The engineers are doing everything they can to get them out, but it's not good timing.

'Brigadier, I want you to launch your warbird, have it land on the surface among the mountains above the entrance to the Grand Canal. You leave it there and make for Earth as quickly as possible. Give the pilot free rein to engage the locusts at whatever they judge to be the optimum moment to disrupt any attack.'

'Very good,' said the brigadier. 'You know it's probably a one-way ticket for the warbird crew.'

'I know. I hate it, but that's the mission, I'm afraid.'

'General, you should know... Fay came on board an hour ago. She's rostered as warbird pilot right now.'

Dower winced, screwed his eyes tight shut for a moment. Suddenly, he was glad he'd moved away from the technicians to the top of the Goliath. 'Thank you, brigadier... Please, tell her I know she'll do her duty.'

He cut off the call, bit his lip hard. Wiping tears from his eyes, he hurried for his quarters and his wife – she needed to know. He wanted her to get to safety on the observer that would shortly take off, but deep-down, he knew she wouldn't leave.

Chapter 42

Primo Main Base

Steph and Kingston hurried into the main control room. She noted Captain Besinski was there with a squad of men, all fully armed. Two technicians flitted between the Goliath and one of the regular LPAs. Beyond them was the general and his wife.

'Steph, Kingston, over here. Come see,' said the general.

They joined him. Steph paled, then began an interaction with her sleeve and the Goliath. 'No doubt, that's the cone Colonel MacMillan recorded at Pardamax. Odd though, it seems bigger.' She continued to interrogate the information stream. 'I think there are more components than we previously thought.'

'Components?' said Dower.

'Attachments. Vessels. It's carrying more than our earlier data suggested.' She looked round the group. 'It's an armada of the same attack vessels that first chased the colonel at Pardamax.'

'How the hell did it get here? And so quickly?' said Dower.

'Somehow, they've got the folddrive working in the sampler they captured. I don't know how,' said Steph.

'Where the hell is the Perseus Squadron? How did this cone get past them? And I don't understand why it didn't show up in the Goliath when it was travelling in the Fold – all the other samplers do.'

'They must have overridden the position beacon release. If they can incorporate the sampler into their ship, stopping its beacon launches would be a cakewalk.'

The general half-turned away to listen to a message. 'Okay, thank you. And good luck to you too. Do not return without direct confirmation that it's safe to do so. Get Earth sealed. Then fold away, all of you.'

He turned back to his audience. 'The Leviathans are leaving now. We're on our own here.'

They nodded acceptance.

'Now, tell me – what news of the warbirds?'

'I've detailed crews to every craft; they're familiarising themselves right now. They've all had plenty of simulator practice, so they'll do great,' said Kingston. 'The warbirds' bots have activated, and it's organised chaos in the hangar while they all work to get the ships out of mothballs and functioning. Stocking, rearming, whatever they need to do to get them ready for flight after so long. But we're still stuck in the hangar. It won't open. Three full squadrons. If I can just get them out, we'll make mincemeat of the locusts.' He could hardly mask his frustration.

'I've tried every trick I know,' said Steph. 'Our top engineering teams are working on the hangar doors. Whatever is keeping them locked, it's not in the regular IT system, so it must be a unique block that they just can't find.'

'Keep them on it. Meantime, we need to fall back from here. If those locusts arrive before the warbirds are freed up, I don't think we can be certain of defending Primo Main Base. It's too open, we don't have enough troops.'

'What do you suggest, sir?' said Kingston.

'I've got Besinski and his teams standing by to shield us, but we don't know what the locusts' combat capability is. Main Base has dozens of hangars that will offer possible access points to the enemy – we only have the numbers to defend some of them. Unlike the Deep, not every hangar up here has heavy armoured doors. The best we'll be able to do up here is delay them. The Deep is just more defensible.

'I want you to make sure all those hangars we opened to release the old sample craft from the Deep are closed again. Then the one access point to the Deep will be by the gravlift, which only operates to Steph's and my command. The people will be safe in the Deep.'

'That's no problem,' said Steph. 'Those hatches closed themselves once the sample craft had gone. Already done – sealed.'

'I just wish we could open the warbird hangar,' said Kingston. They all nodded in agreement.

'If the engineers are on it, there's nothing more we can do,' said Dower.

'Sir, there's a warbird on S-1. Have you sent it away? It's long odds, but it would be something to put up a fight with,' said Kingston.

'No, I've positioned it up in the mountains above the Grand Canal's entrance. The pilot has the discretion to attack at the time they judge most beneficial.'

Kingston looked at Mrs Dower, and his face fell. He understood her reddened eyes. 'Sir, Fay's the duty pilot.'

'Yes, I know.'

'But general, she'll have no chance against that lot,' said Kingston. 'Call her in, let me take over while there's still time. I'm a way more experienced pilot.'

'Thank you, captain. I'm afraid that's not possible. Fay has her duty and so do you. We need you to marshal those warbirds. Break them out of that hangar fast. Get Fay the backup she needs and make a fight of it. Give those locusts hell – that's an order!'

Chapter 43

Base Primo: Beyond the Grand Canal

Fay scanned the scene ahead from her hidden vantage point high in the mountains above Primo's entrance. Events were not playing out as anticipated. The cone had adopted a position high above the plain that spread before Primo. For fifteen minutes that seemed to stretch into eternity nothing happened. Then the cone had deployed twenty vessels.

Having broken from the cone, the locust vessels assembled into squadron formation. Just as Fay readied to power up, the locust vessels split into two flights and began to manoeuvre away in different directions.

'That's odd,' said Fay, turning her head to look at her co-pilot.

Johnny grimaced back at her. 'Yes, why aren't they attacking?'

'Let's sit tight and see what's happening.'

'I think they're going after the Leviathans, trying to get them before they can fold. They're defenceless without a warbird to support them. What should we do?' said Johnny.

'The Leviathans have speed. If push comes to shove, they'll outrun those locusts. Our job's here. Let's hope the Leviathans stay alert and see the locusts chasing after them.'

'But S-1 is heading for Earth. It will lead the locusts directly there.'

Fay sucked her cheeks in and tutted. 'I know. But these locusts seem to know plenty about everything, so they probably know all about Earth too. Hopefully, S-1 will have the sense just to run on.'

As the enemy squadron disappeared into the distance, the dark skies of Planet Nine became still again. The warbird crew waited for the looming outline of the cone to make its next move.

Chapter 44

Primo Deep

Standing in front of the first warbird in line – his – Kingston looked along the rank of warbirds, all a familiar black and each still carrying the strange insignia of a lost era. Every craft was crewed and ready, though a smattering of bots still scuttled about individual warbirds, finishing last-minute tasks. For the most part, the hangar was quiet and the warbirds ready. Ready but trapped.

'How you doing, guys?' said Kingston, crossing to the engineers who were desperately trying to understand and release door mechanisms that had not shifted in millennia.

'No joy yet, sorry. Still working on it,' said the chief.

Kingston nodded, biting his lip in frustration. He turned away, touching his sleeve to call Steph who was working on the same problem at the Deep's Goliath. 'What's happening, professor?'

Steph's reply sounded in his collar. 'It's still proving difficult. I've got every speck of processing power working on it, but there seems to be no engagement with the locking process. I'm trying to dig through layers to uncover what's needed. It's not easy, but I'm working on it. I've actually left the Deep's Goliath to its processing; right now, I'm up in the Main Base, heading to the reserve control room to see if Lily and I can link the two Goliaths, double-up the thinking power. I believe that's our best chance.'

'I think we're out of time,' said Kingston.

'Yes, but we must keep trying.'

'Steph? Kingston? Dower here. Get those hangar doors open. I don't care what it takes! I'll be leaving the main control room shortly, heading for the gravlift to start evacuating the last of our people into the Deep. Besinski's teams are about all we have left up here. Steph, did you say Lily is still in the reserve control room? She should have been pulled back into the Deep by now.'

'Yes, general. I'm heading there now. I passed a lot of technicians heading for the gravlift. You'll meet them there. Lily was trying to wrap some calculations on the Earth atmosphere job. I'll pull her back with me as soon as we hook up the two Goliaths.'

'Okay, but don't linger. I trust Besinski will hold the locusts off, but we have no idea of their capabilities. Quick as you like now.'

'Message received,' said Steph.

'Sir, how long before contact?' said Kingston, once again surveying the rank of warbirds.

'Contact is imminent. The cone has begun shedding more combat vessels; they were forming up as I left the main control room. If we have any time before contact, it's only minutes. I want your warbirds active and launched ASAP.'

Kingston could hear the general gasping for breath as he ran along the moving travelator, heard the pounding feet of the technicians and scientists who ran with him. 'I'm on it, sir.' The chief pilot cut the call and slammed fist into palm as he turned back to the engineers. 'I need that hangar door open!'

Chapter 45

Primo Main Base: Reserve Control Room

Steph rushed through the secret doorway leading toward the reserve control room. Several scientists hurried in the opposite direction, making a dash to link up with General Dower at the gravlift to the Deep and what they hoped was safety.

'Ma'am, wait one,' said Earl.

She paused and looked back.

'I'll stay guard here at the entrance. Be as quick as you can – Captain Besinski and the troops should hold them off, but we just don't know.'

Steph nodded. 'Okay, thank you.' She hurried along the passage toward Lily and the Goliath, passing the last of the exiting stragglers on her way.

By the time she reached the Goliath, there was nobody to be seen. It had returned to the stillness she remembered from her first visit. Except, within the Goliath, a billion light spots were flashing in excited unison.

'Lily! Where are you?' Her shouted call prompted Lily's head to pop over the crest of the Goliath.

'Steph, I'm up here, almost done, come see.'

Steph beckoned her down. 'No, leave it. We've bigger fish to fry. I need to link this Goliath with the Deep Goliath, need their combined processing power to open the warbirds' hangar door.'

Lily joined her. 'It won't take me long to finish now–'

'No, you're finished. The locusts are here. Stop what you're doing, and let's link the two Goliaths up.'

'Right, what do we do?'

'The Goliaths are hubs, each with their own network of localised LPAs. It's our last shot. I'm going to try and join the networks, establish a direct connection between this one and the Deep's Goliath. I've set up the Deep end already. You need to stop all your Goliath's current tasks, clear it, ready for something new. I'm going to use this regular LPA as a router of sorts. It will be the interface between the Goliaths. If all that goes to plan, we'll just need to activate an inter-Goliath connection. Let's get started – we don't have any time.' Both women immediately set to the task.

Chapter 46

Base Primo: Beyond Grand Canal

'Here we go again,' said Fay, watching more combat vessels begin to peel away from the cone. They counted, and a sense of trepidation grew with each launch.

'I'm seeing forty now,' said Johnny.

'I think a little more,' said Fay, her hand poised to activate the warbird. 'They're lining up on Primo.'

'How did they know where to come? It's like they have a spy. But you couldn't smuggle a locust into Primo… could you?'

'Doubt it. I'll leave that for boffins like my sister to sort out. Right now, it's down to the likes of us to face off. Seal suits.' They deployed their helmets and deftly flicked out the gloves from their suit cuffs. Sealed and ready for action, Fay's fingers gently stroked across her sleeve. Around her, instruments flashed into life. The warbird's joystick controls nudged from the arm of her bucket chair and nestled comfortably in her hand. 'Here we go.'

Far below, a rank of twenty combat vessels flew toward the mouth of the Grand Canal. A second rank stood off, waiting. As the warbird's power signature built, it was detected, and from the first rank, a flight of half a dozen vessels peeled off. They began to climb, flying up the mountainside that loomed above Primo.

'They're onto us,' said Johnny.

'We're off. I've got the laser; you have the missiles. Take targets as you can,' said Fay.

The warbird rose from the natural ledge jutting from the mountain face. It edged forward to clear the mountain then tilted its head down. The flight of combat vessels was powering up to meet them but did not immediately fire their missiles, perhaps taken aback by the sudden appearance of the warbird so close by or because of the shielding offered to the warbird by a mountainside overhang.

Johnny was not so slow and immediately released two missiles, firing them into the mountainside ahead of the onrushing attackers. The missiles exploded on contact, splintering off surface rocks that spun out into the path of the onrushing attackers. Three were damaged in the debris shower. The first exploded, a second lost control and veered into the mountainside where it was consumed in a blast, and the third lost a wing, backing off toward open space, only to begin an uncontrolled spiral toward the ground below. The other three came on and, at last, fired their missiles.

Fay powered the warbird away from the mountainside as she activated the laser, using its high-energy beam to swat down the missiles that exploded harmlessly under its searing ignition source.

Driving out and down, she passed the surviving attack vessels still heading up the mountain face. Bending her course gently back in toward the mountain, Fay was suddenly staring into the gaping mouth of the Grand Canal. Directly ahead was the first wave of intruding locusts.

'Missiles, Johnny, fire your missiles!'

'But Primo. We're in the Canal.'

'Hell with that. Fire, fire now.' She activated the laser beam and swept across the sterns of the two nearest locust vessels, slicing them into parts. From one, strange dome-headed beasts tumbled into the void. The second craft exploded in a ball of orange that engulfed many of those escaping from the debris of the first.

Just a twitch of her finger had the warbird bowling round and beyond the spreading plume, heading deeper into Primo's main artery.

'Missiles away. Acquiring more targets,' said Johnny. His voice was calm, almost matter of fact, as he loosed a further salvo. Less manoeuvrable and caught from behind, suddenly the locusts' overwhelming numbers mattered less.

'This one's mine,' said Fay, allowing her eyes to settle on a vessel that was closing on an open hangar. The laser beam crossed its tail section, melting it away. Out of control, the attacking vessel careered off course and away from the open hangar, crashing into the Canal's side wall.

'How are they opening the hangars? It shouldn't be that easy for them,' said Johnny.

'God knows, they must have access codes.' Fay pulled the warbird into a tight turn, making for mid-channel. She lasered another enemy vessel during the manoeuvre. In the process, she only absently registered Johnny's reports of further missile strikes.

She swerved to evade a vessel that rushed past. 'That one tried to ram us.' Adjusting the heading, she brought the nose round to face out toward the mouth of the Grand Canal.

They had made plenty of kills, but she knew in that instant she had failed. A row of open hangars had allowed at least four combat vessels to berth. Others were moving toward steadily opening hangar doors. Meanwhile, the second wave was entering the Grand Canal.

'Christ! Like flies in the Outback. You'll never swat them all.' Johnny released a pair of missiles that streaked out toward the oncoming wave.

'We can try,' said Fay, guiding the laser beam onto an approaching missile. Flying directly down the beam, it vapourised.

'Let's go try then.'

With no friendly craft in the vicinity, Fay set the laser beam to automatic proximity defence. It would kill anything that came close. She focused all her efforts on piloting the warbird toward the oncoming locust wave while ramping up the speed as far as she dared. If she could get through and turn on them from behind, her greater manoeuvrability and firepower might just deliver an advantage.

It took only seconds for the warbird to reach the line of attackers. Already, several had fallen to Johnny's missiles. As the warbird powered through the battleline, the laser took out two more vessels. Fay immediately began a tight turn to strafe the rear of the enemy.

All the while, the Grand Canal's automatic cleaning system was working overtime to keep the channel clear for navigation. It generated focused bursts of gravity to snare all debris, force it aside and propel it out and away, Planet Nine's insignificant gravitational pull easily cancelled out by the power of the cleaning system.

'Aw hell!' said Johnny. 'That's not good.'

Fay's moment of elation at breaking through the line vanished in a second. She saw a third wave closing on the Canal's mouth. Then they vanished from her sight as the warbird's continuing turn brought them round to face back into the Canal behind the second wave.

Fay chanced a glance toward her co-pilot. 'I'm sorry, Johnny. I think it's over for us.'

'You only think? Well, I tell you, that one's coming with me.' Johnny released a missile. 'Him too!' He fired another.

As Fay powered the warbird back into the Canal's mouth and the rear of the second wave, its laser swept up, flashing its beam to intercept a vessel approaching from above.

'Wow! Where did that one come from?' she said.

Then they were back in the dogfight. More vessels downed; the locusts couldn't cope with the agility of the warbird nor its close-quarters laser.

'Behind us. Behind, behind!' Johnny was turned in his bucket seat, half-looking at the mini-LPA, half-peering up and back.

Fay didn't have time to react. A tight group of three vessels were closing on them from different angles. Clearly intent on collision. Tumbling out from behind each were lines of dome-helmeted beasts – like paratroopers deploying from a plane.

The laser took out the first vessel cleanly, before swinging on to slice through the nose of the second and, as it cut open the third, a severed wing smashed into the warbird's hull, tearing a gouge across the fuselage to rip open the pilot's screen. Power lost, the laser cut out and lights died. An oxygen pocket fed a burst of fire that expired almost before it had begun; the craft drifted lifeless in the Canal. Bursts of gravity from Primo's channel cleaner immediately began to propel the hulk out and away.

All resistance destroyed; the third rank of locust vessels lined up to berth in open, welcoming hangars.

Chapter 47

Primo Main Base

'Run, run! Get out of here!' Besinski jabbed a finger at three technicians who had suddenly emerged from a side chamber. 'What the hell? You should have been long gone. The general's waiting at the gravlift. Get there now.' He stroked his sleeve and alerted Dower to more late-coming evacuees. Then he turned his attention to a viewing port.

He had witnessed the start of the Grand Canal action. Fay had been putting up a good fight, but it was quiet now. He knew what that meant.

A call came through his collar-phone. 'Captain, they're in the base. I don't know how, but all the hangars are opening in front of them. I'm seeing them now; they're exiting the berthing doors.'

'Same here, sir,' reported another team. 'There are dozens of them. They've got the berthing door open… They're in.' As the words sounded in his collar-phone, Besinski heard bursts of accompanying rapid fire. He signalled his squad to follow him while he hurried forward.

As they advanced, the forward defence teams' status reports and further gunfire began to mix with screams of injured men. The cries growing quickly to replace the gunfire, then silence.

'Corporal, report. What's your situation?' said Besinski. Silence. More gunfire broke out, echoing toward them down other passageways.

'They're through our berthing door too, captain. It's not good.' The sound of gunfire sounded simultaneously in collar-phones and from a nearby passage.

'Sergeant, report.'

It's bad, sir, our weapons don't touch them. They're bullet-proof. Rounds just have no impact...'

Besinski knew his men were stretched too thin. He'd chosen to cover the first twenty hangars. Even with just four men to a hangar, they were covering less than half the possible invasion points in this area alone. And it seemed his men had nothing to hit the invaders with anyway.

More gunfire and screams reached him from another passageway. He looked toward his roving support squad of a dozen men. Not enough. He activated his collar-phone. 'All units fall back now. Rally on me outside the main control room immediately.'

He signalled his squad to about turn, and they retraced their steps, the short journey punctuated by distant gunfire, screams and silence. He was losing men at every turn.

Reaching the main control room, he saw a little over thirty men gathered outside in a defensive huddle; he pumped out an all-stations call. No replies. In less than ten minutes, his company had been butchered, and he didn't have any handle on the event. Besinski knew nothing except his soldiers didn't stand a chance.

'Dower here, captain. What's happening?'

'Sir, we've taken a hammering. Anyone who engaged is dead. We have nothing that hurts them. Must have some special armour.'

'Captain, can you get out? Can you make it back here?'

'I don't know, sir. There are none in this immediate area. They are certainly getting through the berthing airlock doors further back. Whether they're getting in ahead of us I don't know.'

'All right, captain. I want you to fall back on me at the gravlift. I'll stay here to keep it open for you. Come now.'

'Yes, sir. Moving now.'

Besinski waved all his troops toward the travelator. 'Let's move out now. The general's standing by at the gravlift. Everyone move, and keep moving. Fast as you like.' As the last of his soldiers hurried onto the travelator and began the long run for safety, he looked about ruefully. How had the locusts got in and berthed so easily? Why didn't his men's weapons stop the locusts? Just before he stepped onto the travelator, a group of stragglers arrived, supporting one soldier with a bad leg wound. 'Come on, we're falling back,' he said, and guided them onto the travelator.

***

The dash along the travelator had been uneventful so far, but as they passed the reserve control room, Besinski saw Earl guarding the entrance. He jumped off and hurried across to him.

'Come on, Earl, what are you still doing here?'

'Professor Simpson's inside, sir. And General Dower's daughter.' Earl's voice betrayed concern, and relief that Besinski was on hand to take control.

'What the hell are they still doing here?'

'Don't know, sir.'

'Right, I'll go and get them. The locusts are coming – you get on that travelator and run for the gravlift.'

Earl saluted. 'I'll wait, sir. The professor's my detail.'

'Okay, Earl, good man. Stand by here. I'll be as quick as I can.' Besinski hurried inside, and Earl braced himself for whatever might come.

***

Steph looked round from the Goliath in response to the distant shouts of her name. The sound of running boots closing fast preceded Besinski who burst into the reserve control room.

'Ma'am, we have to go now,' said Besinski.

'Not quite yet, captain. Lily and I are almost done. We're trying to link two Goliaths. I've done everything, but the process just won't kick in.'

'Begging your pardon ma'am, I don't give a damn. You and Lily must come now. The locusts are in the base. We can't hold them off.'

Steph blanched. 'We've failed then.'

Lily looked anxiously at Besinski. 'What do you mean, they're in the base?'

'I mean we go now or we're dead. Primo Main Base is lost; we've nothing to touch these monsters. The Deep should be secure while we work out how to fight back. But we've got to get there. I insist you come with me at once. Leave whatever you're doing and come.'

Steph nodded. 'Come on, Lily. We can't activate the link between the Goliaths. Let's go, we'll have to think of something else.'

Besinski turned for the exit as the sound of gunfire echoed down the passageway and into the reserve control room.

***

Earl fired again as the monster continued out from the tunnel into the open concourse. A locust, its yellowish hued body supported on great legs, its back encased in a black-and-red streaked carapace. Little arms carried something, a weapon, though it made no attempt to fire at him as its great black eyes considered the source of the gunfire. For a moment Earl froze. This was a nightmare. The beast's head was encased in a transparent dome from within which the enormous eyes had focused on him. Above and around the eyes, two sinuous antennae twirled and swirled.

A clacking sound from the carapace signalled action, and the monster began to advance. One by one, more locusts followed the leader from the tunnel and spread out in a line abreast, all matching the leader, step for step.

Earl raised his weapon and fired. Fired and fired. He could see the locusts' bodies waver as his rounds hit their targets, but there was no significant effect. They kept coming. Earl emptied his magazine. Still, they came. He stepped back, falling through the doorway. Catching his step, he retreated while forcing a fresh magazine into his weapon. A dozen paces in, he turned again. One locust was already through the door, and a further two were entering. He kept firing while stepping slowly backward. The three leading locusts matched him step for step, seeming to almost enjoy his failing attempts at resistance.

In desperation he threw his weapon down and pulled out a grenade. Removing the pin, he hurled it along the passage toward the locusts, then he threw another before flattening himself on the ground.

Two blasts sounded in quick succession. The sound deafened Earl. As the ventilation system sucked away the smoke, he felt a moment's elation. The leading locust had lost its legs. Waving arms were haloed by torn wings, freed from their carapace to flap forlornly against the side of the passage.

The blast's reverberations cleared from Earl's head. instantly replaced by angry hissing and clicks.

Beyond the dismembered locust, a second stumbled forward, disoriented. It's helmet shattered by shrapnel. It was unsteady, in discomfort but determinedly closing on him. Yet further back, the third locust was slowly climbing to its feet, equally unsteady but seemingly unhurt.

Earl pulled himself off the ground and ducked aside as the stumbling locust lunged for him. It twisted its head as it fell and caught his left hand, biting hard. The clamped hand began to drag him down, and Earl jerked his arm back. A spurt of blood marked the severing of four fingers, but Earl was still upright. He stamped on the back of the locust's head, pressed it hard to the floor. It hissed, antennae waved back and up, trying to sense his position as strong legs braced to force itself upright.

Biting back the pain, Earl pressed the stub ends of his severed fingers hard into his torso to stem the bleeding. He sensed the insect's ferocious power building beneath his leg and instinctively knew, once the locust began to rise again, he wouldn't have the strength to resist. From the corner of his eye, he saw the third locust was up and turning its attention to him. He had to run.

An antenna whipped across his thigh, and he grabbed it. Jerked it, pulled, and ripped it away. Beneath his boot the locust erupted from the floor in pain. It launched him away, and amidst a torrent of raging shrieks struggled to its feet. Spinning in agony, it blocked the path of the third locust that had commenced a charge.

Beyond the pair, at the passageway's entrance, Earl could see more locusts peering in, trying to assess what had happened before following the leaders in. He took another step backward and saw the entrance door slide shut in response to his suit's proximity sensor moving away from the entrance. In that short moment, he laughed to himself. By now, the doorway would be fading, and the locusts outside would be staring at a blank wall. They'd never find the entrance again.

As the two surviving locusts in the tunnel disentangled, Earl turned and ran. He hurried for the reserve control room, leaving a trail of blood behind him.

'Captain Besinski, sir. Breach! They're in. I'm falling back on your position.'

'How many?' said Besinski.

'Three in, then the entrance shut. Big beasts, sir. Bullets don't touch them. One's down, grenade. One's injured, the antennae are very sensitive. One unhurt, closing fast. Urrgh…'

'Earl? Earl, report!'

Through the still open collar-phone, Besinski could hear Earl's laboured breathing. Some gasped breaths and a strange crackling sound. Then the fast-stepped approach of a heavy legged attacker. A moment's silence, then a rattling carapace, hisses, and a blunt thud.

'Earl?' Besinski looked at Steph as another thud carried to them. 'That's not good.'

She shook her head. Blanching, she averted her gaze and held out her arm for him to see the data display. She had accessed Earl's bodycam feed.

Besinski gripped her wrist to steady the sleeve. Steph was shaking. He saw why. Each collar-phone thud was reporting another great thrusting bite from Earl's rapidly dismembering body. 'They're eating him alive! God! We can't let these monsters win.'

'Where can we go?' said Lily. She allowed Steph's arms to encircle her. 'What can we do?'

'Earl said bullets have no effect. Grenades do, but I've none with me.' He let Steph's sleeve go as the picture feed broke up then blacked out. 'I'll think of something. But I need to get you two safe first. Is there any hideaway down here you can use?'

Steph shook her head. 'There's the sarcophagus room, through the door at the back of this control room. But every space here is linked. If they're in, they'll find us eventually.'

Besinski suddenly raised a finger, silently blowing a shoosh against it. He pointed back toward the entrance from where the sound of approaching footfalls reached them, punctuated by hissing and clicks from the wounded locust. Steph pressed her hand gently against Lily's mouth to mask the gentle sobs.

'Come on, let's get into your sarcophagus room. They'll find us, but at least we'll have a little time to think.' He hustled Steph and Lily through the door, closing it just as the first locust entered the reserve control room.

'Can you seal this door?' said Besinski.

'Yes, but it's not heavy like the main access door. No armour. It's designed to stop casual interruptions, not an attack. Judging by their legs, they could kick it in easily.'

'Do it anyway. Every moment will count.'

Steph triggered the door lock as Besinski cast about. The greatest Goliath dominated this room, its dulled display all dark and glowering. Beyond it, the sarcophagus. Nowhere to hide. He hurried to the sarcophagus, closely followed by the others.

Steph activated the controls, and the lids became transparent to expose Weeman's lifeless body in one chamber, alongside the other empty one.

'Can you both get in there?' said Besinski.

'There's not room for two,' said Steph.

'What about in that one?' Besinski nodded toward Weeman.

'No! I don't care what happens – he doesn't deserve to be desecrated. Weeman stays there until we can give him a proper send-off.'

'If you don't hide, you'll likely not be here to give anyone a send-off.'

'I'll take that chance.'

Besinski shook his head despairingly. He didn't agree, but this was Steph's domain. Taking a deep breath, he called the general while Steph guided Lily into the empty sarcophagus chamber.

'I'll be trapped inside. What about you? Where will you both hide? Shouldn't I stay with you both?'

'You'll be fine inside, Lily. Your suit has sufficient enhanced access that you can open the lid from the inside if needs be. Don't worry about us, I'm sure Besinski's got a plan. He's calling your father now.'

Even as Lily formed another question, Steph triggered the sarcophagus to shut over her.

***

The general broke off from gravlifting soldiers to the safety of the Deep and took the call. 'Besinski. Where are you?' He listened to the brief report, all the while marshalling newly arriving soldiers into line. He took several steps back along the passageway to find some privacy.

'Thank you. I understand your position. But Besinski, right now, we have nothing that will hit these locusts. Grenades will only get us so far. I can't send an extraction team for you – I'd be sending them to their deaths. Do what you can to keep Lily safe. Steph too.'

'Understood, sir. I'll do the best I can.'

'I know you will, captain. Right now, we're taking a hammering. The only plus is most of your surviving men are already back and transferred into the Deep. I think there's just another two squads to get back here, and yourselves. For now, I'm stuck at the gravlift so I can get stragglers out of harm's way.'

'Very good, sir. Thank you for getting the men out. We need to find something to hit these beasts with.'

'We will. Meantime, Steph went there to link the reserve Goliath with the Deep's, to create some massive processing power to try and get the warbirds' hangar door open. Has she managed it?'

'No, sir.'

'Besinski. We're losing Main Base. The locusts have control of the Grand Canal and are berthing craft at will. If we can't get the Deep's warbird hangar doors open, the base will be overrun. Main Base is just about theirs. She has to link those Goliaths. And she needs to do it now, or it's all over. You keep Professor Simpson alive until she can get the Goliaths linked. No matter what!'

'Yes, sir,' said Besinski.

'Okay, it's over to you and Steph now, captain. Good luck.'

'Thank you, sir.'

The general was sure he heard a banging sound behind Besinski's voice as the call ended and he returned his attention to the lengthening line at the gravlift.

***

Another bang sounded against the sealed door. Then another. Then silence.

Besinski jogged Steph's shoulder. 'You get behind the Goliath,' he whispered. 'Stay tight in its shadow and keep close to one of the corners. If a locust comes round, you keep retreating. Stay out of sight. Whatever happens.'

'What if one comes from the other direction at the same time?'

Besinski shrugged as the door reverberated under an enormous blow. 'You let me worry about that. Now get behind the Goliath. I'm going up there,' he said, pointing to the Goliath's top. He pushed her and ran for the corner stair as the door caved in.

Pressed tight behind one of the Goliath's corners, Steph peeped round to see what was happening. She was almost sick. A locust entered the room, way taller than a man, its head encased in a great transparent dome from within which large black compound eyes scanned the room. A pair of antennae turned and writhed within the helmet, sensing, and feeding detail to the beast. The mouth parts were bloodied, as was the yellow colouring of its abdomen.

Behind the first, a second shuffled in. This one had no helmet and only one antenna. An oozing stump twitched to signal where Earl had done his work. The locust was in distress but sported the same blood-red muzzle as its partner. Wings drooped from a half open carapace, and all the while, the shuffling locust kept up a stream of clicking and hissing. The leading locust rattled its carapace briefly and silence fell.

Lying flat on the Goliath's top, Besinski was out of sight but also unsighted. He had his combat knife gripped tight as he waited for his moment, straining his ears to follow the locusts' movements. He knew they had split up. The steady clicking of scaley feet on floor signalled the bigger one moving slowly toward the sarcophagus at the far end of the room. A click and drag sound signalled the second locust was limping round the base of the Goliath.

As the big locust approached the sarcophagus, Steph eased backward and away from the Goliath's corner. If the locust turned around at the sarcophagus, as it surely must, it would see her. She slipped round the next corner and continued to back away, praying the other locust was not circling the Goliath. It was. She could see a growing locust's shadow looming across the floor from behind the further corner of the Goliath. It was coming. Where was Besinski? She wanted to scream but kept it in.

Taking a nervous step backward, she stumbled, letting out a little gasp as she lurched. Her arm plunged into the chilling fog of the dormant Goliath. It felt cold. She tried to pull her hand out and suddenly her terror doubled. Her hand was trapped. No, more than that – it felt like it was actually being gripped by the chilly murk, and she was being drawn steadily into the gloom. Pulling back, trying to resist, her head was still clear as she cried out in fear. Glancing to her side, she saw the stooped locust just appearing at the corner, the predator hurrying in response to a victim's distress call.

By the time the locust had rounded the corner, Steph had been dragged right into the Goliath and was gone from view. Frustrated, the locust limped along, determined to find the source of the cry.

Meanwhile, Steph struggled against whatever had dragged her in, but she was no match for its strength. No matter what she did, she could not break free. Completely disoriented, she stopped struggling, and as she did so, the grip on her arms eased. With visibility extending only inches, she could see no one and nothing. It was as though the grey fog of the Goliath itself had gripped her. Attempting to move a leg induced immediate restraint; moving an arm produced the same response. She stilled again and the controlling pressure eased once more.

The cold seeped and rolled around her face, and she squeezed her eyes tight shut to shield them. Why hadn't she put her helmet up when the locusts came? At least she would have been sealed in safe. Biting her lip, it occurred to her this was no locust-inspired incident.

Standing quite still, Steph waited and wondered. Seconds may have elapsed, perhaps minutes. Deprived of all senses, time effectively stopped. Then she thought she was seeing things. Stars flashed in front of her closed eyes — bright points flickered and faded then returned.

She opened her eyes and blinked. The lights were still there, a cluster steadily gathering. Combining tightly together, the lights were little more than football-sized. Close up, it was bright, but she instinctively knew if she pulled away the light would immediately be lost amidst the grey. She stared at it.

'What is this? What are you doing?' she said. The light dropped and vanished from view. 'No, don't go,' she whispered, suddenly doubly alone.

Then she felt movement against her arm, lifting it close to her face. She stared intently at the sleeve, the little lights dancing around it. She felt instructions being keyed, and the display messaged her:

It's me. Don't be frightened.

The light cluster began to move, tracing up her sleeve to the shoulder, then across her collar, disappearing from view at her neck. Trapped, immobile, she could do nothing as the lights burrowed beneath her suit collar, sliding inside, and circulating against her body. Then, one by one, the peculiar sensation of the lights moving against her body vanished, and her senses returned to normal. But she was still held tight within the Goliath.

'Hello, Steph,' said her collar-phone.

'What? What's happening? Who is this?'

'I told you, Steph. It's me.'

'I don't know what your game is, but just cut it out. What is this?'

'I don't have time to speak right now. I'm studying your suit's data. It looks as though you have reached a critical juncture. You are going to need some help, again. Please wait…'

'Who is *me*?'

Her arm was still held locked in front of her face. The sleeve display changed, and she gasped at the picture on display. 'Weeman? It can't be you. You're dead. What is this?'

'No tricks. Don't you remember you placed me in the sarcophagus and set it in motion?'

'I did, but you died.'

'My body did. But you uploaded me into the Goliath. Well, just the essence of me. To have uploaded me would have demanded the Goliath be fully functional. It contained only the smallest of holding charges, a pilot-light if you will.'

Amidst all the danger, Steph suddenly felt euphoric. 'You're alive, Weeman, alive!'

'No, just a part of me, everything else has faded. But quiet now – I need to work.'

In the silence, she sensed information streams processing through her suit.

'Steph, we need to engage now. I need you to have Captain Besinski act. Tell him to do as you say. Not to think, just to do... For now, perhaps best you don't think either.' Weeman gave a concise briefing.

'Really, you want us to do that?'

'Exactly that. You are free to move now. Please call him and start the process immediately.'

Steph moved her arms. Lifted a foot. She was free. Her suit squeezed her, prompting, almost like a gentle nudge, and she called Besinski.

Concealed high on the Goliath, Besinski watched and listened. Steph's instructions seemed foolhardy, illogical. But she was the brains of the operation. If that's what she wanted, he'd try his best. The big locust remained at the sarcophagus, determinedly pulling the controls and trying to open it.

On the far side of the Goliath, the injured locust still hovered around the spot where it thought it had heard a human. Not sure of the murk, it had thrust its head in and immediately withdrawn. It was cold and stung the antenna stub viciously. Angrily it started to move along the back of the Goliath, aiming to join its companion.

Besinski pulled himself up to a crouch, gripped his knife all the harder and perched on the edge. It was a fair drop. Directly beneath him was the wounded locust, out of sorts and largely desensitised to its surroundings. A single antenna twitching, the beast was clearly very angry. He jumped.

Landing on the locust's back, his legs thrust beneath the half-opened carapace where they tangled with the partially deployed wings. He stopped his slide by wrapping an arm round and under the locust's jaw.

It hissed and clapped its jaws together in a rattling call. Meanwhile, the attempt to clap its carapace failed with human legs wedged into the wing casing. It tried to turn and bite, but Besinski was fixed behind it, just safely inaccessible.

Following Steph's instructions, Besinski brought his combat knife against the locust's remaining antenna; it understood what was happening and dropped to the ground. Rolling, trying to dislodge its attacker.

Besinski held on for just long enough to slice the antenna off. With what must have been a scream, the locust rose, turned, and desperately flapped its wings. It careered into the wall, bounced, and dropped, unable to function.

Besinski turned and ran, calling Steph as he sprinted for the broken exit door. 'It's done. I'm on my way now. The other one's coming.'

Besinski broke cover at the far end of the Goliath, and the big locust jumped into the air, landing halfway across the room. It jumped again, landing at the door, immediately after Besinski had passed through. It followed him.

'I'm here; now what?' said Besinski, halting at the row of regular LPAs flanking the Goliath. He half-turned back toward the broken door.

'I can see, I've accessed your body cam.'

Besinski flinched and dropped to the ground as the leaping locust grazed just above his head, landing further into the room.

'It's here.'

'Yes, I know.'

'So, what do I do now?'

'Keep the LPA between it and you.'

'Really? Is that all you've got? Come on, you put me here – give me something to fight with.'

'It's under control, just do as I say.'

Besinski swore quietly.

'I can still hear you.'

'And can you hear that?' Besinski pointed toward the locust. Steady steps clicked on the floor as it closed in. Straightened legs raised it to its full height.

Gripping his knife in one hand, Besinski drew his pistol with the other and fired. The locust paused as three rounds thudded into its thick and scaly body, with no discernible impact. The locust advanced again, relishing Besinski's futile attempts at resistance.

He switched target, aiming for the dome. The locust paused again – it at one end of the LPA, Besinski at the other, little more than six feet apart, just out of arm's reach. He kept firing, and the rounds kept deflecting away. He could tell the locust was toying with him. 'This isn't working for me, professor!'

'Not long now.'

Then a lucky contact and a crack appeared in the dome. The locust suddenly stopped its game and rattled its carapace. Effortlessly, it hopped onto the LPA and advanced toward Besinski.

Magazine empty, he hurled the pistol at the locust and transferred the knife into his fighting hand. The locust rose high above him, tilted its head to look down at its victim, savouring the moment before feasting.

'Besinski, drop! Hit the deck!'

Besinski would not go down without a fight and slammed his combat knife in toward the locust's lower leg. His heart sank, last card played and lost. The blade deflected away. The locust flicked its foot almost contemptuously to propel him away from the LPA and down onto the floor.

Flat on his back and momentarily immobilised by the kick, Besinski looked up at the locust. Standing on the LPA, still drawn to full height, it was frighteningly impressive. He saw it bend slightly at the knee, readying to jump and knew this was the end.

'Stay down,' said Steph in his collar-phone.

Before Besinski could return a final pithy response, his eye was drawn to the Goliath. The lights within it were suddenly churning in a frenzied turmoil that far outshone the room's steady ambient lighting. The locust too noted the change and twisted its head to look toward the source.

A ripple of light passed across the side of the Goliath, bulging outward slightly. The locust's antennae twitched, focusing on the strange light pattern just as a plume of light erupted from the heart of the Goliath, jetting out like a stream of plasma to envelop the locust. It struggled to jump away but was held tight, locked in the glowing power that flowed out and around it.

Besinski sat up, trying to understand what was happening as the lightshow continued around the locust.

'Are you hurt?' said Steph, kneeling beside him.

Besinski looked round and grinned at her. 'Sore but living. You've nailed that one for sure. What's happening? How did you do that?'

Steph looked at the locust with undisguised distaste. 'Yes, it's finished now. Cooked in its own shell.' She touched her sleeve, and the beam immediately receded, releasing the locust from its grip, letting it fall to the floor.

She straightened and gave Besinski a hand up from the floor.

'I didn't know your Goliaths could do that,' he said.

'No, nor did I.'

Puzzled, Besinski looked at her as she walked beyond the fried insect to peer into the Goliath.

Steph turned and headed for the broken door and the sarcophagus room beyond. 'Let's get Lily out. I might need her help.'

Chapter 48

Primo Main Base: Gravlift

'They're right behind us, sir.' A rising tone told of emerging panic in the owner of the voice reporting through General Dower's collar-phone.

'All right, soldier. Keep moving. I'm waiting for you. Report your status.'

'Three of us. One wounded. There's no one else, sir. They're all dead.'

'I see you now. Keep moving.' The general could also see the chasing locusts. For whatever reason, they did not seem to like the travelator and were running along the side track, the roof too low for them to use their jumping ability to get ahead. His men were just about keeping in front of the swarm. Only just.

Dower pointed toward a little cluster of grenades he had taken from soldiers before gravlifting them up to safety. 'Corporal, take some of those, get forty paces up the passage. Once the wounded party is past you launch all the grenades down the tunnel. It's the only way we'll buy enough time to get them transported up, ahead of the locusts.'

A look of fear flitted across the corporal's face.

'Don't worry, man. I'll wait for you here. Go for it now. Hurry.' He clapped the corporal on the shoulder.

The young man suddenly snapped into action. 'Yes, sir.'

Dower watched his corporal sprint up the passageway. Passing the retreating party and reaching the prescribed distance, he knelt at the tunnel's side. More forms were hurrying toward him, their nature betrayed by an inhuman gait.

The retreating men reached the end of the travelator and stumbled off. The middle man sported a torniquet sealing his stump, the leg lost below the knee. The other two were exhausted, having run their comrade the whole length of the travelator.

'Good men, well done,' said Dower. He stood one soldier to the side and manoeuvred the wounded man and his other supporter beneath the gravlift. He glanced at the third man. 'Stand clear there… Up.' The beam came down and spirited away the two. Dower waved the third man forward. 'Come on, get into—'

His words were cut off by a blast as the first of the corporal's grenades detonated. Another blast deafened them, then a third. As smoke swirled back toward the gravlift, the general grabbed the third soldier, pushed him into position and shouted, 'Up.' The man went, and Dower turned his attention to the passageway.

The super-efficient ventilation system was clearing smoke, and already he could catch glimpses of his corporal amidst the swirls. The man had fallen back, now kneeling perhaps only twenty paces up the passageway.

'Come on. We're ready to go!' Dower shouted at the top of his voice, unsure how the blasts had affected the corporal's hearing. He saw the corporal's arm swing once, twice, hurling more explosives toward the onrushing locusts. Then watched him stand and allow something to drop at his feet before sprinting back toward the gravlift.

Further down the passageway an explosion was followed by a second. 'Get down!' the corporal yelled and threw himself flat on the floor. Dower dropped too. A second later, the dropped grenade exploded.

Amidst the swirling smoke, they jumped up and made the two steps to the gravlift. Beneath the gravlift's beam, the general took a moment to make sure they were within its footprint.

'Sir,' said the corporal, 'we're too late.'

Dower looked up, a locust had emerged from the smoke and stood only an arm's length away. Anxious for the feast, it had removed its helmet in the final steps of its advance. Mouth parts opened wide, and with a rattle of carapace, the head jutted forward, its mouth closing over the general's arm.

'Up. Up.' The general shouted as the locust bit.

Immediately, they rose in the kaleidoscopic tunnel of light to stand in the upper passageway.

They had made it; they were in the Deep. Dower fell to his knees, dragged by an irresistible weight. He looked at his arm, weighted to the floor, and the pain began to register. He knew his arm was broken. The spread of blood told him the flesh was cut through. But it was still attached, thank God.

'Christ!' said the corporal, kicking violently toward the general's arm. His boot made contact and dislodged the locust's head, propelling it across the passageway where it rolled a little way down the slope before coming to a halt, still twitching, mouth parts dripping red with the general's blood.

Dower supressed the pain and, grim-faced, looked up at the group of soldiers who had gathered round. 'Thank you, corporal. Now you all understand why I told you to keep your arms within the beam when gravlifting.' He gave a gruff laugh. 'Kick it again, corporal.'

Chapter 49

Primo Main Base: Reserve Control Room

'I need to go into the light array. I won't be long,' said Steph.

'Wait, you saw what that Goliath did to the locust. Don't go in – it'll kill you,' said Besinski.

Steph smiled at him. 'Don't worry. I've got this.' She turned to Lily. 'Call Kingston, tell him to have his warbirds standing by. I know how to open the hangar doors now. We still need to link the Goliaths, but not as we'd first thought to boost analytical power – it's a safety mechanism, quite unrelated to what we were trying to do. The warbird hangars require a double Goliath instruction to unseal them. Weeman did it to unlock the first squadron's hangar doors, using the main control room's Goliath together with this one. We didn't know about the procedure then; we didn't need to.'

'How do you know now?' said Lily.

Steph smiled again and tapped her sleeve knowingly. 'Call Kingston now. And your father. He needs to know that I can open the hangar, and that you're safe.' She turned to the Goliath and stepped directly into the light array. The lights swirled about her, becoming ever more agitated as she went deeper. Besinski and Lily watched anxiously and caught occasional glimpses of her amidst the whirling lights. Her arms seemed to rise and fall. Touching and stroking light sequences that formed and reformed around her.

Then the tumult subsided into a more regular pattern, and Steph emerged from amidst the lights to rejoin them.

'It's done,' she said.

Chapter 50

Primo Deep

Sunk deep in the walls of the Grand Canal, concealed bars slid away to unbolt a hangar door. Then unseen mechanisms activated, bit by bit, winding back internal locks. Finally, freed from constraint, the hangar-door indicator showed live access.

With a whoop, Kingston triggered the opening and the hangar door swung away as smooth as though it was its first day of installation.

'Stand by, warbirds, I'm going to check it out first.' Gingerly, Kingston edged his warbird through the open hangar into the Grand Canal. Here, at its furthest depth, there was no movement. He turned to face up the Canal. Miles ahead, its mouth was silhouetted against the pale twilight that represented Nine's brightest time. He saw scores of vessels moving about the entrance, ferrying back and forth to Main Base's many berthing hangars.

Turning to his co-pilot, he gave a dry smile. 'They don't know we're here.'

'I'm guessing they will soon,' said the co-pilot.

'Believe it.' Kingston moved his warbird into mid-channel and called the others out to form on him.

All thirty warbirds assembled, three flights of ten, together in a single formation. One tight disc. On his order the warbirds advanced very slowly, jockeying for position, fine-tuning their formation. Then they flew faster.

It may have been overconfidence or bloodlust, but whatever the reason, the locusts had stopped looking for danger, had stopped scanning for warbird power signatures. The jet-black warbirds had advanced three miles up the Grand Canal before an attacker registered their presence. From there, with so few miles before contact, the locusts had no time to respond.

The warbirds were paired and allocated a designated firing arc. In each pair, there was one to hit enemy vessels, and one to take out inbound missiles. Kingston and his partner were in the middle, aiming directly ahead, the adjacent warbirds aiming at a slightly wider angle, and so on, until those at the formation's rim found themselves aiming almost at right angles to the direction of flight.

'All warbirds, match my speed. Laser beams only, take out everything that crosses your firing path. Nothing survives.'

Kingston activated his laser. All around, others flashed into life, forming a prickling hedgehog of laser beams that would burn everything in its path to nothing. 'All warbirds, I want every one of these devils brought down. Today, we're fighting for humanity. Burn them all to hell.'

One incoming locust attack vessel happened to be pointing in the right direction and loosed four missiles in quick succession.

The forest of beams flashed, and the incoming missiles melted into nothing.

Then the warbirds were abreast of Primo Main Base. A firework display erupted, with every locust vessel in the Canal under attack. Dozens were sliced and carved. Some exploded, others tried to turn and run. A few made the turn, many colliding with others, releasing great sheets of flame as oxygen pockets flared. With every passing moment, Primo's debris-clearing system stepped up its efforts, working far beyond its design capacity.

Beyond the mouth of the Grand Canal, other attack vessels could be seen marshalling into a screen, as the distant cone, now devoid of its attack vessels, began a turn to run.

The squadron continued its advance along the Grand Canal, destroying every vessel in front of it. Everywhere, locusts abandoned damaged vessels: swarms of locusts.

'Listen up. Flight One, break from formation. Stay in the Canal. Any and all locust vessels that emerge from the berthing hangars are to be destroyed immediately. Meanwhile, I want all these locusts abandoning their vessels lasered. Vaporise every one of them. No survivors. Understood?'

Kingston's collar-phone filled with messages of assent as Flight One slowed, peeled away from the main formation, and turned to begin the clean-up operation.

'Flight Two. When we leave the Canal, you are to engage that screen of combat vessels. Destroy them all. Flight Three, on me, we're going after the cone. It must not escape.'

***

General Dower walked slowly into the Deep's control room. Each step reverberated into his wounded arm to ensure the pain was always with him. He had rejected analgesics – right now, only a clear mind would do. Time enough for proper treatment later.

'Sir, we're all glad you made it,' said a young captain, throwing him a smart salute. 'And… and my condolences over your daughter. She was very brave.'

Dower winced: a different pain – one he knew analgesics could never touch. He'd just shared the news of the loss of Fay's warbird with his wife. He should have stayed with her but… there would be time for grieving later. 'Thank you, captain. Where are we now?'

'Excellent news, sir. Captain Kingston and his warbirds have cleared the Grand Canal of invaders. He's going after the cone while others are commencing a mop up.

'Your daughter Lily is safe in the reserve control room with Professor Simpson and Captain Besinski. But there are big problems up in Main Base.'

'Tell me,' said Dower, lowering himself gingerly into a seat.

The captain took a half-step back, deferring to the scientist who had assumed temporary control of the Goliath.

She stepped forward. 'General, Professor Simpson managed to link the Goliaths. That enabled the hangar doors to open, somehow. The Grand Canal has been cleared, but a lot of locust vessels had already berthed. Consequently, there are many locusts up in Main Base. It seems a good deal more than you have soldiers in the Deep.'

'How many locusts?' said Dower.

'A lot. The Goliath in the reserve control room is using various scanners and sensors up there to get an accurate count. It's channelling the information down to us, and the Deep's Goliath is mapping it now. Then we'll know exactly how many and where they are.'

'Sir!' said a technician working at one of the regular LPAs. 'Sir, a Leviathan, P-1, has just dropped out of the Fold. Colonel MacMillan is asking to speak with you.'

'Great. Patch him through,' said Dower.

A swift exchange made clear to MacMillan his cone-attack warning had come too late. News of how they had fought off the locusts at Secundo was welcome. As would be the experience of the marines MacMillan had on board.

'Hurry in, colonel. We'll need your troops. I'm trying to build a plan to clear the locusts out. We can't begin to consolidate until they're all gone.'

Dower returned his attention to the scientist. 'Let me know as soon as you have a full disposition on the enemy.

'Captain, I want a full count of surviving troops in the Deep. Let's get them mustered and rearmed; I want them all briefed with Colonel MacMillan's intel. Let's see how we can create weapons to hurt these monsters. When we go in this time, I want us on the front foot.'

The captain immediately began collar-phoning instructions throughout the Deep.

Looking into the Goliath, Dower noted it was displaying a layout of Main Base. There were hundreds of red indicator lights spread across the plan.

'Red are locusts,' said the scientist.

'How many exactly?'

'Present count is seven hundred and sixty-four. But the Goliaths are still analysing and transferring information from remoter parts of the base. There will be more.'

Dower nodded an acknowledgement while pointing into the display. 'Seems the greater part are gathered around the main control room and the berthing hangars.'

'Yes, sir. You see the yellow marker lights there? That shows the locust vessels that are still berthed. Nineteen. They can't go out into the Canal because the warbirds will pick them off. Some locusts are still disembarking. Others are heading back toward their vessels. It's certainly very confused around there.'

'It is. I tried to contact Professor Simpson a little while ago. Why is she offline?'

'Not sure, general; she's thinking about something.'

Dower glanced at her. 'That stops her speaking?'

The scientist shrugged and looked at General Dower blankly – she had no answer.

Dower activated his collar-phone while heading up the Goliath's corner stair.

'Hello, Lily. Thank God you're safe.' His daughter immediately began to share a little of her experience, and he cut her short. Bad news needed to be delivered. Standing alone on the Goliath's top, he told her of Fay's loss. For a short while, he allowed Lily's emotions to have their release. But – and the general hated himself for the brutality of bringing his daughter to focus – he had to move on: events did not wait upon pain and loss.

'Lily, this is very important. Can you speak to Steph? Tell her we have news from Secundo, and Colonel MacMillan has provided some information about how to fight the locusts. Tell her the information's being sent to her suit. She's to take a look and consider if there's anything that could be applied for taking back Main Base.

'It's urgent. I'm going to have to send soldiers to clear the locusts out. I really need her input.'

'I'll tell her. She's busy thinking through a bunch of new information she found. I'm not sure what; she's gone quite quiet.'

'Okay, tell her now. And you stay brave – we have to beat these monsters for Fay. Now, I need to speak with Captain Besinski. It will take a little while to get to you, but you're safe there. Do as Besinski says. Meantime, speak with your mother too.'

Chapter 51

Beyond Base Primo

Kingston led two flights of warbirds out of the Grand Canal. Ten and ten, each one ready for action and revenge. The retreating cone was far off in the distance. Between them and it, a formation of perhaps forty locust attack vessels was deployed in a defensive shield.

Kingston glanced to his co-pilot and grinned. 'That's step one complete. Now for the big one.' He activated his collar-phone. 'Flight Three, on me; we're going direct for the cone. Flight Two, break off and engage the locust screen. Remember, no survivors. None.'

Looking across his formation he saw Flight Two break away and make for the screening locust vessels. He set a direct course to follow the cone and all the while kept a close watch on Flight Two's attack.

'Something dead ahead of me,' reported a warbird on the outer edge of Flight Two's formation. 'Oh, hell. It's ours. Dead in the water.'

'It must be the warbird Fay and Johnny were flying. Any signal, any signs?' said Kingston.

'No signals. The fuselage has been torn open: it's finished,' came back the deadpan response.

Silence reigned for several seconds.

'Flight Two, mark that location. I want that warbird recovered. Meantime, take those locusts apart. Fay and Johnny were our own folk.'

The ten warbirds of Flight Two seemed hopelessly outnumbered, but none of the pilots were concerned. They all knew that the flight analysis had their warbirds way ahead on speed and manoeuvrability. Now to put the knowledge into practice.

The flight closed into a tight line abreast as they rushed toward the locusts' massed ranks. Laser beams flashed and glowed as they swatted down incoming locust missiles. At the same time, the warbirds launched salvo after salvo of missiles.

Kingston stood in his cockpit, turning to look up and back, keeping the conflict in view, following every aspect for as long as he could. He could see the enemy missiles were not getting through, and they had no defence against the warbirds' own missile salvos. The locust lines were thinning amidst the exploding missiles.

The Flight Two warbirds were quickly so distant that Kingston could hardly discern them, their presence marked only by the burning light of their laser beams cutting through the dark like searchlights. A flash of light signalled the explosion of a fleeing locust.

'Cakewalk!' shouted Kingston. 'No contest! Take that, why don't you?' He glanced to his right and found his co-pilot standing, looking back and cheering.

'Well done, Flight Two. Get them all,' said Kingston into his collar-phone. A round of cheery responses came back.

Kingston consulted the LPA. Most of the locusts were gone. It was clear that those that were running would not get far as half of Flight Two chased them down. The second half of the flight had peeled away on his order and set off in hot pursuit of those locust attack vessels that had earlier departed to chase the Leviathans. He looked at the cone's signature light and smiled – they were closing. Not long now.

'Flight Three, you saw how it's done. Now let's do our bit and take down the mothership. Come on!'

Ahead, the cone appeared bigger now. It was racing for a place to fold. Powered by the commandeered sample craft's gravdrive, it should have been able to maintain its distance on the warbirds. It couldn't. The vast cone framework within which the sample craft was fixed drastically slowed it down.

Kingston channelled a call back to Primo. 'Primo, we are closing on the cone. Please confirm your destroy order.'

There was a short delay as messages crossed the growing distance. 'Stand by, warbird leader. I'm putting you through to Professor Simpson.'

'Captain Kingston? Hello, Steph here. Your pilots have done well.'

'Thank you, ma'am. We can be in attack mode shortly. This cone is their command post. Do you want us to disable it, bring it back so you can study it?'

'Kingston. You must destroy it totally. When you think it's just debris in space, hit it again and then again. Nothing must survive. No life pods, no hull sections that might harbour life, nothing…'

'Scorched earth it is, ma'am,' said Kingston. He turned to his co-pilot. 'She really, really doesn't like these locusts.'

'No, and she's in good company.' The two men laughed. 'What's the attack plan, boss?' The two men fell silent as Steph resumed her transmission.

'Captain Kingston, be advised, while the sample craft was in proximity with Primo, automatic data sharing took place. We know there is a locust queen on board the sample craft. Under no circumstances can it be allowed to survive. I repeat again, destroy everything. Everything. This is Professor Simpson signing off, over and out.'

Kingston looked at the nearing cone with distaste. Shed of its attack vessels, its only defence was speed, and it didn't have enough. 'Flight Three, we're going in. Orders are we must completely destroy the cone. There's a queen on board. We'll approach from the stern, hit the sampler with missiles to stop it folding, then rain fire and brimstone. We're not going home till the whole thing is matchsticks.'

Chapter 52

Primo Deep

General Dower looked at the little group of officers. 'Well, we have to go in. But how? We can shuttle troops up the Grand Canal and attempt to land in the berthing bays. But we'll be very exposed, and I'm thinking that will be costly. We can go back down by the gravlift, but that's going to be slow, and if they get wind of it, whoever's sent down will be outnumbered in a confined space – difficult. I've asked that Professor Simpson think of some way to adapt Colonel MacMillan's experiences for application here.'

'We'll give it a go, sir. You say the word,' said a lieutenant, forcing a brave face.

'We have Captain Besinski up in the reserve control room. When the time comes, he'll create a diversion. But it's still long odds, even if we wait for P-1 to arrive with its soldiers. Problem is, every hour we wait, the better established they'll be. We must act but can't afford to push them without forcing them out entirely. We need to regain full control of Main Base – no mistakes.'

'Do we know how many there are for sure, sir?'

'Just over eight hundred. Eight twenty-five at the latest count.'

Dower turned away from his officers while raising a hand to his ear. 'Go ahead.'

'Hi, it's Lily.'

'Honey, this isn't a good moment, sorry. Can we speak in ten?'

'Yes, that's good. I need to speak, desperately. I want to know exactly what happened to Fay. But right now, I'm calling for Steph. She said to tell you not to attack, yet. She needs to do something first.'

'What? What does she know? Why can't she speak with me?'

'I'm sorry. Steph's being super weird. Most of the time she's sitting or wandering around inside the Goliath. It's like she's speaking with herself, but some of the lights sort of flurry like they're speaking back.'

'Is she all right? Was she injured by one of the locusts? What does Besinski think?'

'She seems fine. Captain Besinski is waiting to hear from you. All I can tell you is what I've already said. Oh, hold on, she's coming out now. I'll transfer this call across to her right away. Bye, love you. Speak in ten.' And she was gone.

'Steph, what's happening? Speak to me.'

'General, don't attack. Not yet. I've been making arrangements.'

'Expand.'

'It's not a nice comparison, but we've got an infestation. I can force them out if you have your warbirds ready in the Grand Canal to get them there.'

'I'm listening.'

'From here, I can use the reserve control room Goliath to take control of all the berthing hangars and inner airlocks in Main Base. I'm going to apply zero gravity across all Main Base, then I'll open the hangars and airlocks to vent it all to space. Some locusts will manage to get on board their vessels and lock down. Mostly, they won't have a chance, they'll be sucked directly out into the Canal.'

'Are you sure you can do that?'

'Yes, I have it set, ready for your word.'

'That'll certainly move the odds in our favour.'

'More than move them, general. But there will be plenty locusts tucked away in various chambers and passageways who'll be able to hold on and avoid the suction.'

'We'll take care of any remainder.'

'I don't think so. I've got control of the ventilation system. Once we've vented Main Base's atmosphere, I can selectively power up the ventilation and use it like a leaf-blower. I'll target individual locusts, flushing each one out and blowing them to the exits.'

'Steph, this is brilliant, are you sure? Will you be safe in the reserve control room?' The general beamed and his officers knew something good was afoot.

'We'll be fine. I've already isolated the reserve control room's atmosphere from the rest of Main Base, but it will just be simpler to manage the artificial gravity control as a single setting for the whole living quarters up here. When I start the process, we'll lose gravity in here too. You should all be fine in the Deep, as it's completely separate. I'm sure I can do this. It's going to use up a lot of our atmosphere reserve, but not all – we'll have enough, and it can be replenished afterwards. You just need to have the warbirds pick off the locusts as they emerge.'

'That we can do. It'll be like shooting fish in a barrel. Captain Kingston has left Flight One in the Canal – they'll manage that.'

Chapter 53

Primo Main Base

Steph and Lily stood between two of the regular LPAs close beside the Goliath. Besinski joined them, watching intently.

One LPA was set to display the camera feeds from various parts of the base: berthing hangars full of attack vessels, promenades, tunnels and chambers – all crawling with locusts. The locust were mostly milling about – clearly, none had yet worked out how to respond to their change of fortunes in the Grand Canal.

The second LPA showed a detailed layout of Main Base, populated by a host of indicator lights, each one shining red for locust.

'You know what to do, Lily. Once we start, you'll need to direct me – it needs two sets of eyes to make a success of this.'

Lily nodded.

Steph squeezed Lily's arm. 'It'll work out. We just need to stay focused, not miss a thing. Are you okay with this?' She took Lily's silence as agreement. 'Good. Now Captain Besinski, your LPA, is carrying video feeds from across the base. You can monitor how effective our plan is as it plays out – call out any problems you spot. I have to go now. Remember, hold tight to your LPAs. I'm about to deactivate the gravity stabilisers.' Turning, Steph walked directly into the Goliath.

Lily could see how a small cluster of lights gathered around Steph as she began stroking and signalling the Goliath into action.

'There! It's starting,' said Besinski, gripping the edge of his LPA as the gravity in the room suddenly lowered at Steph's command. Lily grabbed her LPA too, and they were weightless.

Still holding tight, Besinski looked to the LPA. The display showed locusts floating away from the floors, jumbling together in struggling clusters, all individual purpose lost. Then the berthing hangars opened onto the Grand Canal. At the same time, inner airlock doors slid open.

In that instant, Main Base transformed into a swirling vortex that sucked anything and everything that could be moved out into the vacuum.

Within the Goliath, Steph's hands glided about tweaking and adjusting.

Besinski watched the video display with a sense of satisfied horror. Locusts were flying out through the hangars, grabbing what anchor points they could: fellow locusts, doorframes, the hulls of berthed vessels, but few stuck. Most of those that did get a handhold were soon dislodged, bumped by other locusts hurtling past.

Lily, too, held tight. In the LPA, she saw red indicator lights vanishing in droves as they emptied into the Canal. 'It's working,' she said.

'Hello, you two, I'm ready for the next phase. Can you guide me now?' said Steph.

'Go ahead, Steph,' said Lily.

'I want to start at the furthest point and begin flushing through, get every last one. We'll start at the gravlift access to the Deep. It's at the end of a passageway that doesn't show on Primo's main plans. I've adjusted display arrangements, so it should show up on your LPAs. Can you see the gravlift?'

'There are two red lights there. Two locusts showing on the plan,' said Lily.

'I have visual on the passageway,' said Besinski. 'Two of them. They've braced their backs against each other, legs against the walls.'

'Clever,' said Lily. 'But they can't stay like that forever.'

'They won't need to. Once the atmosphere leaks to full vacuum there will be no exit suction. I'm going to activate a single vent now. Just up-tunnel from the locusts. Tell me what you see,' said Steph.

Besinski stared intently at the video display. For a moment, nothing happened. Then he saw the locusts redoubling their efforts, bracing themselves harder, struggling against an unseen force.

'It's working, Steph, but they're fighting it. Can you increase the air pressure?'

'Will do. How's this?'

The two locusts pressed harder against one another, fighting to lock themselves in position.

Lily triggered the audio feed, and the sound of rushing air stormed through her collar-phone. Then the locusts' lock-grip waivered. One moment, rock-solid; the next, a slipping foot. Then they were gone from Besinski's video feed, blown down the passageway.

'That's it,' said Lily. 'I see their light signatures moving. Moving fast.'

There's another signal in the tunnel ahead. They're closing on it at speed.'

Besinski had just selected another camera feed in time to see a solitary locust clinging to an open archway. It was cannoned into by the two hurtling locusts, and all three bundled away, joining others as they careered along.

Inside the Goliath, Steph's hands worked fast, opening and closing air vents to keep maximum pressure on the targets, sweeping them along toward the open hangar doors and a rendezvous with the warbirds waiting in the Grand Canal.

'They're on the move now! It's working,' said Besinski.

Chapter 54

Osarus c.: S-3

The shock every crew member had felt at the brutal death of so many animals was beginning to ease, as such things must, but the underlying horror remained.

'We've been studying the hopper's video feed of what happened downstream, and it's thrown up something interesting. Now we know what we're looking for, the same things feature on other upstream footage taken earlier by the drones and on S-3's own recordings,' said Ossie.

'Go on,' said Jamie, while gratefully accepting an offered beaker of coffee. The only consolation he had found after the slaughter was that many herd survivors were now appearing safe on the far side of the river. Clearly, many animals upstream had survived the bloody river crossings to continue their migration.

'Watch,' said Ossie, waving toward the screen. 'See, this is where a part of the herd forks away from the main body and follows our side of the river downstream. Look above the leading animals.'

'I don't see anything,' said Jamie.

Ossie rewound the sequence. 'Watch again, above the animals. See the birds.' He set the pictures running.

'I see them,' said Jamie. 'Wow. Are they doing what I think they're doing? Run it again, please.'

They saw big black birds swoop down in formation. Several lighted on the backs of the big males leading their family groups. The birds fixed themselves behind the animals' shoulders. Talons tightly gripped thick skin, then the birds began a rhythmic pecking on the animals' right shoulders. The lead animals turned left, trying to get away from the pecking sensation, so leading their families and a whole swathe of the following herd into the valley mouth.

Other black birds swooped behind the lead animals and vigorously pecked at their hindquarters, forcing the animals to speed up, accelerating the change of direction.

'If you think they're herding the animals, I think you're right,' said Ossie.

'God save us! What's happening out there?' said Browning.

'See, once the herd is in the valley, the birds stop steering them. It's quite deliberate. An intentional action. I think we have to assume these birds are far more intelligent than we've given them credit for.'

'But why are they driving those animals to their deaths? That's not intelligence; it's sadism,' said Browning.

'How intelligent?' said Jamie.

'My team are going to need to look into that. But capability? It looks as though around fifty or so black birds cut out and marshalled a herd of many thousands of wild animals for a purpose that we don't yet comprehend – we couldn't do that. Whatever their purpose, it was premeditated.'

'Are they a danger to us?' said Browning.

'I can't say. They've been around us since the day we landed, and they've never attacked or done us any harm. Probably no, but I can't be sure. These birds are clever; they act with purpose.'

'What do you mean clever? Like having smart instincts?' said Jamie.

'No, I mean clever. Intelligence clever, and they clearly acted in a coordinated way, which indicates structured communication and leadership.'

'So, these are no Earth-type birds,' said Jamie.

'I'm not so sure. Earth studies show some crows use rudimentary tools; others work together to teach and learn techniques. Best of all, it's been shown crows can learn to recognise a particular individual human as a danger and avoid contact with them. The following year, their young will recognise that specific person as a threat, even though they have never had any previous contact with them nor experienced them as a personal threat.

Meanwhile, they were markedly less wary of other humans – that points toward complex communication, the ability to teach their young about specific conceptual risks.'

'Are you telling us these birds speak and learn?' said Browning.

'No, I'm telling you birds can be clever. Watch this.' Ossie tapped his sleeve and the playback continued.

They watched the herd still a little upstream of the perimeter wall, again advancing at grazing pace. Suddenly, a dozen black birds swooped down behind the leading animals and began to peck at their quarters, forcing the pace on.

'Look into the distance. See, way off – little black specks, you'd miss them unless you were looking for them. That's the rest of the birds dropping into the middle of the herd. They disappear from view but watch now... the herd suddenly moves forward as one from that area.'

They watched the leading animals continue toward the wall where they found themselves trapped by the onrush from behind. Jamie looked away. He'd seen it in real-time, didn't need a re-run to know what came next.

'So, intelligent birds, where does that leave us?'

'I don't know, but we should be careful. And talking of being careful, having reviewed the video feed from the thicket, it's clear there is one bit of good news – we can be very glad that trees are rooted to the ground. We've been watching for serpents and guarding against intrusion since day one, but it's quite clear now, whatever we choose to call them, they're not serpents. These are carnivorous trees.'

'Is that even a thing?' said Jamie.

'On Earth, there are lots of plants that get their nutrients from trapping and killing insects, even small amphibians and rodents. The principle is sound, but the scale here...' Ossie gave a shrug. 'My team needs to do more work before I can give anything approaching a coherent explanation. As long as we stay out of the thickets, there's no danger from that source. I need you to lift the curfew. Now we know what we're facing, we really need to collect the science. I'd like to get a team to set up a remote observation post near the thicket.'

Chapter 55

Osarus c.: The Birds

Hands on hips, Ossie nodded enthusiastically and turned to his botany team, made up of Louise and Jay – it was their observations that had brought him hurrying from the lab to within a dozen paces of the thicket. 'You're right, it's fascinating.' said Ossie.

The weave of boughs had fully re-knitted, and their budding leaves had begun to fill out, covering everything in a dense and striking grey–green. But it was the ground level that had his attention. The mound of carcasses beneath the canopy had visibly reduced in height. Close up, the reason was clear. Stout, yellow-hued tendrils had emerged from the ground, and having looped around dead limbs and bodies, they were slowly drawing the carcasses down into the soil.

'Those are roots, I'm sure. They're dragging their food underground. I'm thinking the killing wasn't a one-off feast – it's a gathering of a whole season's high-energy fertiliser,' said Louise.

'Louise, this is fascinating.'

'Professor! Look up here, you'll want to see this.' Sergeant Grant's voice sounded in Ossie's collar-phone. He glanced up toward the hopper cab from where the sergeant was pointing to the tree canopy.

'What is it sergeant?'

'The black birds are here.'

Ossie clambered up to the cab and stood on the shotgun seat, his head and shoulders protruding through the top hatch.

'Well, I'll be damned,' he said, almost to himself. He stood in silence, watching the big birds purposefully hopping about the newly closed canopy.

Sergeant Grant squeezed his broad torso through the top hatch to join Ossie. 'What's happening, sir?'

'What's happening? I'll tell you! I believe this is a nesting site. Look – the birds are coming in pairs, working together. Some have brought in twigs and branches – I'd think that's to start building nests. This must be a breeding colony.'

For a minute, the men watched the birds' activity in silence. Then the sergeant nudged Ossie and pointed to where several of the birds had gathered to observe the hopper's occupants. 'They don't look too friendly, sir.'

'No, they don't. Perhaps we should back off a bit.' Ossie pointed to another group of birds that was peering down toward the botanists. 'I don't like the look of this.'

'Very good, sir.' Grant slid down into his seat and readied to retreat.

Ossie touched his sleeve. 'Louise, we're pulling back a bit. I'd like you both to fall back too. You can set up your observation kit further back.'

Louise looked up to the hopper. 'We're nearly done here. Just need a couple more minutes.'

'No, fall back now. The birds in the tree canopy don't look happy.'

The hopper arms scooped up the botanists' kit, and the two scientists moved into its shadow, and all retreated as one. A halt at thirty paces allowed Ossie to reappraise the situation. 'Those birds still look pretty agitated.'

'They do,' said Grant, eyeing the row of black birds perched on the edge of the thicket. 'I think we should be further back.'

'Agreed, take us back another thirty – they can set up there.'

At the chosen spot, it took Louise and Jay only minutes to reset their kit.

'We're done, everything's working down here,' said Jay.

'Let's go. And quickly,' said Ossie.

The hopper resumed its retreat, and the botanists walked briskly alongside, all the while throwing cautious backward glances.

Amidst the row of birds, one with a yellow flash on its breast squawked. At once, a bird launched from the thicket and flew to the camera rig. It circled, then landed. Approaching carefully, it pecked inquisitively at the tripod. Then hopping up, it peered into the lens and tapped it gently before launching back into the sky with a shrieking call.

The yellow-flashed bird responded with a series of deep croaks, and at once the whole flock took flight.

'They're up! Let's pick up the pace,' said Ossie, looking over his shoulder. As the birds reached the camera rig, several swooped down and began attacking it. Their aggressive assault quickly had the kit rocking then falling. The rest of the flock continued their flight, closing on the retreating crew, fast.

'Sergeant, we're not going to make it. Can we lift the botanists into the cab with us?'

'Will do, sir. It'll be a tight squeeze with four on board.'

'Do it,' said Ossie, alerting the pedestrians to the change of plan. He saw their nervous glances toward the fast-approaching birds, saw the hopper's arms lift the pair up. Throwing open the hatch, he extended a hand to guide Louise on board as the birds circled.

She squeezed in and Ossie reached out toward Jay, gripping his outstretched hand as the first bird attacked.

Jay wriggled to distract the bird. Undeterred, it latched onto his arm, talons gripping tightly for stability. The bird needed only one short step, and the assistant's face was within range. The black head pulled back then thrust forward in a practiced motion. As it struck, it adjusted direction, responding precisely to the victim's evasive manoeuvre, ensuring the beak struck with maximum effect. Jay's scream displaced every sound in the locale. Pulling back, the black bird's glistening beak drew with it an eyeball.

A single flick back of the head, and the eye was swallowed. Jay squirmed in distress and fell from the hopper arm's grip. His whole weight transferring to Ossie's arm.

Leaning its head forward, the bird struck again. Jay's free hand was up now shielding his remaining eye. It required only three pecks to successfully move the hand aside and access the remaining eye. Terrified and totally blinded, Jay hung from Ossie's arm, screaming and waving his free hand, his legs kicking in uncontrolled distress beneath him.

Every jerk threatened to dislodge Ossie who could do nothing to distract the bird. One hand gripped the botanist's, the other was braced against the hatch rim. He held the wounded man for all he was worth.

'Get him in!' shrieked Louise. 'Get him in!'

Ossie was struggling to keep his grip. More birds were mobbing the defenceless man whose terrified screams continued to fill the air. The original attacking bird displayed the deftest of hops to reverse its direction on Jay's arm. Now it faced Ossie and hopped forward, switching onto the chief scientist's arm, moving toward his unprotected face.

'Sergeant! I'm stuck. For God's sake, do something!' said Ossie.

The bird hopped again, bringing it into striking range. Defenceless, Ossie ducked his head down hoping to avoid the butcher's practiced strike, knowing it was a futile gesture.

Jay's cries were momentarily overwritten by the report of Grant's pistol. The bullet punched through the bird's body and instantly swept it off Ossie's arm.

Grant leaned across Ossie, trying to take a reinforcing grip on Jay's arm. As he reached out, it was already clear nothing could be done. Another bird had alighted on Jay's arm and immediately pecked at the wrist below Ossie's gripping hand. It cut muscle and tendon, a severed artery, and Jay dropped like a dead weight. On the ground, he was immediately lost beneath the flock, their beaks slicing at face and body.

Louise screamed. The wrist-cutting bird had not followed its victim down. Instead, with a screeching call it flew into the hopper's cab. Landing on Louise's shoulder, one clawed foot gripped tight, penetrating her uniform. The other foot tangled her hair, jerking her head back, exposing her neck and eyes. Its neck arched back, giving a loud call, it struck hard for Louise's eyes.

Her protective hand blocked the blow at the cost of a bone-deep wound to her fingers. A second blow almost severed her little finger, and instinctively she pulled her hand away from danger, leaving her eyes open to attack. The bird cackled in triumph, pulling back its head to strike a third time and pluck its prize. There was no time for any evasive manoeuvre, Louise could only watch the striking beak rushing in.

As she screamed, the bird stopped in mid-strike. Its big wings flapped desperately, scattering feathers as it struggled to free its claws from her hair. Around its throat was the gripping hand of Sergeant Grant, squeezing harder, harder, crushing its neck and life.

'Shut the hatch,' said Grant as he grappled with the bird.

Ossie hesitated. 'But he's still out there-'

'Shut it now!' Grant swung the bird, and it died, neck broken under his crushing grip. Immediately, he used the lifeless body to beat out another bird entering the hatch. 'Now!'

Ossie overcame his paralysis and slammed shut the hatch, just as more birds thumped against it.

Grant looked at the dead bird, threw it down at his feet and slid back into the driver's seat. 'Best see to her hand,' he said, nudging Ossie with his elbow. Numbed, Ossie barely registered his words.

Grant gave his arm a firm shove. 'Come on, it's always hard, but you'll get over it. See to the girl.'

A deep sob from behind them had Ossie suddenly springing into action. He grabbed the first aid kit and squeezed into a position where he could tend Louise's wounds. She was shivering, crying and speechless. One hand was clamped down hard on the other hand's wound, both hands extended far from her body in a shocked denial of ownership.

Gently, Ossie pressed aside her protecting hand and applied a pressure pad to contain the bleed. 'What's happening down there? Can you scare the birds off? Get Jay?' said Ossie, while continuing to dress Louise's wounds.

Grant had been trying to work out how he might recover Jay and had just come to the conclusion it was impossible. The task was beyond the capability of a hopper's arms. With every passing moment, the problem grew. He shook his head. 'We have to leave,' he said.

'You can't leave him here,' said Ossie.

'I can't pick him up either; we have to go.'

'What do you mean? I insist we lift him up.' Ossie turned from the patient to look down at the ground. The flock of black birds were all around Jay, all over him, their heavy beaks cutting and stabbing, scissoring and expertly slicing. 'Oh God.'

Jay's body was already divided into a dozen pieces, taking more cuts every second. Grant knew, by the time he had manoeuvred the hopper's arms down to retrieve the body, there would be no parts big enough to lift. He shook his head. 'Butcher birds. Let's go. I need to get you two back to S-3.'

Ossie nodded.

'What's happening? How's Jay?' said Louise. The seriousness of the situation still submerged beneath her own shock.

'Don't worry,' said Ossie, putting his arm round her shoulders. 'Let's get you back to S-3, get you seen to properly, okay?'

Louise began to ask after her assistant again then paused, closed her eyes and nodded.

Chapter 56

Osarus c.: S-3

Ossie straightened up from an LPA at the back of the science lab and gave Jamie a curt nod. His supporting team of scientists stepped back a couple of paces to make space for the commander who was hurrying across the lab, closely followed by Browning, Martha and Casper Wills.

'Well, Ossie, you called us down. You've got news for us.'

'I think so. Whether you take it as good news is another matter.'

'Go on then, what have you got?'

'My teams have begun to put together a picture of what happened out there.'

Ossie began stroking his sleeve. 'See, in the LPA. We think we're looking at a symbiotic relationship. No idea how it's evolved, but it seems when the birds guide the herd toward the trees, they're actually feeding the trees. And in return, the birds nest in the trees – as safe as they could wish from any disturbance or predation.'

'But why did the birds attack? There was no threat to them,' said Jamie.

'We're thinking they become territorial when breeding – it's quite a common trait in nature.'

'There's nothing natural about those monsters,' said Martha.

'Indeed, but it explains the attack on our botanists,' said Ossie dryly.

'All right, Ossie. Thank you. That's useful to know but doesn't help me lift the lockdown. If the birds are likely only territorial during their breeding season how long is that?'

'Sorry, I've no idea. Three weeks, three months? I just don't know. If you'd allocate me one of the marine hoppers and a driver to monitor what's going on down at the thicket, we might get a better idea.'

Jamie turned to Browning. 'Will you organise that, please, Baz? Right away.'

'Consider it done,' said Browning. 'But why not let my marines go on the offensive? With our firepower we'd rub those butchers out in no time.'

Jamie frowned. 'First off, it's their planet. And then, how many of them are there? Thousands? Millions? They're intelligent, and they communicate. How many will you have to kill to make us safe, and then what else do we have to kill? No, let's see if we can fit in with their natural rhythms first. Make it work for us and everything else.

'For now, only the marines on hopper patrol and the hopper allocated to Science for monitoring the thicket are permitted outside S-3. And nobody gets out of their hopper cab for any reason, period! For all other purposes, without exception, the lockdown continues. No one leaves S-3.' Jamie looked around his leadership team. Each nodded agreement.

Martha gave a little shiver. 'We're locked in.'

Chapter 57

Above Earth's Atmosphere

Celine looked down on Earth. Seen through S-1's viewscreen, it seemed peaceful, quite serene, and lonely as ever. Yet, knowing what she did, the danger was very real. Any survivors on the surface were blissfully unaware of the new threat that loomed. She had to make sure the atmosphere was sealed again. Leaving it open would render the planet accessible and undefended – a locusts' larder to be visited and fed on at their leisure. That wouldn't happen on her watch.

But... she'd spent every hour of the journey back to Earth musing, working and reworking the closure options and all the variables. Once in Earth's orbit, the brigadier had allowed her more time to think through the options, and she still wasn't exactly sure whether theory would translate into practice.

O-2 had long since vanished into the distance, making for the nearest folding point. Now S-1 stood alone over the remarkable column of sample craft. One job: close the atmosphere. Then they too would run for the Fold.

'Celine, we haven't got long. Those locust vessels have almost caught up while you've been running the simulations – they're only minutes behind us. Whatever you're going to do, do it now,' said Brigadier Smith-Brown, glancing toward Harding, the Leviathan's captain, who nodded in agreement.

'Can't you do what you did with the virus delivery craft? Just fly the top craft right down the gravlift tube, then fly the next down and so on? Collapse it from the top,' said the brigadier.

'No. A craft can't travel down its own gravlift tube. The only way seems to be a four-step process,' said Celine, frowning. 'And there's a problem. I still can't resolve for certain if it's even possible to reverse the gravlift direction while maintaining the tube's integrity during the moments when the reversal process implements. Then I'll have to move all the sample craft down to the surface, if it works, as it's the only sure way to keep them all out of reach of the locusts, but it's not a simple process to programme.

'One: reverse the gravlift direction so it's powering through the gravlift focus-face on the hull's topside. So it projects upward, not down – fingers crossed that actually works and we don't lose any samplers to debris during the reversal process. Two: move to one side the lowest craft that's at the bottom of the atmosphere's debris field, and park it. Three: drop the whole column by one. Four: move the new bottom craft aside and park. Rinse and repeat until they're all down. That's the only way to ensure the top craft doesn't get left for the locusts.'

'So just do it. What's the problem?' said the brigadier.

'First: time. Guiding all those craft down is not going to happen before the locusts arrive. Second: when we eventually come back, the atmosphere will be closed again and all our samplers will be on the wrong side of the biggest chaff field you can imagine, with all the communications problems that entails; I'm not sure we'll have the ability to communicate with any craft on the surface to remotely implement a column rebuild.'

'So, what do you suggest?' said the brigadier.

'Let me think again.'

'No time for that. They're here! We have to go now,' said Captain Harding.

Celine turned to the brigadier. 'Just a few minutes more?'

'No time left,' said Harding.

'Captain, once we start to run, we'll out pace them. Let's buy Celine a little more time – take us on an orbit of the Earth. They can chase us all they like. If by the time we get back here, Celine still has no certain answer, she's just going to have to move the upper craft out of the column and into the general debris field.

'Brigadier, that will certainly result in the destruction of the craft almost at once – the next craft down will be unprotected, so it will be picked off and destroyed by debris, then the next... they'll all be destroyed, one by one.'

'Yes, and that's better than leaving an open larder door for the locusts to get down to the surface. Start thinking of an alternative. You have one orbit.'

'And then we run?' said the captain.

'Then we run.' The brigadier looked up to the screen. 'Captain, any signals from Primo yet? What's happening.'

'Still nothing since the report of locusts getting into the berthing hangars. No signals at all.'

'My people are still working on that,' said Celine, her eyes fixed on the data displaying on her sleeve. We don't think it's an equipment problem. Our kit's all good, and Primo has multiple options to broadcast to us. It seems we're being blocked.'

'The locusts can do that?'

'Yes, if they know how, and they clearly know plenty. They're directly between us and Primo. Our best guess is they are beaming out a localised signal that's cancelling any messages Primo might broadcast to us. It's odd – somehow, they know the frequencies we transmit on, even our reserve emergency channels that aren't ordinarily active.'

'How the hell can they do that?'

Celine shrugged and turned. 'They shouldn't know, but they are certainly clever. Right now, I need to get to an LPA and run one last test of the theory for safely closing the atmosphere, the one that we can reverse.' She hurried off the bridge.

'If these locusts can second guess us so easily, is it wise to do anything that's reversible. Shouldn't we just seal and go?' said Harding.

'Captain, we must move immediately, or we will be within missile range,' came the second officer's voice from his position at the LPA. 'They're on us now.'

Captain Harding thrust his hand forward in a sign to the first officer. 'Let's go now, full ahead.' Immediately, the Leviathan broke its position and set off on a circuit.

'Incoming! Incoming missiles. Four closing from astern...' The second officer had hardly raised the alarm before calling it back. 'No threat, no threat. They'll all fall short. Out of range. They fired too early.'

The brigadier looked toward Harding. Let's keep them out of range.'

'I intend to, sir.'

They watched as the flock of pursuing locusts assembled into two ranks of five and began to give chase. On the move again, S-1's gravdrive provided the power and speed to pull away from the chasing locusts.

'We're in the clear.' The second officer reported.

'Thank you, captain. That was close,' said the brigadier.

'It was, sir.'

'Captain, something odd in the LPA,' said the second officer. 'That second rank of locusts is dropping back from the leading rank. I'll lose their signal in the Earth's shadow shortly.'

'Have they altered course?'

No, sir, just moving slower than the lead rank.'

'Okay, thank you. Let us know if there's any further change.'

The brigadier settled to watch the Earth spin away below as the captain engaged in an earnest conversation with his first officer about preferred exit routes once Celine had done her work.

A little while later, Celine returned to the bridge. Her glum face delivered the message before she could speak. 'I'm sorry, no new clever ideas. I can't do anything that doesn't either endanger the column of samplers or risk leaving the route down to the surface open, or possible for the locusts to reopen.

'I'm going to have to do as I'd first outlined. I've got the program ready, so once the first is on the way down, the rest will follow automatically, letting the atmosphere close behind them as they descend.'

'That's it? Then we can go?' said the brigadier as the Leviathan slowed slightly.

Celine nodded, and they all watched the column of sample craft appear in the distance. 'We'll just have to pray we can get a reactivation signal through the cluttered atmosphere to trigger reassembly of the column when the time comes.'

'So run your program now,' said the brigadier.

'Okay, give me a moment to get things going.'

'Dead ahead! Breaking the horizon, locusts.' The second officer's alert sounded from the LPA.

'Hell's bells, that second rank has doubled back; we're caught in a pincer movement,' said Harding.

'Locusts closing, ahead and astern,' said the second officer.

'We can't leave until the column begins to descend,' said the brigadier. 'How long, Celine?'

'Loading the program now. Two minutes max and we're done.'

'Too long, we have to go now,' said Harding.

'No. If they know all our broadcast frequencies and capture my signal, perhaps they will be able to reverse the instruction. We must wait until the gravlifts reverse direction and the column actually begins to drop,' said Celine.

'We'll be over the column in one minute,' reported the second officer.

'The LPA's transmitting the program to the samplers now – I can send the gravlift reversal signal to commence the process imminently,' said Steph.

'Captain, I'm running our exit routes. The locusts ahead are too close now. We can't get clear before coming into range of their missiles. We can't turn because the chasing locusts will be on us.' The first officer's voice was terse. 'No matter what you do with the column, we can't escape.'

The brigadier stared toward Harding. 'Whatever we do, we must see Celine's column begin to close first.'

Harding nodded in acknowledgement.

'We'll be over the column in thirty seconds,' said the second officer.

'Nearly ready to trigger the program,' said Celine.

'Twenty seconds to column.'

'Incoming missiles fore and aft,' reported the second officer.

'Evasive action options?' said Captain Harding.

'Second salvo launched, all en route.'

'None,' said the first officer. 'We're done.'

'Not on my watch, mister,' said Harding, jabbing a pointing hand toward the gravlift column where it showed centred on the screen. 'Hard to starboard and dive, dive now. I want us in that stack and down before it's closed.'

'Will we fit?' said the brigadier.

'Ready to trigger collapse program command now,' said Celine.

'Celine, hold that command,' said Harding. 'I need downward gravlift in the tube.'

'You won't make it,' said Celine.

'Who won't?' said Harding, touching his sleeve and assuming manual navigation. 'No time to programme this; I'll go in by eye.'

One of the lookouts covered his face and leaned against the bulkhead, shaking his head in despair.

The Leviathan thundered down, swooping so close by the top sampler that it almost filled the whole screen. Captain Harding stood alone in the middle of the bridge, eyes fixed on the screen while the fingers of one hand danced across his sleeve controls, every movement tweaking the Leviathan's trajectory.'

'We're in the tube!' said the second officer.

The top craft was above them; below, the next in column loomed large.

'Great. Now let's shift this descent into auto-mode,' said Harding, all the while fingers continuing to dance.

'Programming auto, sir,' said the second officer. 'Autopilot on… now.'

The captain's hand dropped from his sleeve, and he looked surprised at a spontaneous round of applause from the bridge team. Harding grinned then turned his attention to the screen. The next craft in the column was close now, the Leviathan was descending steadily. It was clear they would pass safely. 'Give me a split screen, let's see what happened behind us.'

The screen split. Half now displayed the action in the tube above them – all quiet.

Harding pointed to Celine. 'The instant we're at the bottom of the tube, trigger your program. If anything manages to follow us down, it'll be spewed right back out when the gravlift reverses direction.

'Where are the missiles?'

'The sudden descent foxed them, sir. The missiles altered course to intercept us and ran through unprotected space. They came unstuck in the debris field,' reported the first officer.

'And that's not all!' The brigadier raised both arms, pointing to a screen, image frozen on the last complete atmosphere frame displayed as the Leviathan powered into the isolating shroud of the tube. 'Look at the locusts.'

High above the atmosphere, the locust attack vessels had altered course. Having seen the Leviathan dive toward the shimmering tube, they'd mirrored their missiles' action and altered course to intercept the Leviathan at a lower altitude, to cut it off. Like two ranks of diving pelicans, in synchrony, they had banked and dived for the kill. The frozen image told of attackers thrashing directly into the atmosphere, all with only one goal: destroy the Leviathan. And all the while, they were oblivious to the destruction they were racing toward.

Everyone on the bridge held their breath. For a moment not daring to believe their luck.

'Okay, everyone. Let's make sure we get down in one piece,' said Harding.

'Once we're through the tube, Celine, immediately trigger the gravlift reversal program and collapse the whole column to ground level. If there are any locusts left up there, they won't get in. We'll be safe.'

'Will do. Though it'll take a little while to reassemble the column for upward transit,' said Celine.

Spark's voice sounded from the communications room. 'Captain, brigadier, I've received signals. Primo has the locusts on the run. And I had fleeting contact with warbirds nearing Earth. That's all I got before losing signal as we dropped deeper into the tube.'

'Thank you, Sparks. Did you manage to acknowledge them?'

'Yes, captain, I notified them of our descent, but sorry, it ended there. Once we moved deeper into the tube, it messed the signal completely. All silent now.'

The brigadier shrugged toward Captain Harding. Today, that didn't matter. The atmosphere was closed, and with warbirds in the vicinity, any locusts that had escaped their dive would be easy targets.

Chapter 58

Primo Deep

General Dower stood rigid, one arm around his wife's shoulders as they waited anxiously outside the warbirds' hangar. Here, at the deepest point of the Deep, they were clinging on to a strand of hope that Steph had brought them. They watched through the viewing port as an observer nudged the wrecked frame of Fay's warbird into the hangar. It came to rest beside Kingston's craft.

'Is it back now?' said Kingston, hurrying to join the couple at their viewing port.

'It is,' said Dower.

Gail Dower hugged Kingston.

They watched the observer back out and the hangar doors swing shut, allowing the atmosphere inside to normalise. 'There's the medics,' said Dower, as four figures rushed toward the hulk.

The medics surveyed the craft and didn't even try to access via the shattered stern airlock door. Instead, they clambered directly up onto the torn fuselage. From there, one by one, they dropped through the gashed hull directly into the cockpit. Then everything in the hangar was still. The watchers all turned toward the sound of running feet that heralded the arrival of Steph and Lily.

Amidst the rush of hugs and babbled family exchanges, Steph managed to hook Kingston aside. 'What news?' she said.

'Nothing yet. How did you even think there was a chance?'

'It's the suits. They're more than just fashion statements. We first saw it when Weeman literally crashed into our lives. He was injured, but helmet up, the suit is a little protective cocoon. It can preserve the wearer in a sort of stasis while their body recovers from shocks, like a personal life support machine.'

'Why didn't I know about that?'

'You combat types take enough risks without thinking you've got an Ironman suit on.' Steph patched herself through to the chief medic's collar-phone. How's it looking, doc?'

'Still assessing the situation. Working out how to move them.'

'By that you mean?'

'You were right about the suits. Both unresponsive, clearly lots of body damage, but we have vital signs in both pilot and co-pilot. Trying to work out how to get them out safely.'

'Okay, I've got engineers standing by to do some localised gravity control. That will minimise physical stress as you move them. I'll send them in now.' Steph pulled back from the melee and ordered her specialist gravity engineers forward. Then she reached out her arms to embrace the Dower family as one. 'She's alive. Broken but alive.'

Kingston kissed her cheek. 'Thank you, professor.'

Having hung back to make sure of the news first, Colonel MacMillan busied in. He swung a bag off his shoulder.

'General, I'd kept this on P-1 for a special day. Today seems as special as we could all hope for,' he said, producing a bottle of the general's own favourite Scotch whisky from a bag. Amidst a murmur of approval, he produced beakers, and in moments, a toast was called.

'We came through,' said Gail.

'We did, by God,' said Dower. He clinked glasses with all the party, then instantly drained his glass. 'Set up another round. Today is special, very special.'

They drank another toast while watching the gravity engineers begin the delicate task of raising the survivors from the wreckage.

Steph took the opportunity to draw the general to one side. She looked into his smiling eyes.

'It's not over, you know,' she said.

'I know. We've got Celine and the brigadier marooned on Earth. But Earth's safe, the counter-virus distributed, and we'll get the atmosphere open again, soon enough. And Steph, we blew those damned locusts away.'

She nodded her head while he was speaking then shook it. 'I know all that, general. But there's stuff I haven't had time to tell you. While it was near Primo, the sample craft embedded in the locust cone transmitted information to the Main Base Goliath.'

'Yes, I know.'

'You know they flew that sampler into the Fold by controlling Weeman's friend. It's sick...' Steph scowled. 'When they captured the samplers out in Perseus, they captured Weeman's friends too. They do something to them. I've seen bridge-monitoring recordings from the sampler. They take control of their victims. Those long antennae, they slide them into the body through cranial orifices, behind the eyes, through the ear drums, both – penetrating, connecting with the brain. That's how they learn. They don't just eat their victims, they take their knowledge, their minds. Right now, they know more about Primo and its purpose than we do.'

Dower took a step back. 'That's disgusting.'

Steph looked sadly at the general. 'Disgusting doesn't begin... I've seen the bridge feed – Weeman's friend trussed up, immobilised on the bridge, a locust behind him, antennae behind his eyes, controlling him: his mind, his body his arms, sleeve controls. Everything. Poor soul.'

Kingston had joined them. 'Jesus Christ! The evil devils. But Steph, you had me destroy the cone, I killed him. We could have saved him. Why?'

'You couldn't; he was beyond saving. He was in a living hell. They'd stolen control of his mind. He was only kept alive so his body would operate the ship. His suit was the interface with the ship. When he died, their control ended. He wanted to die. Needed to.'

The general put his arm round Steph's shoulder. 'It must have been hell to see. You did the right thing. If nothing else, the locust threat has been destroyed.'

Steph shook her head. 'Four of Weeman's people went into the Perseus Arm. I've learned they experimented on one; he was killed. Three were kept. We've killed one. That leaves two more alive, piloting cones in Perseus.'

'Oh hell, no,' said MacMillan, who had crossed to find out what was so interesting.

'Oh hell, yes. The fight's not over by a long shot,' said Dower. 'And that explains how they could open our berthing hangars so easily.'

Steph inclined her head slightly, turning away as she listened to a message coming through her collar-phone. 'Are you sure?' she said. 'Have you crosschecked the codes? Repeat for me...' Then she looked round. Her eyes were filled with tears.

The general was confused, concerned.

Gail put an arm round her. 'What is it?' she said.

Steph spoke into her collar-phone. 'Hi, I'd like you to repeat that message for the general, please. I'm opening your channel to my party. Go ahead.'

'Hello, general – sir. Science Communications here. We've just received a message from a position beacon that has dropped out of the Fold. Somehow S-3 has managed to return a homing message. They are safe and well, and awaiting rescue, sir.'

Steph leaned across to General Dower, and while carefully avoiding his slung arm, she pressed the palm of her hand against his chest. 'This time I'm going for him, no matter what.'

Dower swallowed, his throat suddenly dry. 'Steph... you *are* going.' He pressed his free hand over hers. 'And that's an order!'

Books by D. C. Macey

THE POST CONTACT SERIES

Set tomorrow. Post Contact is a near future action series that carries humanity to the heights of new opportunity and down to the brink of extermination.

- ➢ Post Contact: First Days
- ➢ Post Contact: Holding On
- ➢ Post Contact: Breaking Back

THE TEMPLE SERIES

Contemporary archaeological action thrillers unfolding through a weave of historical facts, mystery, secrets and contemporary action.

- ➢ The Temple Legacy
- ➢ The Temple Scroll
- ➢ The Temple Covenant
- ➢ The Temple Deliverance

About the Author

D. C. Macey is an author based in the United Kingdom. For more information:

contact@dcmacey.com and visit: www.dcmacey.com

Post Contact: First Days

(Post Contact - Book 1)

Today a new order is forming across the galaxy. Will humanity be at its centre or lost as victims of change?

A chance encounter offers humanity the opportunity to instantly progress from moon shots to galactic travel. But the exciting opportunity comes with a heavy responsibility that humanity may not be able to bear. As Earth balances on the cusp of a brilliant and unexpected future, age-old human failings assert themselves when greed, betrayal and violence undermine everything.

Even as Earth's leaders fumble humanity's greatest opportunity, first contactors Steph Simpson and Jamie MacAulay rally a few good people to join with the last remnant of an ancient species and face out to the galaxy with its unknown challenges.

Embark on a new enthralling and sometimes frightening adventure, read this first in series book, ***Post Contact: First Days***.

Post Contact: Holding On

(Post Contact - Book 2)

Outnumbered, unprepared, inexperienced: redemption or extinction?

Fierce adversity can bring out the best of human traits. Today it must. Through sweeping space battles to vicious hand to hand combat with cruel alien species, everywhere mankind is beset. Everywhere humanity's remnant is desperately holding on.

Stunned by Earth's calamitous collapse, the few survivors are kept going only by a grim determination that humanity must continue. With resources stretched paper thin, they face daunting tasks. Against the clock, Professor Steph Simpson and her team struggle to unravel the puzzles of the new technology in a desperate race to rescue any who may survive on Earth.

That same technology is needed elsewhere to fend off terrifying alien attacks and fulfil the responsibilities that accompany the new technology. Meanwhile Jamie MacAulay is marooned, lost in the furthest reaches of the Orion Arm. He and his crew struggle amidst an alien nature and environment. Everywhere the threats grow, and everywhere the price of resistance rises.

Follow humanity's journey to the edge in this second in series book, ***Post Contact: Holding On.***

Post Contact: Breaking Back

(Post Contact - Book 3)

Success, Failure, Betrayal. Humanity must stand against the odds.

The survivors at Base Primo continue their struggle to save humanity, desperately striving to turn the tide of adversity that threatens them all. Backs against the wall, they grapple with the turmoil of old foes resurging, the appearance of new enemies, space conflict, and the gritty cruelty of close quarters combat.

Amidst all the conflict, efforts to unpick the new technology continue. But danger lies in the least expected places, and as humanity's old failings resurface, emerging betrayal is the bitter reward. For Steph, Jamie and General Dower, overcoming alien foes may ultimately prove the least of their problems.

Humanity's struggle for survival continues.

Temple Legacy

(The Temple - Book 1)

Seven hundred years ago, in a time of war and betrayal, Europe's greatest treasure disappeared amidst a frenzied and brutal grab for power. The men who guarded it vanished into history.

In Edinburgh today, former élite British Military Intelligence officer Sam Cameron has turned to the quieter world of archaeology. Together with young church minister Helen Johnson, he leads his students on a field trip. What they unearth raises exciting questions. What are the mystery objects? What is their connection to the Knights Templar?

But others are asking the same questions and the thrill of discovery is quickly clouded by the brutal killing of a retired church minister and a spreading rage of violence and death.

Now Helen and Sam must race to unravel an ancient mystery, find how it links to the murdered minister, and fend off a very modern threat. Failure will cost their lives and the lives of many more. Success will answer the greatest unresolved mystery of the medieval world.

The Temple Scroll

(The Temple - Book 2)

A lost treasure, an impenetrable puzzle and a psychopathic killer: a deadly combination.

The Temple Scroll is a rollercoaster ride of danger, mystery and murder. From New England to the islands of the Mediterranean, it follows the deadly hunt for the Templars' lost treasure.

Archaeology lecturer Sam Cameron and church minister Helen Johnson thought their old problems were done. They were wrong. Killers are set on finding the Templars' treasure and they believe Sam and Helen hold the key.

As the psychopathic Cassiter directs his team of killers towards their goal, the calm of summer vanishes in an explosive bout of blood and suffering.

Under pressure from every side, Sam and Helen must draw on all their instincts and professional skills to stay alive as they attempt to crack the puzzle that protects the Templars' treasure.

As the search for the Templar hoard moves inexorably to a conclusion, Sam and Helen must risk all in a frantic bid to save their friends, the treasure, and the priceless holy relics of the early Church. Now there is no mercy and no escape - there is only win or die.

The Temple Covenant

(The Temple - Book 3)

A quiet sabbatical spent visiting archaeological sites in the Great Rift Valley offers Helen Johnson and Sam Cameron the perfect opportunity to unwind and put the violent climax to their recent adventures behind them. But where they go trouble isn't far away.

Disturbing alarm bells start to ring when Helen attracts the attentions of the mysterious Bishop Ignatius of the Ethiopian Orthodox Tewahedo Church. He is desperate to meet with her and will not take no for an answer.

Elsewhere, news breaks that senior British Intelligence Corps Colonel Bob Prentice is missing in Nairobi and security chiefs have cause for concern. Concern turns to panic when it's realised an operational prototype of the British Army's latest super-weapon has vanished too.

In a last gasp attempt to retrieve the situation the British Government turns to former Intelligence Corps officer Sam, hoping that his civilian status can keep him under the radar and his old skills might just be enough to turn the problem round.

Meanwhile, Helen is co-opted into a role that goes against her every belief - a role that her patriotism demands she fulfil even as she struggles to evade the determined attentions of Bishop Ignatius and his men.

Far from the cloudy skies of Edinburgh, a frightening and bloody hunt plays out beneath the burning sun of the East African bush. Racing against the clock, and with scant support, Sam and Helen must risk everything to resolve the challenge of the enigmatic Bishop Ignatius while fighting to preserve the West's place in a dangerous world.

The Temple Deliverance

(The Temple - Book 4)

Jolted out of their holiday season calm, Helen Johnson and Sam Cameron find they must play one last hand in a deadly game.

The final hunt is on to unpick an ancient code that hides the incredible nature of the Templars' greatest secret. From the depths of northern winter to the sun-kissed beaches of North Africa, Helen and Sam must hurry to piece together the final clues in a race against time to save themselves, their loyal friends and Christianity's greatest heritage.

Beset by danger, they must contend with the return of old foes who are hell bent on vengeance and determined to snatch the ultimate prize they have coveted for so long. As violence and death sweep across the continents, innocence is no protection; knowledge and grit are the only currencies of survival. Calling on trusted allies, Helen and Sam struggle against the odds, knowing that this time only one side can walk away.